The Other Anna

BARBARA ESSTMAN

The Other Anna

HARCOURT BRACE JOVANOVICH, PUBLISHERS

New York   San Diego   London

HBJ

Parts of this novel originally appeared, in slightly different form, in
Lear's, *The Union Street Review*, and *Iowa Woman*.

Requests for permission to make copies of any
part of the work should be mailed to:
Permissions Department,
Harcourt Brace Jovanovich, Publishers, 8th Floor,
Orlando, Florida 32887.

Library of Congress Cataloging-in-Publication Data
Esstman, Barbara.
The other Anna/Barbara Esstman.—1st ed.
p.   cm.
ISBN 0-15-170410-4
I. Title.
PS3555.S69087   1993
813'.54—dc20   92-33107

Designed by Trina Stahl
Printed in the United States of America
First edition
A B C D E

For my parents,
Helen Culbertson and Robert Beste,
who always carried me in their heart.

And for Mark,
who helped me find my own.

My thanks to the National Endowment for the Arts, whose support enabled me to complete this novel.

Thanks also to Mark Farrington, Jody Brady, Ellen Stone, Barbara Bass, Audrey Fleming, and Miriam Altshuler for their help and support.

If he goes there in the middle of June, the long light which never fades at that time of the year, but ebbs and ebbs until, before one can tell how, morning is there again, will charm and tease him; he will lose his sleep for a few nights and be discontented during the day, and feel that he is not quite in the real world. If he has an eye for such things, he will be delighted by the spectacle of the quickly changing skies and the clearness and brightness of all the colors. But he will not come to know much about the place unless he lives there for quite a long time, habituating himself to the rhythm of the life, and training himself to be pleased with the bareness and simplicity in all things.

EDWIN MUIR (1887–1959)
on the Orkney Islands,
from *Scottish Journey*

Part One

Part One

Prelude

THE PRUSSIAN NEVER FORGAVE ME for dreaming of seals. Though I knew she thought them dangerous, I once told her about them. It was the year I turned sixteen, the summer Edwina died, one morning when the iceman had delivered the new block and given me a handful of the extra chips. I filled the largest mixing bowl with ice and water and dipped my hands in, at first just to cool myself. But the water brought back the Old One's sea stories, and my hands turned to seals hurtling through infinite ocean, parting and closing continuously around them, the two sliding slick through the cold and keeping in unison through secret cues between them.

Though my hands were awkward in the crowded bowl, the seals curved back in graceful loops and bends, spiraled in a seal ballet, turned in all the impossible ways creatures can move under the water but not on land. They lifted their chins, tucked their flippers to them, and fell through the ocean, not in the frightening way one falls from sky but in the water way where falling becomes floating.

Then they skimmed over the bottom, signaled each other, stroked once and rose to the surface, signaled again and submerged. Somehow I never imagined them wet. The Prussian owned a seal coat that fell past her knees in rich folds, and when I was small I loved to touch the dense black pile, the softness more velvet, more butter, than any other. Whenever she wore the coat I stroked it and rubbed my cheek against it, until she forbade me to touch and I had to sneak into her closet to run my fingers down the sleeve. Father had told me water would bead and run off the fur so it never became soaked the way cloth coats did. I believed him, and my seals stayed dry and never ran out of air.

Pools of water laked the counter, and a band of wet soaked my front. The coolness was refreshing, and I was delighted at remembering how it felt to play as a child. The seals swam back and forth in semicircles around the rim until the water emptied out of its center and sloshed over the sides. And suddenly the Prussian said, "Anna!" and my hands drowned to the bottom.

"Anna," she said again, "what are you doing?"

The Prussian always demanded explanations. When I was small, she'd stand over me, digging in the dirt or, as then, playing in the water, and ask, as if it were the most aggravating but perplexing question in all existence, "Anna, what are you doing?"

And I, not thinking I was doing anything especially complicated or unusual or secret, forever wondered what exactly was so strange and confusing about myself that even my own mother had to ask. That day was no different. I turned to look at her and in my turning pulled my hands from the water and dripped on the floor. Even in my fear of her, I thought in the moment when I first turned that she was beautiful, small and well-made, with dark chestnut hair and brown eyes. She wore a cream-colored dress with green trim like braided grass, and her hair was neatly twisted and knotted at the crown of her head.

I was grateful my mother was pretty, since I believed I would grow up lovely only if she was. And she was as delicate and finely made as my father's pair of bay Morgans, the most marvelous real creatures I knew of at that time. The greatest compliment I could give my mother was to compare her to them. Yet I could never tell what one of the Prussian's looks meant, any more than I could figure out what the horses were thinking as they watched me with their great brown eyes rolled back to show white. And I was always anxious that I would be stepped on.

"What is this, Anna?"

She held one of my wet wrists, her wedding band pressing against the knob of bone. I shrugged. The question was confusing, the answer obscure. Wrist, water, Anna, or seal?

She took a precisely folded towel from a drawer and began rubbing it roughly against my wet middle. She held one arm about my waist so I could not back away from her.

"What did you think you were doing?" she asked. "You're too old for this."

I held out my hands, red from the cold water.

"Well?" she asked again and dried them.

"Thinking about how seals swim," I told her finally.

She stopped mopping. We were almost the same height, our faces so close I could see the perspiration on her upper lip and the faint spray of freckles over her cheekbones.

"Seals?" she asked, still holding me loosely around the waist as though we were dancing.

"The Old One used to tell me the stories," I said.

"Which?" she asked.

"About the seals who shed their skins and became

men." I lifted my bare hands as if to show her the naked, transformed bodies. "About the ones who change."

"Carline Selchie is insane, Anna." She trapped one of my hands in hers. "We never discussed it at length, not with all the upset over Edwina and all, but you should never have been around her at all."

The Prussian blew out an exasperated breath. Her eyes widened the way they always had when she was about to warn me not to touch the stove or dead animals, not to play with strange children or speak to drunks. There was no use arguing when her voice took on that warning edge and she began to explain to me how I felt and what I knew.

"The stories she told you were not fitting for young girls." The Prussian released my hands and clamped my chin between her thumb and index finger. "And your father was wrong to encourage you."

I wanted to step back out of her reach then, but instead I held very still and refused to blink.

"Promise me you'll forget that woman and her stories."

I studied my mother's face. Something soft and wincing about her eyes contradicted the forcefulness of her voice.

"Promise to forget," she said again.

I nodded, and she released my chin with a soft pinch. "Clean up the water now," she said and left the room.

Afterward, whenever she asked me what I was thinking, I'd say "Nothing," then return to my work with such movement and purpose she couldn't help but know I'd lied. Yet she didn't press the issue. That was our agreement: I pretended to be only as wide and deep as my visible surface, and the Prussian pretended that was all there was of me.

Edwina was dead before I realized the Prussian allowed our arrangement because she was afraid of the dream seals and where they swam. The Prussian afraid: a most amazing thought—but I forget I haven't always known these things and still don't know all. In the beginning I was barely more conscious than a cat, only five when the Old One came to work for us.

What I'm sure I remember from that day the Old One arrived and haven't invented later is that when I first saw her, I thought she was another child. She sat on the stool in the kitchen, hugging her knees and watching the fire in the open belly of the wood stove. When she turned from the flames, she hunched her shoulders the way children do when they are delighted. Yet her hair was white, pulled back in an old-lady bun at the nape of her neck, and her skin finely lined. I thought with alarm that it was possible for children to suddenly become old.

There was nothing to upset me—not really. The Prussian simply took me by the hand and introduced me in the same way she had pointed out where we kept the button box and skillets so the Old One and her grand-daughter Edwina, newly hired, could locate what they needed for our housekeeping. But the stove door, always shut in deference to the Prussian's caution with fire, was wide open, and the child-sized woman crouched so close that one side of her face glowed red with heat. She took my hand between hers. Her touch was sure, her skin dry. I liked the way she felt, how her eyes were green like the inside of a wave, the way she tucked herself on the stool so she seemed my size.

The Old One slid her hands around mine and played with my fingers, as if that were the proper way for two people to meet. She lifted one hand, rubbed her fingertips in a circle on my cheek, and smiled so I could see her gold tooth.

"Sweet baby skin," she said. "Sweet baby."

I wanted to touch her back, explore the strange calluses on her fingers, the smooth nails with the very white half-moons at their base. When I hesitated, half hypnotized by the fire and the circles the Old One was drawing on my skin, the Prussian pulled me backward toward the hall.

"Today I'll take Anna with me," my mother said. "When you're more settled, you can take her over."

The Old One stood up and smoothed her apron. Then the door swung shut behind us and I heard her whistling, the way birds do in the gray light before sunup.

The Prussian towed me up the stairs and told me, "You must listen to Mrs. Selchie when she tells you what to do, but she is just your caretaker. There's no need to be affectionate with her. Understand me, Anna?"

I never let the Prussian know I disobeyed her. At first I drifted through the kitchen, always keeping a table or chair between the Old One and myself, but gradually I came closer, until I spent afternoons sitting with her and Edwina while they sewed or peeled vegetables for dinner. The Prussian, impressed by the efficient way the women produced hot meals, clean rooms, and ironed linens, trusted them with me and gladly went about her own business without the distraction of a child. By the third week of the Old One's reign, I spent all day with her, from the time she and Ed arrived in the morning until they served the evening meal and returned to the house they shared with Ed's father, a widower.

I sat on the smooth wooden floor under the kitchen table, stacking my blocks in different-sized towers and studying the terrain. The Old One's black shoes pointed out under the hem of her black dress, the mourning outfit for her husband, who died before her son had been born, fifty years earlier. She replaced our darning in the small wicker sewing basket on her lap and took her quilt patches from the burlap sack she always carried with her. For all the time I knew her, she ceaselessly patched quilts while telling her stories, Scottish folktales or outright gossip.

The Prussian gave her our discarded clothing, and the Old One sewed patches cut from my summer dress and rearranged pins with quick, sharp stabs.

On the other side of me, Edwina's feet were planted wide apart, and she dropped snippled beans into the apron hammocked between her knees. She was nearly as big as a man and wore men's work boots, but from my vantage point under the table I could not see her large breasts or the jut of her hip, which sloped from her waist like the bluffs to a river. When she first arrived in the mornings, she acted as a lady's maid and fastened the dozens of hooks and snaps and buttons on the Prussian's slips and skirts and corsets, but after that she got on with the real work of laundry and sweeping, dusting and cooking. By afternoon her sleeves were rolled up, her collar was undone, and a tangle of red hair escaped from her combs and hairpins. Sometimes Edwina stopped working and became curiously becalmed, as if she were watching a play being acted in the air in front of her. I didn't like Edwina's eyes then. They were not the soft color of the Old One's, watered with age, but were bottle green, the clean color of newly sprouted wheat, sharp green to cut myself on. I wasn't sure what they saw and was happy when she came back from where she'd been and returned to her sweeping or dusting.

The women told stories then while I sat blocked in on either side by their knees and listened to their voices like the wind rising and falling, one story running and twining into another until I couldn't tell them apart. While the Old One shaped the newest patch and Edwina peeled carrots, they discussed the origin of their name— Selchie—the Old One repeating the legends of the magic seals of the Orkney Islands, where she had been born, the stories of powerful selchies who ruled under the sea. Occasionally these selchies shed their seal skins, took human forms, and begot children with those people of the land. But while on land, they were in mortal danger from hunters, possessive of their own kind.

"They had a great kingdom under the sea, they did," the Old One would say, and what was left of her Scottish burr vibrated softly on the underside of the words. "The selchies' rich lands stretched across the ocean floor, all theirs what they could swim over. But every now and again, a strangeness would come over one of them, some desire there weren't not a cure for. Then the others would have to let that selchie go to land, while they could only wish for his safe return."

The Old One went on at great length, one story reminding her of another and linking together in a great chain. Edwina often interrupted to remind her of a part she'd left out or told differently from the time before. They argued over whether the captured selchie was ever released; whether the Scottish lord's daughter returned with her selchie lover to the sea; where the selchies hid their seal skins while they walked on land. Every once in a while, the Old One leaned sideways and peered under the table at me. She shook her finger and said, "I know these stories. They tell true, and you must remember them."

The Old One and Edwina argued about the selchies with the same intensity with which they debated if Edwina should obey her father and marry Marshall Schmidt, the runty little son of a widowed farmer. They decided she should not, since the offer came not from love but from need of a woman to keep house for two bachelor men. Then they sang the ballad of the Great Selchie of Sule Skerry. The Old One with her wavery voice and Edwina, soft and slightly off key, sang how he begot a son and predicted his own death to his mortal woman. "You will marry a hunter good," they sang. "He will shoot both my young son and me."

Then after a moment of quiet the Old One sniffed— in either sorrow or indignation—and said, "And you know, Edwina, last names come from what our ancestors did, what they were. I married your grandfather because I wanted selchie blood in my children's veins." She snorted. "The man took after the human side of the family, surely as your father did."

"And you're praying I'll be the one to turn into a seal and swim off across a cornfield?" Edwina laughed and snapped a bean in two.

"You're barely seventeen, girl." The Old One yanked and tugged on the quilt patch so that a pooch of material suddenly turned in on itself and took its place flat on the pattern. "Who's to say what you'll be?"

Then after a moment of quiet, their hands moving continuously at the work in their laps, Edwina started humming the Selchie's song and the Old One invented a counterpoint, until another story crossed their minds or one asked the other if either had remembered to stir the soup.

Their images shifted in me like thunderclouds, and I made their stories into my own shapes. In the beginning I believed the Old One turned Edwina into a seal, and because I didn't know exactly what that was, I saw her woman's head on a massive animal body that was at once eel and cow and snake and cat. And because I had never been out of the flat midlands of Iowa and had only seen the ocean through the Old One's words, I imagined my house submerged at the bottom of a giant bathtub.

Then the Old One peeked under the table again, her head tilted sideways, and the whole room seemed turned, with the wall now the floor. She asked if I was sleepy, reached under the table, and held me tightly under my arms. She swung me up and out, dipping me slightly so I wouldn't knock my head on the table, whirled me in the air, and held me suspended, her arms not quite strong enough to hold me steady, so I wavered above her as if we were drifting in current or tide. I looked down on her bright old face and liked the way she looked, worn and comfortable, and liked the way she had sped me through the air as if I were flying or swimming, and liked the way she lowered me into her lap, tucked me in the crook of one arm, and laid the other over my hips like a blanket.

At first I was anxious, so sure the Prussian would not like me to be held by the Old One. But the Prussian was not here and the kitchen not her territory since the Old One had taken over. I rested my face against the Old One's shoulder. She smelled like cedar and lavender, and her touch was like a quilt. She hummed so softly that I felt the song more than heard it, and between hummings she explained the parts of her stories that I might not have understood. How seals have faces that are a cross between dogs without ears and babies with fur. How the ocean is green or blue or black, depending on its temper, or all those colors at once. How it gives up both nets of fish and the bloated bodies of the drowned. How the waves swell and rock, the lulling and never-ending rhythm stretching and rocking as far as one can see and feel.

Then the rise and fall of the Old One's breathing became that swell and rock, and with my head cradled against her chest, my mouth slack and eyes dazed, her voice became part of my dreams. Curled in her lap, her hands clasped around my waist, one side of my face sweaty from sleeping against her shoulder, I dreamed water covered the tops of the trees and steeple of the Episcopal church and ran past the miles of wheat and corn fields outside the town to the shore of a place where I'd never been.

In my dream, the water parted in front, closed in back of me, and then disappeared. I wore the Prussian's coat and waited for another, from the water, to meet me. But there was only bare, flat land, the ocean now only heat shimmers on the horizon, and the sea voices calling and singing were so distant I couldn't distinguish the words. I was sure the other should be there, one from the sea who understood it as I did the land, but there was no place for that other to be, save inside the earth I stood on.

I held more tightly to the Old One's finger. She tucked a lock of hair behind my ear and ran her fingertips across my forehead so lightly that I felt her phantom touch after she took her hand away. Wood scraped against wood, and imagining in my dream that it was the Prussian coming to chide me for stealing her seal coat, I struggled to sit forward. It was only Edwina scooting her chair away from the table. The Old One pulled me closer.

"Hush," she said. "Don't you worry."

She tucked me against her body, and I lay back in the circle of her arm, so close I smelled the coffee and warm milk on her breath and saw one white, bristly whisker on her chin. "I promise," she said and pressed her palm against the side of my face, "I'll stand the watch."

Then they were all gone—the hunter who would kill the seal, the deserted shore with no sea, the Prussian who would find me here. Just the Old One watching for intruders while I curled against her. Just her waiting to come get me if I became lost in my dreams. Just us together where my mother would not go.

Chapter One

❧

*M*Y PARENTS AND I LIVED in New Marango, Iowa, halfway between Storm and Spirit lakes, just east of the Little Sioux River. We lived in a big house where my father also had his medical office, two blocks from the private girls' academy where I attended school. My mother was beautiful, and our housekeepers, the Old One and Edwina, were my friends.

This was my nursery life until the summer I was twelve and Hailus Tucker came to stay. His coming marked the beginning of knowing, even of what I didn't want to know.

He was the son of a woman Mother had gone to boarding school with, and he planned to live with us until Christmas. Mother said he came for a rest, but the Old One told me she'd overheard my parents say that he'd had trouble he hoped wouldn't follow him to Iowa.

The week before he came was filled with extra cooking and cleaning. On the day he was to arrive, Mother, not Edwina, woke me. She stood holding a bundle of fresh sheets, though this was not the regular day to change linens. Her hair was neatly coiled, a blue and white apron tied over her dress.

"You have just enough time to get ready," she said. A pulse point throbbed under the lace collar hooked tightly around her throat. "We're late."

Then she disappeared into the hall. From downstairs came the smell of sausage, the soft clink of dishes and skillets ringing against the range. Across the street, the neighbor's dog yapped at the iceman.

I looked sleepily at the room as it was reflected in the mirror carved with dark scrolls of wood, at the green drapes and the wallpaper that at one moment appeared to be endlessly curling vines and in the next seemed to be a wall of faces, all with their tongues stuck out. It was too early to be late.

Then my mother returned, carrying my Sunday dress, though it was only Tuesday. "Get up now, Anna," she told me. She waited with her back turned while I put it on, and then with sharp precision she did up the long row of hooks and buttons down the back. "Tell your father it's time to eat. Please do that for me."

I passed Edwina, carrying a mop and bucket up the stairs. She pushed a lock of red hair off her forehead and made a face. "Your mother's making me clean behind and under the furniture, as if that young man will get down on his knees to inspect. She'll make us all crazy, she will."

She trudged up, banging the mop against the bucket more than was necessary, and I slipped into my father's office. Even he seemed unusually busy for so early in the day, glancing up from the records and files spread out all over his desk. "Good morning, Schatzie," he said.

I settled in the crook of his arm and pressed my face against his neck, his man smell mixed with lime toilet water and his beard pleasantly rough against my skin.

"We must be quick before the eggs get cold and your mother scolds us."

So we straightened the desk, and as we walked together down the hall to the dining room, he told me about the new baby he'd delivered the night before. How tiny and wrinkled she was, how she squalled in anger at being disturbed from the quiet sea of her womb.

"This baby had a caul." He sat down at the table. "Red hair and a caul." He shook out his napkin.

"A what?"

"A cap of membrane on her head. Like a hat of skin.

When I told Mrs. Selchie about it this morning, she said she'd seen only half a dozen in all her years of midwifing, but it means the child will be lucky and 'have the sight,' as she puts it. That means she'll have the ability to know more than the rest of us, to see what others miss. She said Edwina was born with a caul."

"That proves it's a foolish Scots superstition," my mother said, coming out of the kitchen to set a toast rack on the table, her white skirts flying. "Edwina can't see the dust she's to clean, let alone the furniture."

"Edwina said if you stand in front of a mirror at midnight on Midsummer's Eve, the face of your true love will appear behind you," I said. "But you can't turn around, or you'll both be cursed and terrible things will befall you."

"Edwina is telling you fairy tales. She no more can see a face than you can turn into a fish." Mother brushed invisible crumbs from the cloth with the back of her hand.

"There's no harm in folktales, Etta. They can't hurt the child."

"As long as she realizes they are untrue."

"Did I have a caul when I was born?"

"I don't think so," my father said.

"But weren't you there?"

"It makes no difference whether he was or wasn't, or you did or didn't," Mother interrupted. "There's nothing to see but what's directly before you."

What was before me was a cup, a spoon, and my father's hand beside mine on the cloth, my mother like a queen at the head of the table, and the sun beyond the windows so bright the air shimmered like water.

"Serve the plates, Will," she said and returned to the kitchen. My father and I watched the door swing until it ran out of momentum.

"Can the baby really see that way, with the sight?"

"Babies can't see much of anything, Schatzie."

Mother carried in the claw-footed coffeepot and set it on the silver trivet. Father said grace and then went on about the new baby's delivery for so long that finally Mother set her knife across the edge of her plate with a click.

"Please, Will, the breakfast table is not the place."

He looked up, startled. "It is what happened, how life is."

"Not now." She lifted her chin slightly in my direction. I pulled streams of yolk out of my egg's eye and drew their tendrils across the face of the plate. Father leaned back, his eyes narrowed as if he were trying to diagnose a difficult case. "All right, no more talk about babies, I promise." He buttered another piece of toast. "I spoke to Mrs. Geising yesterday, and she wants to stay on the farm."

Three weeks earlier Mr. Geising had caught his arm

in some machinery and bled to death before one of his sons found his body in the new wheat.

"But they cannot winter out there alone." Mother broke a biscuit in half.

"She insists on it and claims she can bring in the wheat with the help of the older boys. Besides, they must decide for themselves."

"Not when they don't know what is best." Mother rang the small bell standing at the rim of her plate, and Edwina appeared, to pour coffee.

"May I have some?" I asked.

"You're too young. It will stunt your growth."

Father motioned to me to scoot my chair closer to his and pushed his cup between us so I might take spoonfuls to sip.

"I've left the afternoon free to help you," he said.

"The train's expected at one, so perhaps you could leave at twelve," she answered.

"That doesn't seem necessary."

"What if there are only strangers there when he arrives?"

"We're strangers to him, Etta."

"Oh, no, Will. His mother was like a sister to me, and we've kept in touch all these years. He will be like family, I'm sure."

"Perhaps, but six months is a long visit even for a relative."

"Is he nice?" I asked.

"His mother is; I'm sure he is also."

"But what's he like?" I persisted.

"I haven't seen him since he was an infant, but he was a darling child with lovely dimples."

I began to think of the visitor as the little brother I'd occasionally half wished for. Then Mother left with Edwina to finish the guest room, Father kissed me and went off to his first patient, and I was left alone, counting the bongs of the kitchen clock striking nine. Almost five hours to wait.

I sat on the lowest step in the dark-paneled hall. A pier mirror hung at the bottom of the steps and reflected the Oriental carpet blooming red and blue flowers all the way to the second floor. I sat quietly hugging my knees and thought of each room of the house containing one person. All doors opened into the hall, and I was the only one to know what went on everywhere.

When I was little I would not sit here. I thought there was something I could not imagine the shape of at the top of the steps, something like night wind, which made a sound like voices I could not understand. I would not go upstairs by myself, afraid I would accidentally look into the face of the shape the wind had taken.

I shook off the chill of remembering and went out back to the outside entrance of the cellar, where the Old One was doing laundry. Two doors opened back over a mouth in the earth, and spiders crawled on walls that smelled damp and clammy, even under the fresh soapy steam that rose from the washtubs. I picked my way down the open-backed steps and found a spot to sit away from cobwebs that might brush my arms and face. The Old One bobbed up and down over the scrub board, a long white tendril of hair escaping from her bun and her forearms red from the water.

"Did you come to help, Anna Berter? We've enough work for an army of housekeepers today." She stopped to squeeze a pillowcase through the wringer and glanced at me. "Why are you dressed so soon for company, girl?"

"Mother told me to wear this."

"And what does she expect you to do all day, getted up like that?" The Old One dried her hands on her apron and took an everyday dress of mine from the basket of clothes to be washed. " 'Tis not all-out clean, but will do for the morning. Here," she said, and undid the buttons down my back. I held up my arms, and she skinned the Sunday clothes from me, the way she always had when I was little, and dropped the old dress over my head.

Edwina came down with a wicker laundry basket braced on one of her formidable hips and touched my head as she passed to set her load on the worktable. "Even with all this commotion over the visitor, Mrs. Berter's just told me Father will come tomorrow so they can both speak to me again."

"The woman thinks because your own mother's dead that she can step into her place." The Old One slapped a wadded-up sheet into the tub so hard the water sprayed up and sloshed over the edge. "You'd think Marshall Schmidt were their own son, the way they push him at you. But they're not the ones who'll roll over every morning to his pockmarked little face that not a single woman will have."

Ed sorted the clothes into piles. "We'll have the same conversation over again, I know we will."

Even I knew it by heart, Mr. Selchie's argument that Ed should marry his friend's son and my mother's agreement with him. They would tell her once again that there weren't many men of her station and she'd better marry this one, available and willing.

"Stick to your guns, girl. Don't be forced into taking what you won't have." The Old One slapped another sheet into the water.

"I just can't stand to think about him, Grandma." Ed dropped her large hands and moved close by the washtub.

The Old One touched her cheek with one wet finger. "He's naught but a little weasel, with nothing to recommend him."

"But Mrs. Berter frightens me, all her talk of me dying alone with no one to care for me."

"Look at your grandfather. What good was he?" The Old One pulled a sheet from under the water. "Taking me from my islands and leaving me nine months pregnant in a foreign land. I had to take care of myself, and I did."

"But she says I'll have no children if I don't marry now."

"You can always get children. Mrs. Berter were older than you when she were wed."

"Twenty-six," I said, "the same age as the visitor and two years older than Edwina."

They both turned to look at me, on a wooden box by the shelves of preserves lining one wall.

"See, Edwina, the young one knows." She smiled and nodded, then took two hobbled steps toward Ed and reached up to cup her face in her hands. "Will you die if you don't have a man? You're existing by your own self right now. That won't change. Look at all three of us here, at all the ages of life. Which of us could be made greater with the addition of Marshall Schmidt? He's subtraction, my girl. Did you not learn your sums at school?"

Then Ed began laughing, and she stooped to lean her face against her grandmother's. I moved nearer until the Old One pulled me close, her bony arm around my neck and Edwina's large breast pressed against my face, the smells of sweat and soap and wet sheets and water all around us.

"Don't let that Prussian woman get to you, child," the Old One said to Edwina. But I thought she was talking to me, the way she spoke low, the way I felt the vibrations of her words through her body touching mine. "Her people came from Prussia, and she was born rich, believing she's in charge of what's around her. She's had her sorrows to make her what she is. But you're not hers, and she has no right to tell you what to do. Do you hear me, child?"

Ed nodded, and so did I.

"You must do what you feel in your heart is true, and don't let none of the others stop you. Do you understand?"

The Old One hugged us more tightly to her. She and Edwina went back to their work, and for a time I stayed near, reading the labels on the preserves, the dark fruit shapes floating in their juice and bumping up against the glass when I tilted the jars. Then to pass the time I stuck clothespins together in different patterns. I sat in the sun and drew in the dirt with a stick the outline of the German Empire, the place where my grandparents had been born. I stood by the horses' stalls while they ate oats from their mangers and listened to their swish and stomp and huff. I drifted through all the rooms of the house and tried to see them new as Hailus Tucker would, and finally I lay facedown on my bed and watched purple-blue blotches swim in the dark behind my eyes.

When Mother called me for an early lunch, she ran her fingers over the red streaks on my face, left from lying on the spread, then pinched the collar of my dress between her fingers. "What have you done with your clothes, Anna?"

"I changed."

"Change back before we eat. You can't sit down at my table like that."

After Father left for the train station, the Prussian changed into a salmon-colored dress and waited in the parlor, frowning in concentration over a book in her lap. I stared out the glass panel on the front door, covered with a gauzy curtain that made the summer lawn look hoary with frost. I smoothed my skirt over my knees and pretended it was winter. I tried to imagine what a caul would feel like on my head. I sat up straighter and watched my face surface in the glass, my brown hair pulled back in braids, my eyes large and blue-green. I could not decide if I was pretty; certainly I was not in the way my mother was. I did not know if I thought the new baby would have the sight or if Ed should marry or if the Geisings should stay. The thing I was positive of was that I was tired of waiting for Hailus Tucker, and whoever he was, he had better be worth all this time spent on his behalf.

Chapter Two

$\mathcal{H}$AILUS TUCKER HAD SMOKY HAZEL eyes, the color of sky before a tornado, and a scar like white silk threads across his cheekbone. When Mother introduced us, he bowed, brushed my hand with his lips, and said, "A beauty, just like your mother."

I could feel the phantom pressure of his touch long after he'd released my hand. He made me feel grown up and beautiful when I was not.

Then Mother sent me to tell Mrs. Selchie we were ready for refreshments. The Old One looked up from the lemon half she was grinding over the cone of the squeezer.

"The look on your face, Anna Berter," she said and shook her head.

I blushed and fled to the parlor, not sure why I wanted to escape her sight. Mother and Father and Hailus talked interminably about trains and weather and the new motorcar Hailus's father had just purchased. My feet could not reach the floor flat, nor could I rest my back against the chair, but while they talked I sat smiling at him all the same, until the muscles in my face and back and legs hurt. All the while I squirmed inwardly, wondering how soon I could show him the house or walk him down to the stable. Several times he turned to me and asked about my schooling or pets or friends. He listened intently as I told him I had no pets, not many friends, and was a failure at spelling bees. Then Mother turned the conversation back to her topics, and Edwina brought in the lemonade. Her apron bow was coming undone, and her petticoat dipped in points of white beneath her hem. She presented the silver serving tray to Hailus and, when he looked up at her, belatedly remembered to curtsy.

He was no taller or older than Marshall Schmidt but was handsome and well-dressed and the only man I'd ever seen who wore a ring other than a wedding band. He didn't have a job, I found out, and talked about having traveled to Europe and South America, about seeing wild parrots and French cathedrals, Mayan ruins and Shakespeare's home. He described his last Atlantic crossing with schools of dolphin following the ship and immigrants crowded into steerage. Mother said she didn't know what we were to do with all those foreigners, and he explained how they were sorted at Ellis Island and the faulty ones sent back. Occasionally he smiled at me, and once he winked during Mother's long story about when she and Mrs. Tucker were girls. Then Father got up and excused himself to see an unexpected patient, and Hailus settled in.

"I was never a scholar like you, Mrs. Berter. To this day, Mother raves about how quick you were with your schoolwork. In fact, when I was about your age, Anna"—he turned to me—"I contracted scarlet fever and was confined to bed. After I was through the worst of it, I began to think the illness worth the time off. But then Mother hired a tutor, an old skinny man around forty, with a wart on his nose and two on his chin. I delighted in hiding his spectacles, or insisting I'd given him an assignment when there was no such paper in existence. He finally quit in disgust, and I malingered for weeks."

He grinned. "Later that same year I had to glue the pages of the headmaster's grade record together so I could convince him I had gotten a C instead of an F in history."

At first I held my face expressionless, because I did not know which expression was correct. I liked how bad he'd been, how he'd done what I had sometimes wished to do, how he was so engaging. But I was troubled that

I'd somehow be punished for his mischief, the way a whole class was sometimes kept after when one student acted up. Then Mother said, "Oh, Hailus," and laughed in shocked delight.

He went on, smiling and winking, leaning toward me as if I would understand. How it had been the night he and his friends stole privies and lined them up around a statue of Franklin Pierce in the city park. How he packed an iron dumbbell in his father's valise and set off firecrackers under the maid's chair.

Then, to my astonishment, Mother told stories of herself at boarding school, about how she short-sheeted the beds of some girls she didn't like or hid their homework. She leaned toward Hailus and explained how one of the girls cried because she thought her bed was broken and she would get in trouble.

"I know how that is." Hailus laughed. "Once my mother had an immigrant housekeeper who brought her child with her to work. I remember the girl's name was Anna Schalupe. Silly name, wasn't it? She had little beady eyes and dark hair all in a tangle, and she couldn't understand half of what we said to her. She always brought foul-smelling cheese sandwiches for lunch and would sit on the back stoop to eat, even in damp weather. So one morning I took her sandwich and covered the cheese with soap shavings. When it was time for lunch, she bit in and made the most terrible faces and complained in some

foreign language, but her mother berated her in gibberish
and then slapped her so hard I could hear the smack in
the next room. She shouted and hit until dumb little
Anna Schalupe ate all her lunch and was sick half the
afternoon."

The sweat from my glass spread out in a great wet
ring on my skirt that clung to my leg. I shifted the glass
to another spot. "How did you know what faces she made
if you were in the next room?" I asked.

"Pardon me?" Hailus said and turned.

"You said she made faces, then you heard the smack
in the next room. How could you do both?"

"I don't know." He laughed. "I suppose I imagined
part of that. You know how children are."

"Don't be so picky, Anna," Mother said.

"Yes, have mercy on me, Anna! I changed a detail
to make a story better, but I beg your pardon for it."

Hailus struck his breast with his fist three times and
smiled. Then Mother went on about all the parties she'd
planned for him in the next few weeks. I tried to imagine
my mother playing wicked tricks on her friends, but when
I could not, herself in her story became another person,
separate from the one before me. I tried to make excuses
for the soap and how Hailus laughed at Anna Schalupe
even now. She was different and dirty and didn't know
how to act. She deserved what had happened to her. But
all the reasons that would make his actions clever and

smart drowned in my imaginings of how it had been for her. "There is nothing wrong with your food," her mother must have said, as I had heard my own say. "Eat it and don't complain. The problem is all in your head." Then Anna ate, as if the bitter taste in her mouth were all imagination and what she knew could not be trusted. All the solids in her world must have turned to water then, when what was real to her was not to others.

My fingers went numb from holding the cold glass, but I didn't put it down, for fear of making a white mark on the table. Mother and Hailus went on talking and laughing until Father returned and suggested they take a walk.

"One thing first," Hailus said and excused himself. He brought back two packages in white tissue, gifts his mother had sent to my mother and me. When I tried to unwrap mine one-handed, it rolled off my lap and Father took the glass from me. "You're doing things the hard way, Anna," he said and handed me the gift.

Inside the tissue was a small blue velvet box with a tiny gold button that opened the lid. Inside the box were platinum filigree earrings, graceful teardrops ending in opals, soft blues and greens trapped in the milky stones.

I held up the earrings. Hailus leaned his head back against the cushions and smiled at my mother. "They go nicely with her eyes," he said. Then he crossed the room and knelt before me, held one earring against my ear and studied my face. I was so close to him, near enough to see the gold flecks in the green-brown of his eyes, the delicate whiteness of the scar through the ruddiness of his cheek. He looked at me closely, and his hand brushed my hair. "Yes, they are a success," he said, "the way they bring out the remarkable color of your eyes."

I touched the earring gingerly and brushed his hand with mine. He nodded again. "Yes, perfect."

Then he replaced the earring, and Father took the box from him. "They'll be lovely on you," he said and passed them to my mother.

She nodded also. "Lovely," she said, then handed them back to me. "When you are old enough to wear them."

I flushed and hid the box in my cupped hands. "Maybe when you're sixteen," she went on.

"The piercing is a simple procedure," Father said. "I could do it today."

"In time, Will. She truly is too young." Then she turned to Hailus. "But they are beautiful, and she will save them until it's time. Won't you, Anna?"

I nodded, but all the flesh around my smile felt as if it would crack and drop off. She was a Prussian, just as the Old One had said in the laundry a few hours before, taking over what was not hers, what had not been given.

Then she opened her gift, earrings similar to mine but set with onyx and pearl. She exclaimed over them and changed them with the sapphire ones she was wearing. Hailus leaned close to her, inspecting first one, then the other, and touching them in turn. "They were made for you," he told her.

"Exceptional," Father said.

"How kind," she told Hailus and laid her hand on his arm. "Anna, take the earrings upstairs and put them in my dresser."

"Mine too?"

"So they won't be lost," she said. "Then begin your thank-you note to Mrs. Tucker."

I stood at my bedroom window and watched Father and Hailus walk down the long drive to the street. They stopped at a large rose bed filled with yellow blooms and then at the bronze mastiff Mother had ordered the year before from Saint Louis. Hailus held his fist in front of the metal teeth, and I heard their laughter across the lawn. Then Mother came out and linked her arms between them.

I sat down before the mirror at my dressing table and unbraided my hair, letting it fall in crimps to my shoulders. I held one earring in place, its tip pointed to the curve of my throat. It was not fair, the way I had to imagine what the earrings would look like if I could wear them properly. Not right. I stretched one lobe taut and pinched the earring's post tightly between my fingers, pressed the point against my flesh. A quick push and it would be through. The opal dangled by the curve of my jaw and grazed my skin. My breathing echoed in my head like waves sounding in a shell. I couldn't do it, turn the swaying and dancing into piercing. I watched the silver swing against the line of my throat and pulled my hair up in a graceful loop that showed off the strong curve of my cheekbones and the largeness of my eyes. Not beautiful but certainly lovelier than I had hoped, with this sidelong look like a czarina's or my mother's.

I wanted Hailus Tucker to reach out again to touch the opal lightly with his fingers. Yet I couldn't push it through. I could already hear my mother saying to me, "What have you done, Anna? How could you do that to yourself?" I didn't know. I put the earrings back in their case and carried them to my mother's dresser, shut them in a drawer, and turned the key.

Later that evening, when Father came up to tell me good night, he stood at the threshold as he always did, as if he were unable to pass through that door into the territory of my room. "I'm sorry about this afternoon," he said.

"Why?" I asked and busied myself at the dresser.

"That Mother might have embarrassed you."

"No. I didn't want them anyway, not something I have to get holes put in my ears for."

"Oh. It is all right, then?"

"I'd rather he'd brought me a book or drawing pencils."

"Then you are fine?"

"Sleepy."

"I'll see you at breakfast, then."

"Yes."

"Good night," he said. "Sleep tight."

I shut the door then and locked it, something Mother never allowed me. But I felt as if I were changing shape and wished to be out of Father's sight. I was afraid I was turning into something he could not love, but I wanted to change all the same. I lay in the dark and played the afternoon over the way I wished it had happened, my ears already pierced to slip the metal through, Hailus moving close, and Father gone so that he could not see. I did not even know why this was so important or why the peaceful house seemed filled with wind.

Then Anna Schalupe appeared in my dark. I tried to think of her as a character made up for a book, a witch or stepsister. But she kept changing back to herself, the child whose truth had been denied. The images would not hold still that night, and I couldn't stop picturing myself wearing earrings, though I was sure, as I had told my father, there was nothing I wanted less. I lay awake long into the night, not able to straighten the sheets or find a comfortable position to sleep in, trying out conversations I would have with Hailus the next morning at breakfast, imagining how he would look, and half hearing the night sounds outside, a dog baying and a drunk singing so far away I could not understand the words.

Chapter Three

WHEN I WENT DOWN FOR breakfast the next morning, Father was already out on calls, and Mother and Hailus were still in bed. I ate in the kitchen, while the Old One rolled out dough for pies and Edwina mucked out the stable, since the boy who usually did it had sprained his wrist.

"She won't go in those stalls unless the horses are away, you know." The Old One snorted in disgust and rubbed more flour on the rolling pin. "Says the beasts want to step on her and she can see it in their eyes, she can."

"But I thought she had the sight."

"Who told you that foolishness?"

"You told Father."

"I said she were born with a caul, which is not the same as having the sight. What she's seeing in this case is an excuse not to muck out those stalls. And on top of that, she's mooning over that young man of your mother's, as if she could fall in love from just serving him a glass of lemonade."

"A cookie too."

"Well, that makes all the difference."

Then Edwina came in with bits of hay stuck along the hem of her apron and washed her face and hands in the sink. "I won't do that anymore," she said. "She's going to have to hire another boy until the first one heals; I'm not going in another stall."

"The list of what you won't be doing is getting longer than the one of what you will." The Old One shaped a circle of dough to the bends of the pan.

Ed sat down across from me at the table and ran her hands over her flushed face. "It's not just the mucking I hate. It's getting all hot down in those stalls and smelling like dray horses for the rest of the day."

"They're purebred Morgans," I told her.

"That don't make them smell any better." Edwina sniffed. "And would you look at that!" She bent over and picked the hay bits out of her shoelaces and apron hem. "I look like a bumpkin just come out of the fields."

"Since when are you being so particular about your looks?" the Old One asked.

"Can't a woman take pride in her looks?" Ed smoothed her skirt over her lap. "Especially when there's a gentleman around."

"The Doctor's always been here. We weren't needing any spare gentlemen."

"You weren't around Mr. Tucker like I was. When I took his bags up to his room and showed him the bath and all, he didn't treat me like a serving girl. He called me 'Miss Edwina' and bowed and smiled. He told me I had hair like a Scottish queen."

"He's turned your head, he has," the Old One said.

"You always told me my hair was pretty."

"Of course, child. That's not what I meant."

Then I caught a slight motion out of the corner of my eye. Hailus was at the door, holding it open with one hand, his other shoved in the pocket of a maroon dressing gown with tasseled ties. I didn't know how long he'd stood there, leaning casually against the jamb, but when I noticed him, he opened the door wide and came in. His hair was shiny with pomade, and with his straight nose and strong chin he looked like the man in the Arrow shirt advertisements, except for a small nick of blood where he'd cut himself shaving.

"Go on into the dining room, Mr. Tucker," the Old One said. "I'll bring you coffee there."

"No need, Mrs. Selchie. If you'll show me where the cups are, I'll get my own." He began opening cupboards, got down a cup, poured his own coffee, and sat next to me. After a few sips he asked Edwina if she put eggshells in the grounds to get the mellow flavor. She blushed and mumbled that her grandmother did all the cooking. Then before any of us knew it, Hailus was breaking brown eggs in a bowl and talking about French omelets with mushrooms and peppers while he chopped and stirred. The Old One leaned over the skillet and kept telling him it looked like he was just doing some fancy scrambling, until he set a golden-brown pocket before her and she admitted it was indeed special. Then he made more and in turn served Edwina and myself, and we agreed, all chewing and nodding, that there was no more lovely way to eat an egg.

"You should be letting us fix your meal," Edwina said. "It's not right for a guest to be working in the kitchen."

"I'm not like other guests," Hailus told her. "We'll do things differently while I'm around."

"Mrs. Berter told us to take special care of you," she said.

"Then I'll put this right with Mrs. Berter, so don't

you mind. But if you want to help, you can clean up my mess while Anna and I take some air."

Then he took two cups of coffee and stood by the door. "Come, Anna, show me the back garden and stalls, the ones I saw from my window."

He handed me a cup, and I walked with him down the rows of sweet corn beginning to tassel and beans tied to their poles, hot coffee sloshing over my hand until I spilled enough for it not to matter how I jiggled the cup. He asked me to name the zinnias and phlox the Old One had planted and alyssum and squash I'd set the seeds for. Alone with him, I began to feel as if this were my house and yard, and I guided him around the way I'd seen Mother do with curious guests from town, pointing left and right, explaining the plantings in various beds, how first the Emperor tulips bloomed here, to be replaced by the daylilies and then the mums. The Old One did our gardening, except for the heavy work, but I went on as if the vegetables and blooms were all my plan. Hailus and I walked slowly down an avenue of fruit trees, cherry and plum and peach and apple, then under the arch of vine in the small grape arbor and past the round gazebo on our way to the stalls.

As we circled the stable and started back up toward the house, Ed came out to hang towels on the line. "Ah, look," Hailus said. "They look like flags, and Miss Selchie's hair's in flame."

And indeed, with the white towels billowing and the sun behind Ed lighting up the red in her hair, the familiar yard was transformed, and she looked beautiful and graceful as she stretched to fold the towel over the line.

"Is she engaged?"

"Who?"

"Miss Selchie." He nodded in her direction.

I shrugged. "Almost everybody wants her to marry Marshall Schmidt, but she doesn't like him and the Old One says not to give in."

"The Old One?"

"It's what I called her grandmother, Mrs. Selchie, when I was little."

Then he asked me too many questions about them, but I kept answering because I loved his attention and being the keeper of the knowledge.

"What's wrong with the man in question?" he said finally.

I shrugged again. "He's all right. Just nothing special."

"She's holding out on them all, then?"

"Edwina's stubborn. She won't give in to anyone."

As I came up the rise of the yard with Ed standing among the waving towels, I forgot how she worried about not marrying or doing the wrong thing, about how she went to the Old One for comfort and advice. At that moment Ed seemed as strong and sure as I had imagined her for Hailus, and I was as grown up as he had made me believe.

DURING THE NEXT FEW WEEKS, Mother invited all of New Marango society to dinner or luncheon or tea to meet Hailus. The table was set with damask cloths and Haviland china, tiny spoons and dishes of salt at every place, and bouquets of flowers, kept fresh in the icebox. My best shoes felt light on my feet, and our names appeared frequently in the paper: "Mrs. Wilhelm Berter Entertains for Out-of-Town Guest."

Mother and Ed and the Old One were so busy with preparations, they hardly had time for me or Hailus. Until the moment the company arrived, he and I were left to our own devices and most often spent this empty time walking in the back gardens or reading and talking in the gazebo next to the grape arbor. He told me the gossip he'd heard, and I found out more about the people he'd just met than I'd known about them my whole life. Lucy Minchion told him she had had a twin who wasn't "right." Lizzie Ott whispered that her grandfather had "kept" a woman at the hotel until the neighbors ran her out of town.

He also told me what my mother had confided to him, things she would never tell me. She said Douglas Selchie was ready to beat Edwina if she didn't listen to reason about getting married, and in the gazebo Hailus and I discussed this information the way my parents talked over issues at the breakfast table. I told him I thought Ed would be unhappy with Marshall Schmidt but I didn't know how she could convince her father of that. Hailus said he thought Edwina should run away and that he had offered her money and help if she should decide to leave. Then he looked off across the lawn, his jaw set and eyes serious, and I thought of him as Ed's savior.

But then the social motion was reversed, and Mother's guests invited her and Hailus in return to their teas and luncheons and dinners. I wandered restlessly around and couldn't settle into any task. I sat staring out windows at the empty yard or mindlessly watching the household move past me. Gradually I sensed the changes, but I cannot say exactly what I noticed. Perhaps something in the similarity between Mother's and Ed's expressions when Hailus came into a room, or the way they attended to their hair and clothing, or maybe just the bright key of their laughter. I had not yet learned to name what was before me and even now must guess at how I knew it.

But late one morning after I came in from outside, I saw clearly for the first time the shape of the thing that was coming. I thought the Old One and Ed were doing laundry in the cellar and the others were out, but as I started up the stairs I heard soft voices in the hall above me. I stopped on the landing. The afternoon light through the round window broke into rainbows along its beveled edge, and the voices were a rising-falling hum. I shut my eyes and felt the solidness fall away beneath my feet. For a moment I believed the voices were the night sounds I used to imagine as a child, and my old fear of them returned. But as I listened the sound divided itself in two, still soft as fog in early light. Then the voices sharpened and took shape, the way a rabbit in the grass stared at but not recognized suddenly takes form.

She said, ". . . with me, Mr. Tucker."

He said, "Oh, Edwina, you'll break my heart."

The next words were lost in low laughter and the rustle of her skirts. I leaned back against the wall, anxious over being caught eavesdropping, but something else besides, I wasn't sure of what. Hailus and Edwina teasing and joking in an empty hall?

Then Edwina's words began popping clearly to the surface: *No. Not here. I'm not that.* The rustling quicker and sharper. I began to move downstairs step by step, when the Prussian on her way in from an appointment appeared behind the snowy curtain at the front door. She shifted brown parcels from arm to arm, freed a hand, and fumbled with the knob. I scrambled quickly back up. Edwina's broad back was to me, her apron sweeping over the slope of her hips. Hailus rested his head on her shoulder and buried his face against her neck. When he looked

up, he pushed her away, and Ed whirled around, flushed
red as flame.

"Good morning, Anna," Hailus said, moving between me and Edwina.

"Mother's home," I told them.

Edwina stood frozen for a moment, then swooped
down on her mop and pail and vanished into the bathroom. I started toward my room, the wall sliding across
my back as I edged sideways past him and away from the
Prussian. He reached out and grabbed my hand.

"Don't tell her, Anna," he said low under his breath.
"You'll get Ed in trouble."

I liked the touch of his hand on my skin, the dark
curve of eyelashes against his cheek, the flecks of green
in his eyes.

"Please don't tell."

I wasn't thinking of Edwina and I didn't know what
I'd tell, especially not to the Prussian and not about him.
There was nothing but the grip of his hand around my
wrist, the way his fingers circled and his muscles tensed.
Just Hailus waiting for my reply, when I had none.

Then suddenly he took my arm firmly and guided
me toward the steps. "Just agree with me," he whispered.
"Just do it."

He jerked his head in the direction of the steps, then
smiled, though he was clutching my arm so tightly I felt

bruises rising under his fingers. Under the sound of Edwina banging around in the bath, I heard the Prussian's footsteps already on the landing. He was chattering about teaching me to play mumblety-peg, and we came around the corner as she mounted the last steps.

"Etta, you're home," he said. "Anna and I were just on our way out. I was going to teach her a game I know."

Then he nudged me around her and took the parcels from her arms. "Let me take these for you," he said. "Tell me how your morning's been."

I fled down the steps, but as I closed the front door behind me, I heard them talking, their voices losing shape and becoming one murmur from the upstairs hall. I ran out on the sunny lawn and sat for quite a while, leaning against one front leg of the bronze mastiff and listening to insects hum. I tried to look at nothing and think of less, but the image of Hailus's arms around Edwina and his head on her shoulder kept resurfacing. I closed my eyes and pushed it back down under the darkness there. But it reappeared, and this time Mother's figure replaced Edwina's, and Hailus, his fingers in her chestnut hair, looked up over the slope of her shoulder at me standing in the hall filled with voices I didn't want to hear.

AFTER THAT, HAILUS ASSUMED WE were conspirators and always found time to spend with me. At first I was uncomfortable, but Hailus went on as if nothing had happened, and soon I convinced myself that nothing had. A week later Douglas Selchie came to pick up Ed, but she wouldn't leave with him until Father told her that she must. That evening as Hailus and I were playing Chinese checkers by the front window, the sky going dark blue beyond us and fireflies blinking on the lawn, Mrs. Geising came to talk to Father about hiring help to bring in the wheat.

"I thought they were leaving town," Hailus said.

"I don't think so."

"Etta said they were, at least if she had anything to do with it."

I shrugged and moved a green marble closer to the center. Hailus leaned his elbows on the table and hunched over the board. "She also said Mr. Selchie has reached the end of his patience with Edwina. He said it's an embarrassment and a burden to have a twenty-four-year-old daughter on his hands."

His scalp showed fish-white between the narrow comb furrows in his hair. It startled me to find something unattractive, even repulsive, about Hailus, and I looked away.

Hailus shook his head. "Your mother told me Mr. Selchie is going to throw her out."

"But he's her father."

"That doesn't mean he has to keep her, not if she won't do as he says. I told her she should beat him to the punch and run away before he can do anything to her."

I moved my palm lightly in a circle over the marbles, cool and smooth under my hand. "Can she just leave like that?"

"Of course, but we might have to help her."

Then Mother came in and asked if I had finished straightening my closet, as she had told me to do earlier. I accidentally bumped the table, and marbles rolled from one arm of the star to another, the colors mixing and settling into the wrong spots. She looked down at the board and moved two blue marbles back to their correct places. "Close the door on your way out, Anna."

But I left it ajar and listened quietly in the hall.

"It's the same issue I told you about last week," she told Hailus. "Will acts as if he's going out there to take in the crops for the Geisings himself. He's getting as stubborn as Edwina."

"It's out of your hands, Etta."

"I just worry about people who put themselves in danger without half a thought to what could happen. You know about my own parents in a similar situation."

Then she went on about the Geisings and Edwina, the parts I already knew, and I tiptoed upstairs to do my chore as quickly as possible. When I returned, they were laughing, and I pushed the door open ever so slightly so as to hear them more clearly.

"That reminds me of a young man who lived two

doors from my father's house," my mother said. "I can't imagine why I've thought of him after all these years."

"His name?"

"Edward Mather. He long ago moved to Des Moines, and no one's heard from him since, but then he lived too close and dropped in often. I was always polite, and he mistook that for encouragement. During his many calls he began asking if I'd sit on his lap. He always sat in the chair you're in, Hailus, that I brought from my father's house. He'd sit there and pat his knees." She demonstrated. " 'Right here, Miss Etta, give me the honor of sitting right here,' he'd say.

"Well, finally I grew tired of putting him off and one day said, 'Mr. Mather, I've decided to give you your wish.' "

"You didn't!"

"I did," she said. "I sat on his lap. And sat. And sat. And sat." She laughed. "He kept asking if I'd prefer another chair, or if I cared to change position. I told him I was perfectly fine, though I was quite cramped and my right foot fell asleep. With my weight on him, I can't imagine what pain he must have been in. But we kept sitting, it must have been two hours or more." She paused again. "Finally," she said, "he began to cry."

I wanted to see her face then and pushed the door all the way open, pretending I'd just come back from upstairs. She smiled brightly and coyly, even as she asked if I was finished, then abruptly turned to Hailus and suggested a game of whist. I watched them play, quiet but for the shuffle and slap of cards, her hand resting loosely over the edge of the table while she waited for him to deal and their heads inclined toward each other. When Mrs. Geising left, I wandered into my father's office and sat across from him in the chair reserved for patients. A moth fluttered in his lamp's yellow light. I kicked one heel against the chair leg and finally said, "Did you know Edward Mather?"

Father glanced up from the accounts Mrs. Geising had left him. "A school friend of yours?"

"A man Mother sat on."

He looked puzzled for a moment, then smiled. "Oh, yes, she was very proud of that. It was a famous story."

"Where did you hear about it?"

"From her."

"She told you?"

"Mr. Mather certainly didn't."

"What did you think?"

"That I should never ask her to sit on my lap."

He turned a page, and I watched the moth circle.

"Are the Geisings staying?"

"At the farm?"

"Yes."

"Of course," he said. "I've talked to Thomas Rafferty

about giving them a loan on their property to get them through the summer. Do you know him?"

"Mother's said that I shouldn't talk to him."

"Your mother's looking out for your own good. But Rafferty is useful in his way."

"What way is that?"

He glanced over the papers again and made a notation with his pen. "You're full of questions tonight."

"I just was wondering if the loan would make it all right for them."

"What's made you so curious?"

"Nothing. A thing Mother told Hailus about the Geisings."

"Your mother has her own thoughts about them, but the majority goes against her this time."

"Umm," I said and went out to sit on the porch, where yellow light fell in the shape of windows and the thin moon spilled watery white on the lawn. I pulled at a stick of wicker coming unwoven from my chair until I worked it loose to suck on. I wanted to ask my father about so many things I didn't yet have names for, about Edwina in the hall and my mother in the parlor and Hailus all around. About the Geisings and how my grandparents were like them. But I couldn't see shapes clearly or tell if they had substance.

I tried to form the questions I wanted to ask, but the

only thing I heard distinctly was the Prussian and her litany of answers that stopped me from knowing.

What do you mean?

It is none of your business.

Young girls don't need to know such things.

In the dark I could make out the silhouette of the bronze mastiff, its pointed ears and heavy muzzle. If I hadn't already known what it was, I would have wondered if it was a living dog, standing tensed to attack. Beyond it, I could not identify the shapes in the familiar yard to tell if they were bush or shadow or deer, but I stared so long I began to imagine some of the shadows moved like men hunched over and creeping from one cover to another. I began to imagine I'd dreamed all the questions too. If there were anything to explain, Father would surely tell me.

Hailus and Mother finished their game, and she stood at the door in the dark hall. She laid one hand flat against the screen and looked out for a moment. I could not see her face clearly, just the outline of a woman with her hand raised in greeting or farewell or warning. She held the door open for me and stepped back to let me in. "I'll braid your hair for you before bed," she told me. "It'll be cooler off your neck."

Hailus leaned in the parlor doorway, his arms folded across his chest and his shadow falling long into the hall. I reached over quickly and switched on the light.

Chapter Four

FATHER NEITHER TRUSTED NOR WAS handy with mechanical things, but by July Hailus had convinced him to buy an automobile, and they went to Des Moines together to bring it back, shiny black and full of reflections, a silver emblem on its hood. Father was proud of himself for owning such a machine, only the fourth in town, and it seemed the one thing he and Hailus had a common interest in. But although he and Hailus drove around the neighborhood and out in the farmland with both of them in dusters and goggles, he still took the horses when he went alone on calls.

I was disappointed Father didn't take to the machinery with the confidence Hailus did. But Hailus drove us everywhere we needed to go or just around if we couldn't think of a destination. He picked up Ed and the Old One from their house each day, delivered our groceries, and ran errands for Mother. He helped her out at the curb of the dry goods store or dress shop, then waited with one hand draped over the steering wheel, his boater pushed back on his head, until she returned. Later he and I went driving alone, when the town was still in the noon heat and Mother rested in her room.

The first time he backed down the driveway and out into the street, it seemed we moved so fast I couldn't help clutching at the edge of the seat. But then Hailus pulled me next to him. He kept his arm around me, though I had to sit a little sideways to keep my knees from the gearshift on the floor. "It's all right, Anna," he said and squeezed my shoulder. "I wouldn't hurt you for the world, but I must show you how we can fly."

He accelerated to the speed of horses running. I'd gone that fast before, but never for as long as the car could take us. The city limit sign passed by and dust swirled, all behind us lost in the wonderful brown cloud we'd made like a tornado, he and I the wind itself.

We drew even with a farm team and then quickly were past. A hay wagon pulled out of a lane, and Hailus honked and waved at the driver, whose horses reared in fright. Then they, too, were past, lost in the swirling dust, while before us stretched the flat bright fields in the shadowless noon.

"I could drive like this forever," he shouted.

At that moment it seemed as if nothing would ever stop us. The universe was but a great field of green and a greater one of blue, and Hailus and I traveled across the face of Iowa toward the thin line between them. I held my hand out the window to feel the slap of the wind we made. Hailus sang "Barbry Allen" in his pretty tenor and gestured out the window like an opera singer to the corn.

"I don't know what it is," he said, "but I hate to hear about dying for love in these songs. It gives me the heebie-jeebies."

He shivered and chattered his teeth, and we laughed. Later that night, when the house seemed full of whispers and footsteps, the song's words sang heavy and dark inside me.

> *Better for time that you shall never be . . .*
> *I die for him tomorrow.*

But by the next morning I'd forgotten, and when Hailus came down for breakfast, his face swollen from sleep, I pestered him to take me for another ride.

"It's too early to talk about this," he complained.

"Promise you'll take me."

"Not now, Anna."

"Later?"

He peered at me over his coffee cup and kept sipping. Finally he said, "If you leave me alone now, later I'll teach you to drive."

"Yes! Will you?"

"On two conditions." He ran his finger around the inside of his cup handle. "First, you don't tell."

"Never, I promise. Cross my heart," I said.

"Second," he said, "you do me some little favors."

So it began. The wondrous afternoons of sun and flying, the wheel in my hands and Hailus helping me with the gears and clutch, all that solid and magic machinery that I could run and control, or thought I could. Whenever I seemed to be heading toward a ditch, Hailus would grab the wheel and turn us back in the right direction. Then he explained how to be gentle in my movements so as not to "startle the machinery," as he called it, and I gradually learned to steer straight and true. He seemed to understand the car so thoroughly that I began to feel invulnerable and drive more recklessly, snaking down the road in great fat curves, pushing with my toes against the gas, and swooping in circles around the square of a crossroads. When Hailus tired of careening and took over again, I liked to lean back and close my eyes, my hand riding the slipstream outside the window. Sometimes I rested against the door and followed the wires above me that curved between poles, each pole making its own swooshing sound as we passed, and on one of those afternoons, in the middle of what seemed nowhere, Hailus drove slowly down a side road where we'd never gone before. The air was heavy with dust and heat haze, and we felt lazy from the weather. He steered with one hand and looked more at the fields than at where he was going. I pointed to a grove of trees on a rise and beyond that the river, silver in the distance. "That's the Little Sioux and this is Donner's Grove, where we picnic sometimes."

"Donner's? Your mother's mentioned that. She was born close by."

"Out here?"

"On your grandparents' farm. She said it lay between Donner's and the river."

"Grandpa never farmed. He lived in town."

Hailus told me that might be so, but the way he understood it, when my grandparents arrived from Prussia they came to stay on a farm near here. My grandmother Anna was carrying my mother then, and everyone advised her to winter in town since her time was so near. But she wouldn't hear of it, and out at the farm, during a blizzard so terrible cattle were frozen in the fields and the earth was covered over in drifts, she went into labor. By the time the neighbors got through, she was dead, lying stretched out on the bed with my grandfather sitting next to her and holding the baby, my mother, the two of them wrapped in all the blankets and sheets.

Hailus didn't know what had gone wrong. "Female troubles," he supposed, "the baby lying crooked or something." He hadn't bothered to ask my mother the details and told the whole story as if it were one of those exaggerated and horrifying tales that had happened to characters out of Poe.

"The dead one was Anna," I told him. "That's who I was named for."

The car trembled beneath us, and insects buzzed in the fields, an occasional cicada louder than the rest.

"I didn't know they hadn't told you."

"I thought she had just closed her eyes like sleeping," I said, feeling anxious, though she had died again with the telling of the story. I watched out the window at the neat rows of corn, the way I could see straight up to the end of every line. He accelerated and turned into the grove. A strand of my hair lifted in the wind and blew across my eyes.

"Don't tell them I told you," he said. "Not any of it."

"I won't," I answered and looked through the trees for a farmhouse. I half expected my grandmother to be standing in a field or by the roadside, and when she wasn't, I pictured her there anyway beside the tasseled rows of corn and wheat stubble and straw bales. After a while

Hailus began to whistle, and I had a fleeting image of a baby wrapped in a quilt and held by her father in a sky filled with snow, but the image would not stay, in all that sun around me. Besides, it did no good to keep it. I could not tell my mother I was sorry for what I was not supposed to know. I started whistling along with Hailus, and then we sang "Cherries Are Ripe" all the way home.

AFTER THAT, HAILUS TOOK IT upon himself to pass on the Prussian's confidences, but always on the condition that the sharing of the secrets he revealed became a new secret we kept from the others. Mother had told him her boarding school, the one she wished me to attend in two years, had been a terrible, ugly place. She told him her father would not allow her to come home for Christmas vacations when she was there, because he feared her train would be stranded in a snowstorm and all the passengers would freeze to death. She said she disliked the way Father had to leave her in the night to attend to his patients, especially the ones who weren't that sick. But for all the newness of this information, there was something curiously familiar about it, as if I'd known it once but forgotten until Hailus reminded me.

He told me her stories—about boys she had had crushes on, about parties and outings, and about being afraid of a dead cow and calf she had seen while walking with my grandfather when she was seven. But after I'd heard so many stories that contradicted what I had assumed about her or what she had told me about herself, I began to expect her doppelgängers to appear around and behind her. Often during this period she told me to stop staring because it was rude, but I couldn't help waiting for a glimpse of the woman Hailus knew, a break in the facade of the one who was my mother. I began to imagine her opening and opening again like a set of wooden nesting dolls, with other versions of herself inside.

I even tried to trick her, but when I asked about the boarding school, she told me, as she had for years, what a fine education and lovely manners I would receive there, if she could talk Father into letting me go. I gave up trying, though I couldn't get rid of the eerie sense that she had left part of herself at each place where she had been and I would find her in town, at school, and waiting at the grove. Not her as she was in the flesh, of course, but her as baby or schoolgirl or young bride, who would report back to the self who was my mother. I could have no secrets from her—except, by some illogical twist, when I was with Hailus in the car or with the Old One, who seemed to have an equal strength and thus a defense against her.

At any rate, I adored Hailus for telling secrets and claiming me as his. He gave me a kind of power, and at moments I felt myself bigger and stronger than the Prussian and all her others. It was then I became like hawks flying and seals swimming, though often it was the movement of the car that helped with those illusions.

In payment, I became his go-between and lookout. He told me Edwina needed desperately to talk about her "situation" and make plans for her leaving. His eyes glowed, and his chin set in a determined way, like our minister when he leaned forward in his pulpit. So I did for Hailus what frightened me, and felt righteous about it even in my fear. I delivered notes Edwina read with painstaking slowness, and hung on the fence as lookout while he met her in the stable. I turned keys softly in locks or left doors ajar or distracted the Prussian and the Old One with conversation so they wouldn't notice when Ed wasn't around. Quickly the special favors became as frequent as the afternoon drives had been, and my feeling of mission became habit. The week before school started, Hailus asked me if I'd beg the Prussian for a special picnic, just him, myself, and Ed.

"Why don't you ask her yourself?" I said.

"It would be better if you do."

"I don't care about a picnic."

"Anna," he said, taking my arm and drawing me to a corner of the hall, though no one was near. "Ed's father is close to forcing the marriage. Etta told me. We have to act quickly."

Then I felt selfish and mean and went to my room to practice what I would say to the Prussian. I finally told her I wanted to entertain Hailus with a special end-of-summer party, with him as my guest and Edwina as the maid, the way I would have to take care of entertaining when I was grown. The Prussian lifted one eyebrow and said, "Of course. What good practice for you. I'll tell Mrs. Selchie what to pack in the hamper. Or would you rather plan the menu yourself?"

Later Hailus told me she'd asked him to be patient with the "tea party," as she called it. He assured her of his fondness for me, how happy he was, as a member of the family, to do anything for me. "She was genuinely touched," he said. Meanwhile my imagination was filled with scenarios of Hailus riding off on horseback, with Edwina before him and me behind, or us flagging down a prairie train and traveling off to places of our own. None of this had anything to do with what was possible, nor even with what had been planned, but I couldn't stop myself. Even when the Old One caught me alone before we left and asked me to keep an eye on Ed, I promised without hesitation, though there seemed no reason for her caution.

But as soon as we were out of sight of the house, Hailus stopped the car. "Would you get out a minute, Anna?" he asked me. "Let Edwina in front."

She sat blushing in the back seat, her huge hands

grasping the handle of the picnic hamper held squarely on her enormous lap.

"Well, come on, you two," Hailus said.

Edwina glanced at me. I hesitated, then shrugged. She put the hamper down and climbed in next to Hailus. As she passed, she gave my arm a quick squeeze, but I stood beside the car's two open doors and kicked at the dust. "Here," Ed told me and patted the seat. Hailus put his arm over her shoulder and leaned around her to look at me. "Yes, sit with us, Anna."

"There's not room," I said, though there was, and got in the back seat. All the way to the grove, she kept constantly looking over at him, and hummings and laughter drifted between them. Then I was afraid of what I had done. Made up stories about saving Ed and believed them, though when she inclined her head and he brushed her forehead with a kiss, I couldn't help but see what was going on, and I flinched at the touch between them. She cupped his hand in hers and kissed his palm with small hungry kisses. I looked out at the fields.

All through lunch they fed each other bites of sandwich or fruit. At first Edwina had been shy and pulled back from Hailus, but he told her, "Anna knows about us. She doesn't mind."

Then she let him draw her close and take a piece of cheese from between her lips. I picked at my food, and they tried to tease me into a better mood. But when I wouldn't smile, Hailus grabbed Ed and tickled her until tears ran down her cheeks.

"I'll show you what I like, Anna," he said, "a happy woman. If you won't laugh, Ed'll have to shriek for both of you." Then he kissed her soundly, and her eyes went soft. I got up and walked away, but Hailus came after me and put his arm around my shoulder. "Ah, Anna, don't be cross. Ed's had such a hard time, she needs this. A day to get all the attention. Can't you help me?"

He was so handsome, the way the curls lay over his forehead and the thin scar crossed his cheek. He stood square in front of me, resting his hands on my shoulders. "Look, if you go for a long walk, it'll please us both. Please, Anna, can't you do this for me? I'll make it up to you later."

He glanced to the side, just a quick movement he hoped I wouldn't notice, as if he were afraid Edwina would escape. I left them then and walked to the far end of the grove, an island of trees in the flat fields, and stood on its rise above the prairie. Far beyond, the river lay like heat shimmer between patches of field, and the sun hit in quick flashes on the water. I thought of walking to the river, just starting out by myself and leaving Hailus to explain to my parents where I'd gone. But I stood even with the trees at the edge of the grove, the moat of grasses and crops beyond like something to drown in.

The gnats pestered my eyes and I walked the perimeter

of the grove, hoping the motion would stop their biting. I couldn't go back in the direction of the road and the clearing where Hailus and Ed were, but kept retracing the border at the opposite end, which butted up into the fields. I kept my head down, noticing the grasses and underbrush along the trail and thinking on a story my mother had told Hailus recently about when she was small. My grandfather had taken a cabin on a lake, Hailus didn't remember where, and one afternoon took my mother on a walk to a place that I imagined was much like the grove. Along the trail they came upon a dead Holstein, and my grandfather tried to cover Mother's eyes and pull her past. But as they drew even with the cow they could see the half-born calf, still lodged inside her, its hooves pressed up around its head.

She kept asking her father what it was, but he kept telling her, "Nothing." He wouldn't look at her but kept pulling her down the path, yanking her arm and ordering her to hurry. He was never rough with her except then, and she began to cry, afraid of both him and the cow and calf.

As I walked the trail between the grove and the fields, I couldn't help but glance down at the underbrush, half expecting to see a calf, flies clustering on its tender pink nose and closed lids. Sweat rivulets hurried like fingernails tracing lightly down my skin. Finally I sat in the shade with my back against an elm and wished, first of all, that I had never come and, then, that I had brought the lemonade cooler and a handful of cookies with me for the waiting.

I knew from the sun I hadn't been out long, but seconds became years and I blamed their slowness on Hailus Tucker. I watched ants march and a dragonfly rotor by. I peeled the bark from a twig and picked the webbing from between a leaf's veins. The treetops moved past the clouds, and the sun dropped behind the treetops. I fell asleep for a while, but even then I dreamed about Hailus's arm around Edwina, and that somehow mixed in with an image of my mother and the calf. Finally I walked back toward the car, kicking my feet through the leaf meal and snapping branches off as I passed each bush.

The car sat in the middle of the clearing, the blue picnic cloth still spread on the ground and only half the luncheon things packed in the hamper. A dove called and insects chirred and I was suddenly afraid they had left me. "Hailus? Ed?" I called. "I'm here. Stop hiding."

But they didn't answer, and I stood for a moment in the shelter of the trees before starting across the open space. I swung my arms and held my chin high, in case they might be looking. Flies swarming over the open bowl of potato salad rose and resettled as I passed, and my reflection in the dusty car door grew larger as I approached. I jumped on the running board and hooked my arm through the open windows. I'd only meant to get a better look into the woods by standing there, but they were asleep inside, Ed, unclothed and leaning against Hailus in the corner of the back seat, his arm thrown casually over hers and one hairy leg protruding from under her hip.

He was hidden, but Edwina sprawled, one leg up on the seat and the other stretched out straight on the floor, to show the flame of hair between them. I'd never seen a woman naked before, never so much as Edwina now held still in sleep. All her speckled pale skin, the fish whiteness marred with red. The very size of her, thighs like hams and breasts like udders. There was so much, the great curve of belly and hip, the nipples and pubis and dark slit between her legs. All things grotesque and female lay open and exposed, and I studied them in fascination and disgust. Edwina, leaning back against Hailus, covered him with her size and slept with her arm thrown back like a baby's.

Then Hailus stirred, and I ran to the clearing's edge. I meant to sound calm, but I crouched at the perimeter, the veins in my temples feeling tight to bursting, and screeched while I shook the bush next to me.

"Wake up. Now. You must."

Dark shapes moved inside the car. Edwina's face surfaced at the window, then dove back down inside. Hailus replaced her, his face contorted, clutching a shirt up around his neck and waving me off with his other hand.

"Walk slowly to the end of the grove and then come back. Go on, Anna. We'll be ready when you return. Right now. Do it."

He sank inside the car, and I snapped off a branch and turned toward the prairie side of the grove, slapping the branch against my leg with every step. When I returned, all the picnic things were packed and Ed was seated in the back, the front door open for me. Hailus smiled tightly and bowed when I appeared. "Queen Anna, your carriage."

As he escorted me around the front of the car, he squeezed my elbow. "We'll go driving tomorrow. Just the two of us. All the way to Spirit Lake, if you like. How about it, Anna? Tell me yes and make me happy."

I wouldn't say anything or look at him. Edwina sat with her head down and was silent also. But Hailus kept up a constant stream of chatter and whistling, even while he cranked up the car. He tried to get us to sing with him, but we wouldn't, and he went back to talking about everything we passed, as though we couldn't see it for ourselves. How heavy the corn, how rich the fields, how glorious that late August day. But the image of a woman intruded, like a giant sprawled across the farmland, nipples round and red as suns and thighs as broad as wheat fields. I closed my eyes. The car vibrated, and Hailus's voice chirred like locusts on the corn. But that all seemed far away, and only the woman filled my endless dark.

Chapter Five

❱❲

$\mathscr{A}$FTER THE PICNIC HAILUS NEVER asked me to carry messages or serve as lookout, and Edwina kept to the back of the house when I was home. If they were ever together again, I never saw them. To make sure, I left early for school and stayed after. I joined the Camp Fire Girls and attended chorus meetings, though I had never wanted to before. I visited hastily made friends and I did not go home until dinner, after which Edwina returned as usual to her father's house with her grandmother, leaving mine safer for me. In early October, when Hailus and my parents planned a trip to Des Moines for theater and shopping, I did not ask to go.

The Old One stayed with me nights then, sleeping on a cot set up in the kitchen. I wanted her to come upstairs, to one of the beds there, so I wouldn't have to sleep by myself, but she said it was more fitting that she stay in her own place. She was quiet, for her, and distant, the way she was when her arthritis knotted up or the grippe set in. The second night she was there, a storm threatened, and I told her I needed an extra blanket if she wasn't going to sleep with me.

"You won't freeze before morning," she said.

But I couldn't sleep, and when the hall clock struck three I wrapped my quilt around me and crept downstairs. I stood by the foot of her cot while the room flared blue-white out of the shadows. The Old One lay with one hand curled against her cheek and her knees tucked up, like a child.

"It's going to storm," I whispered. "Are all the windows closed?"

She slept on in the flashes of watery light. Then the wind picked up and rattled the panes. I tripped on my quilt and bumped the cot, and she cried out when she saw me.

"Don't be sneaking up on a body like that," she scolded, pulling her wrapper around her. "Nothing worse than waking to a figure at the foot of your bed. I thought it were the late Mr. Selchie."

"I just wanted to ask you about the windows."

She limped over to the sink and stood looking out as the first fat drops smacked against the glass. "The windows? Do you think you're getting too old to admit you're afraid? No one ever gets that old. Now get down the kerosene lamp. Soon there'll be no electricity."

She stoked the embers in the range and heated mugs of milk as the lamp threw our shadows long against the wall. She promised I could crawl in the cot with her whenever we were ready again for sleep.

"Was a night like this when Mr. Selchie drowned," she told me. "No one knew what had become of him until the drought the next year, when the pond dried up. He had worked for the grain dealer and wore a great ring of keys around his neck, the ones to the storage bins and feed sheds. They was still around him when they pulled his bones from the muck."

She was quiet a moment, while the room trembled with light and the rain hit hard and steady on the windows.

"I know he didn't throw his own self into that pond and sink peaceful to the bottom, but when he first left me, I was barely eighteen and big with child. After he didn't come home, I brooded for seven days, and finally

I took a scissors and cut his clothes to shreds. I did that, Anna. All his work clothes and his Sunday suit. I took up a shirt laid out for mending, and a kind of craziness came over me that I didn't care to stop no more. I set in to letting those scissors go wherever they wanted, and they wandered over that shirt like hungry sheep, cutting curves and corners and points. And when they was done, they went looking for all the other man clothes in the house until there were nothing but a pile of scraps before me. Then, when I was done, I laid my face against the pieces and cried like a fury."

"You were so sad?"

"No, child, I was in a fit at being left. He had no right to desert me like that in a foreign land. No right at all. I cried and raged and pounded my fist against the table and was sorry I couldn't strike out against his own self."

"But he couldn't help drowning."

"I didn't know that then. All I knew was I was left alone out there with the baby kicking my ribs so furious I couldn't sleep and the wind banging about. I couldn't stand looking at them scraps nor bear the thought of throwing them away. On the third day I sat down in front of them, at first just feeling sooty and shriveled up inside, every scrap reminding me of a day with him wearing a particular shirt or coat. Then I began seeing patterns, pleasing ways the colors and shapes played off of one another, and I began rearranging the scraps in new ways I liked better. Before long I got out the sewing basket and set in to stitching on them. Laid the patches on my belly like it were a sewing table and kept going so long I had to get out the lamp to work by.

"I took joy in the patterns, I did, and the touch of the cloth and the needle diving in and pulling me out of that ugly place to somewhere beyond. Like the silver needle were a living creature swimming for all he was worth. Then I'd feel strong, I would, Anna, with that same pleasure of going forward through the waves as the selchies had going home to their waterland. It was that feeling of returning to a place I belonged that were more powerful than all my hurt and anger. Do you know what I'm telling you, Anna?" She began clearing the table. "It kept me alive, it surely did."

"Then you had Douglas?"

"A squally little red thing, who weren't happy about being born. Says I forced him too roughly into this world."

"He can remember when he was born?"

"He thinks he can."

"What does he say about it?"

"That he didn't like it at all. But I'm talking too much for an old woman. Let's go to bed."

"I don't remember a thing about being a baby."

"Then it was something you wished to forget."

Outside, the storm crashed against the house, but we curled like spoons. It was almost the same feeling as when I was small and she held me on her lap, save now I was the larger person. My knees stuck out over the edge of the cot, and I held my arms crossed tightly over my new breasts.

"There's hardly room to breathe," she muttered. "You've grown to such a great size."

I scooted closer to the edge.

"Did you see Mr. Selchie after they pulled him from the pond?"

"What were left of him."

"But what did he look like?"

"Not at all like his old self."

"In what way?"

"Now, are you going to talk all night, Anna Berter? If you are, you'll have to be going upstairs and leave me in quiet."

I clung to the edge of the cot and closed my eyes. The storm had settled into downpour, and the Old One's breath was warm on the back of my neck. I dozed and tried to imagine what the Old One's husband had looked like when they found him in the pond, if he was all bones or had some skin or hair left. Then I tried to imagine Douglas Selchie being born, and that was even more difficult, because I couldn't see him without his hairy adult face on the shoulders of a tiny squalling baby. As I drifted into sleep, the images came with me, with rings of keys around their necks and floating in a nighttime sea. Then the sea turned into Spirit Lake, where my family truly went for several weeks each summer, and Mother stood on the bank among the spreading roots of an elm, and the sky and water were such a uniform gray I could hardly distinguish the horizon line between them. Father towed me through the water and pulled me in zigzags and circles while I screeched and sputtered in delight. He and the lake seemed so real I could feel the hair on his knuckles and the water on my skin. Then Mother was suddenly there, tugging my hands from his and pulling me close to her, her arm tight around my shoulders. We began walking farther out into the lake, away from Father, until the water lapped my chin and washed into my mouth. I begged her to stop. The surface rose toward me, and water became all I could see. I clutched at her and tried to pull myself up to the air, but she held her spread palm flat against the back of my head and pushed my head deeper. The water was gray-green and silty, and I could not stop it from coming inside me or her from holding me down. When I half woke, screaming and sweaty all over, I still struggled against the drowning before I realized there was none, only the Old One holding me gently and whispering that it was but a dream.

I lay back, and she put her arm over me. "The vision will not hurt you, Anna. It were only the shape of your fear when it got too big to hide inside you."

I didn't understand her exactly; all I cared was that she stayed near and would not leave me. But still I lay awake what seemed all night, then woke hours late for school. The Old One was gone, and sun blared in the kitchen. At first I couldn't remember why I was sleeping on the cot and wondered if I'd become sick and Father had carried me down during the night. Then the night returned in bits and pieces and confused itself with waking. Ed came up the back stairs. She had a strange doughy pallor and great black hollows around her eyes. A damp strand of hair stuck against her cheek.

"You didn't wake me in time for school." I pointed at the clock.

"Grandma said you'd be too tired to learn and crabby besides if we woke you."

"I'll get in trouble."

"Stop worrying about little things." Ed leaned against the sink and cupped water over her face.

"It's not little!"

"We'll write you a note and say you were sick." She held water to her face, cupping more in her hands when it ran out between her fingers.

"That's lying."

"Well, which do you want to be—a liar or in trouble?"

"I want to be at school."

"It's too late for that."

"It's your fault."

She watched the water run over her hands, then she turned and walked out of the room.

"Ed," I called after her. She wouldn't answer.

When the Old One came in, I was fixing my own breakfast and told her about Ed and missing school. She said we were both too afraid of what others would do to us. Like little rabbits, she kept saying. Then, holding a pencil like a child and laboring over the letters, she wrote a note to my principal, saying I had been detained at home, and she signed it "Carline Selchie on behalf of Mrs. Wilhelm Berter." All the way to school, I feared I would be asked to explain what that meant, and I rehearsed several versions of my story, but after all that, no one asked.

Yet that day marked the beginning of the strange time. I can guess it started long before, but it was only then I began noticing that Edwina wandered lost about the house and that she and the Old One whispered conversations that stopped when I came near. When Mother and Father returned from Des Moines alone, Hailus having decided to stay on for a few weeks, the situation became worse, their angry voices rising like wind behind doors closed tight. Father and the Old One in low conference. Edwina red-eyed and sick-looking. I saw her coming out of Father's office one afternoon during his hours and asked if she was ill, but again she wouldn't answer, just as Mr. Selchie, after his meetings with my parents, looked past me and walked out the door without saying a word. Once I overheard Father tell the Prussian, "This is all Hailus Tucker's fault."

Then one morning late in November Edwina did not come to work and the Old One came only to collect the aprons and things she and Ed kept at our house. When I returned from school, Father called me into his office and I sat in the chair across the desk from him. He fiddled with an ivory letter opener that started as a knife and turned into a woman's shoulders and head at the handle. He told me the Old One and Ed would not be working for us any longer, that Ed was sick and that they and Mother had had a falling-out.

"I know how attached you are to Mrs. Selchie. I thought you'd want to tell her goodbye."

He was so solemn, and the "goodbye" sounded so final, I had the thought that she and Edwina were going back to the Orkneys or at least to where I would never see them again. I could not imagine what they had done to cause my mother to banish them. Something so small

I hadn't noticed, a bed unmade or a spoon unpolished.

"I'm sorry, Anna. I know this must upset you." I waited for more, but that was all he said.

"What happened?" I asked finally.

"Edwina has made a mistake. The worst one a young woman can make in this town. But trust me, Anna, I'll help her out in any way I can."

I didn't understand why that didn't include keeping her, but I was afraid to ask, lest I discover how easily I could also make a mistake and be sent from this home. I went out on the porch, where the Old One had gone to wait for Douglas Selchie. Several bags of quilt patches and belongings leaned against the post, and she stood balancing on the top step, the balls of her feet right on the edge. All dressed in black, she rocked back and forth and watched the sky that spread fat-bellied in the blue-gold light.

She kept rocking, solemn and tight-mouthed, but gradually her expression softened and she smiled ruefully. "Come to tell me goodbye or look at the sky?"

I glanced up at the tall curving clouds.

"Did they not tell you Edwina's having a baby soon? That she cannot stay here because the babe has not a father?"

Then her words made me afraid of the sky that seemed to hide something larger and more formless than itself, which had come shifting and rolling across the flat plate of Iowa. I looked down and studied the laces in the Old One's black shoes, which curled slightly at the toes.

"She won't tell them who he was, though they've tried everything but torture to get it from her," she went on. "She won't even tell me, but I have eyes," the Old One said, "and so do you, I'll warrant."

The Old One put her arm around me, and we stood touching shoulders in the bright light and cold wind. We looked straight ahead, like parishioners standing next to each other at church, and watched the leaves skitter. She cursed Douglas Selchie for deserting his only daughter and leaving her to the mercy of the gossips and the Pharisees. She swore she would not stay in the same house with her son nor allow my mother to send Edwina away, and she promised she would not desert Ed, even now when the others had driven her out.

"Douglas knows when not to cross me, he does, since the time he were a little boy. So he's rented me a house at the far edge of town. I'll take Ed there, since the rest have abandoned her, and deliver her baby myself. They'll have to lock me up to keep me from her."

I leaned against the Old One, her familiar scent of trees and flowers and old woman around us, her hand grasping my wrist so tightly it hurt. I stood very still, afraid this was the last time she would touch me, but more afraid of the baby that had broken the pattern of so many lives and seemed monstrous then, more powerful than the sky and too terrible to ask about, as if she had come to be of her own accord and was under no control.

The Old One stared at the overwrought sky and hummed under her breath. "I'll miss you, my girl. Miss your company. You've been like one of mine, more than Douglas Selchie ever was."

I picked up and swung the bag of quilt patches, bumping it against one knee, then the other.

"I'd stay just for you, if that were possible, but there won't be no peace until she has us all out." She shook her head. "The woman thinks it's all up to her, breaking all the poor creatures around her."

I thought the Old One must be talking to herself and I could hear inside her, where she kept the thoughts she didn't say aloud.

"Remember us the way you know was true, not the way she'll tell you we were." She turned and held my face between her hands, her dry tough skin against my cheek, her strong old fingers holding me firm.

"And don't change to please her, Anna Berter. It will kill you to do it. Remember what I'm telling you, child, though you don't understand it now."

She glanced across the wide lawn. "He's coming," she said. "Don't forget." Then she hugged me roughly, and in a moment her things were lifted into the back of Douglas Selchie's wagon and she sat like a wisp in the seat beside him. I followed them until they turned out of the driveway. When I started back toward the house, I noticed my mother watching at an upstairs window.

"They're gone," I whispered to myself. The words sounded like shouting, and so I did not say them again. Instead I picked up two handfuls of leaves, threw them into the air, and thought it felt like snow. When I looked again, the window was black like an empty eye, and the light shone yellow from my father's office as I ran up the stairs.

I stood in his doorway and watched him read, until he felt me looking and glanced up.

"Mrs. Selchie has left?" he asked.

I nodded, afraid that if I tried to speak I would cry instead.

"The circumstances are unfortunate, Anna."

"She says Edwina's having a baby but it has no father."

Father looked steadily at me for quite a long time, then went to his bookcase and ran his finger down the row of spines until he located the two volumes he wanted. He opened the first on the desk in front of me. He read me the text beneath a drawing of a baby, his index finger moving from word to word. I took the picture to be Ed's baby, the round face, snug nose, and squint eyes, all drawn in black and white. Then he laid another book on top of the first, line drawings of a male and a female

standing on pages opposite each other, the lower portions
of their abdomens open to the tubing and sacs inside. He
spoke very quietly and deliberately, as if he were afraid
of spilling his words, and he pointed to the pictures and
text with the end of his fountain pen, as if they were too
delicate to touch with his finger. He named all the parts
of their anatomy, called off the names and how they fit
with the part of the next name, then how the parts and
names of the female fit with the parts and names of the
male and where the baby grew in the womb and how it
came out where first the seed was slipped in.

My father stood behind me in silence while I studied
the pictures. The image of Hailus and Edwina naked in
the back seat of the automobile rose up like some great
looming thing. Each child has a father, and for Ed's baby
the father might be Hailus. The Old One suspected and
even my own father thought so, or why else would he
show me this? Yet Edwina had been sent away on the
fiction that her baby had no father, and I did not understand why any of them would let this happen.

And churning under this confusion was my guilt that
if Hailus was the nameless father, it had been I who had
lied and deceived and made his meeting with Edwina
possible. If Hailus was the father, then I was his agent.
If not for me, then none of this, and so my fault became
the greatest of all those involved.

At length my father said, "Are you done yet?" I

nodded, and he shut the books, then closed them in the case. He fiddled with some instruments, and I rolled his pen between my fingers.

"Do you understand, Anna?"

"Yes." I uncapped the pen and studied the two parts.

"The baby has a father, but he has not had the courage to come forth."

"You know who it is?"

"I have suspicions and will investigate. And of course, there's been much talk around town, but more than speculation is needed to ruin a man's good name, however tenuous his hold on it. It is a bad business all around, Anna, and I can hardly stomach what's been done to Edwina. She is the victim in all this."

"Then shouldn't we keep her with us?"

He looked at me for the longest time, as if he could not decide how to answer. Then he said, "If all things were easy and simple, Anna, then we could keep Ed with us. But I can only do what seems the best for this household and all involved. I know it's hard to understand, but the tension between the Selchies and your mother was damaging to all, and until I find out who is responsible, it is better like this."

Then I feared ever telling my father about the picnic. If Edwina had been banished for her mistake, then what punishment did I deserve? And all I could imagine was the loss of my father's love.

The silence between us was immense.

"Do you have any more appointments for this afternoon?" I asked finally, glad of a topic that did not make me feel like breaking.

"Not unless there's an emergency."

"Oh, that's good."

"Yes."

Then we heard the Prussian calling me from upstairs.

"Your mother wants you."

"Yes," I said. "I'll go."

He shut the door behind me. I stood in the hall and wondered that with all I had just learned, I still knew so little about what had happened to Edwina, not even something so simple as whether I would ever see her again. I felt the Selchies flying away, pulling part of myself with them, and my held-back sorrow pressed against me. The word echoed and repeated itself: Gone, gone. I could not stand to listen, could not breathe with the sound, and so I went up the stairs to find my mother, her cool voice bringing me back from that place too full of loss, her room bare of what would ever hurt me.

Chapter Six

*H*AILUS HAD PLANNED TO RETURN from Des Moines on the train, but Father went to fetch him in the car. Three days later he came home alone and told us Hailus had gone on to Omaha for a week. Later that evening, when I went to sit in his office, Father said, "I've asked Hailus about the matter we discussed, and he claims to have no knowledge."

Father looked up at me, the lamp on his desk casting hollow shadows under his eyes.

"Do you know anything about this, Anna? You must

tell me if you do. We cannot accuse where there is no proof."

I held my hands out, palms up. "They liked each other, Hailus and Ed."

"Yes, but was there more? Did you see anything happen between them?"

I could only think of Hailus's hairy leg sticking out from beneath Edwina's naked hip, and I could not find the words to describe this to my father. It was what was forbidden, what I was not supposed to know beyond the diagrams, and knowing made me somehow unclean, the kind of female my parents looked down on, and the more guilty because none of this would have happened without my complicity.

"Anna, did you see Hailus touch Edwina?"

I nodded.

"Did you"—he paused—"see him do anything beyond that? Something like . . ." His voice trailed off.

And because I had truly seen no more, I told him no. No. The word shut like a door on what I could not bear to look on.

When Hailus finally returned, he kept up a stream of bright chatter during meals but stayed in his room for hours and went on frequent walks, always moving briskly and fast. Not like Edwina, who at the last had moved as if the air were too heavy to push through, the swelling of her breasts and pot shaping of her belly, the dark circles beneath her eyes, all markers of her secret.

"Well. Here," he said a few days after his arrival. "I brought this for Ed, but since she's not here anymore, you might as well have it."

He handed me a package. I put it, a floral sachet covered with lace and ribbons, still wrapped in its tissue, at the back of a drawer. Later I caught him on the way out for yet another walk and asked if he wouldn't like to visit Ed.

"That's all over now, isn't it?" he said. "We could have helped her at one point, but it's too late now."

He pursed his lips in an expression that was more disapproval than concern.

"She's having a baby," I said.

"Of course. Your father has repeatedly told me so." He drummed his fingers against the screen door and looked out across the lawn.

"Then wouldn't you like to see her?"

"Look, Anna, you obviously don't understand such things, but a woman like Edwina has to look out for herself. There are ways she could've gotten rid of this problem, but since she didn't, it's her business, not mine. All of you in this poor little hick place should learn that's the way it's done."

The door slammed behind him, and I watched his

blank back as he strode across the lawn. I hadn't understood all he said, not about how to get rid of a baby, but
I knew without doubt then that he was the father. I just
knew, and he seemed cruel beyond my imagination. My
father had always said a man who preyed on women was
the worst sort, and certainly Hailus had proved himself
this. But in stupidity and deceit I had gone against myself
for his sake, and that seemed to make me even more
terrible.

The next day a telegram from Hailus's mother arrived, saying she had gotten his telegram and missed him
terribly and, yes, wanted him home for Thanksgiving.
Hailus left within three days, after a flurry of packing.
On his way out the door, he hugged me tight, his lovely
eyes like a stormy sky. "We had some times, didn't we,
Anna?"

As if nothing had happened. And for a moment I
doubted that anything had.

Even Father said nothing about Hailus's departure,
until a few days later when Mother was out at a meeting
and I asked how Edwina was. He told me she was fine.
"About that other matter, Anna," he said, "there's nothing I can do. The gentleman denied everything, and since
Edwina would never name the father, my hands were
tied.

"There was never a question of marriage, just financial support, and that we can make up to her in some way. Don't worry. They will be all right; I will see to it."

I wondered then about the nebulous ties of fathers who claimed their children only when they wished, and because of that I worried all the more that what I had done concerning Ed and Hailus might be enough for my own father to cease to love me, so fragile was my claim on him.

But mothers seemed linked to their daughters with unbreakable steel. A curious vacuum formed around Hailus's absence, which the Prussian filled with me. She insisted I come home sooner after school and start *The Old Curiosity Shop*, taking turns with her reading chapters aloud and for so long each session that we were half done by St. Nicholas Day. She bought a linen runner for me to embroider, and while she read I sat next to her on the couch and bobbled French knots into great messy tangles. She never told me stories as she had Hailus, but only read another's story from a book. During one of our afternoons I asked how my grandmother Anna had died, and the Prussian said, "In childbed." She said it in such a way I did not press for details but simply went on with my sewing, though for the life of me I could not get my needle to swim the way the Old One had described. I eventually discovered how to pierce the thick pad of my thumb's skin so the needle stuck there but did not hurt.

I entertained myself by doing so repeatedly until the Prussian noticed and told me to stop.

As I was helping her get out the silver serving plates the day before Thanksgiving, she said, "I don't know what your father has said to you, Anna, but there isn't any question in my mind that Hailus Tucker was a gentleman to the bone. I wanted you to know that." She handed me a gravy boat and never addressed the issue again.

About the same time the Prussian and I started Dickens, Father hired Frank, the second-eldest Geising boy, to cut stove wood and see to the horses, and the only girl, Margaret, to take over the housework and cooking. The Geisings had stayed on at their farm despite the Prussian's insistence that they move to their uncle's house in Omaha, and Father convinced Mother we needed them as housekeepers as much as they needed the extra money for winter. Frank had brown eyes I swooned over, Margaret fixed my hair as we gossiped, and their talk and laughter filled up the uneasy silence that had been left in that part of the house after the Old One left.

But if Frank cut the lengths of wood too long or tracked in straw from the barn, Margaret was on him in an instant and went on until she started repeating herself and slapping her hand against her hip in frustration.

"Done now?" he'd ask.

"Only because I've run out of words."

"Miracles never cease."

"Get on with you," she'd say. "You let everyone run over you."

Then Frank promised to do better, or brought her a coconut sweet wrapped up in paper and tucked in his pocket when he returned from the store. Or he stacked the wood like soldiers or did one of her jobs before she got to it. Then she doted on him, cooking him special lunches or praising his work, and I saw the love and forgiveness between them.

At first, between Thanksgiving and Christmas, Mother was caught up with holiday parties, packing boxes of food for the poor, and shopping for Father and me. She gave him a silver-backed dresser set engraved with his initials, and he gave her a sapphire bracelet. I got books and games and clothes and tangerines, a music box that played a song I didn't know, and a set of stationery in a leather case. On Christmas Eve we lit the candles on the tree and watched their bright flames for the five minutes they were allowed to burn, while Father stood by all the while holding a bucket of water, lest the branches catch fire.

During this time Mother complained only about small irritations, the napkins not folded the way she preferred or beds not made the way she liked. But after New Year's, when the parties stopped and snows set in in earnest, when Hailus's companionship was most sorely missed in the long gray winter, she had nothing to do but "train" Frank and Margaret, as she put it. She took over the running of the kitchen, standing in the center of the room to oversee Maggie's cooking or the items Frank brought in from marketing. She questioned them about the way the wood was stacked or the amount of soap in the cleaning bucket. She had her small writing desk moved from her bedroom to the wall by the pantry and began doing household accounts by the hour, arching her eyebrows as if the numbers and lists were vexing beyond belief. One afternoon when she caught them laughing and flicking wet dishrags at each other, she asked, "Is that any way to act?"

But most often she told them, "That is not correct." If Margaret was beating egg whites in a circle around the edge of the bowl, the Prussian told her she must beat them in an arc up over the middle. If Margaret swept the kitchen from right to left, she was doing it backward; if she ironed the whites before the darks, it was the other way around. The Prussian enforced a terrible order on the two of them, in that nothing they did on their own initiative ever won her approval. She prescribed every movement, every sequence, and spoke as if their own ways of doing things were not preference but error.

She discouraged me from spending time with them; mostly she kept them too busy to spend time with me, and my hours gossiping and having my hair done came to an end. Sometimes when the Prussian wasn't home,

I sat on a stool by the stove and visited while Margaret polished silver or fixed dinner. Otherwise I only had the chance to tell her hello as we passed in the hall. One day in late February, however, the Prussian asked me to go tell Margaret to season the mutton. When I delivered the message to her, standing at the sink peeling carrots, she wheeled around. She stamped her foot, and I thought she was going to shout at me. Instead she took a breath and pulled the roasting pan from the oven. The savory smell rose with the steam, and Margaret peppered the roast. "This is the third time she's asked me to do this," she said, leaning over the rack. "You'll burn your tongues off."

"Then don't do it."

"She'll get me if I don't."

"Maybe she forgot she told you."

"The woman hasn't forgotten a moment in her life."

The Prussian called from the hall. "Have you told her, Anna?"

"She has, Mrs. Berter, though the meat's seasoned enough for a whole flock of sheep and one bite will put your mouth in flames."

The Prussian pushed open the swinging door and held it ajar at the threshold of the kitchen. "Just do as I say and season the roast." Then she waited.

With one hand on her hip, Margaret stood glaring for a moment. Then, without taking her eyes from the

Prussian, she slowly turned the spice tin upside down. The pepper streamed out, making a black cloud over the roast and a powdery pyramid on its back. When it ran out, Margaret shook the tin a few times to show it was empty. "We've run out, m'am," she said evenly.

There was a moment of silence so immense I imagined the kitchen floor opening up and sucking us, roast and all, into the center of the earth. The Prussian sighed deeply.

"Get your things and tell Frank you're leaving," she said. "Your mother will be disappointed you've lost your jobs when she needs the money so badly."

"No, m'am," said Margaret. "She'll tell us there's some jobs not worth having."

Then Margaret turned to me and said, "Goodbye, Anna, take care," before marching out of the room, down the back stairs to outside. I heard her calling for Frank, who was with the horses, but the house was closed up tight and her voice was barely distinguishable as hers or as a voice at all. The Prussian carefully scooped the black from the roast with a spoon and dabbed the area with a wet towel as she would clean an injury.

"Get me an apron from the drawer," was all she said. At dinner while we waited for Mother to serve the roast, Father told me he was shocked that Margaret had sworn at her. I tried to explain what had happened, but he looked mildly confused, as if I were describing an entirely different incident. Then the Prussian came from the kitchen and set the roast in front of him to carve, and the meat peeled away from the knife like thin slices of skin.

From then until summer there was a long succession of girls who came to work but didn't stay. Most were there a few days; one didn't last more than an hour, while another made it a whole three weeks. Finally the Prussian hired Malina Dvorak, a Czech farm girl. She often held her hand over her mouth to hide her harelip and was so shy and deficient in English that she barely spoke and then only in a stutter to answer what she was directly asked. Unlike any of our other housekeepers, she stayed over during the week, sleeping on the old cot set up at night in the pantry hall, her head against the back door and her feet sticking out into the kitchen. I asked the Prussian if she and her family did not miss one another. The Prussian told me her father had too many children and was relieved to place at least one of them out of his house.

"Her parents can't care for her properly, and she's better off with us," my mother said. "With training, she'll work out here."

But I hated the way she hunched over and kept close to the walls when she moved, and how she wouldn't talk but to answer my questions yes or no. She never looked at me except for quick glances, and her nose was always stuffed up and red. I felt mean toward her and wondered if this was how Hailus was toward Anna Schalupe before he filled her sandwich with soap.

"I wish we'd get the Old One and Edwina back," I complained.

"We can't have people like that in this house," the Prussian said.

The way she said it made me believe that the people I loved and she didn't were somehow bad and if my mother had her way, she would turn them all into creatures like the harelip, sniffling and mute. I did not understand. But the girl was trained quickly to the Prussian's satisfaction, though I thought she made all the soups too thin. After a while she began staying the weekends too.

During the time we changed housekeepers almost as often as bed linen, Mother and I finished *The Old Curiosity Shop* and moved on to *David Copperfield*. I hated Dora and could barely stand to read or listen to her mealy-mouthed sniveling. Mother asked me if I wasn't moved by her farewell to David, and I said no, I was quite glad she was dead and hoped that David would soon follow. She told me I must learn to appreciate great literature. By spring we were deep into *Great Expectations*, and I was equally aggravated by Pip and hateful Estella, all the while wondering why my taste in reading was as faulty as my preferences toward people. One afternoon after Mother and I had finished our chapters for the day and I was wondering if we couldn't somehow send the harelip to clean Miss Havisham's, I came out into the hall just as Father was coming in. He glanced into the parlor at Mother writing letters on her lap desk and quickly pulled me into his office and closed the door.

"I've just come from Mrs. Selchie and Edwina," he said, leaning close and speaking low, the way he did each week when bringing news of them. "They are fine and send you their love. Edwina said to tell you if the baby is a girl, she might name it Anna, and for you to write a note if you find the time."

He squeezed my shoulder and opened the door into the hall. I stood at the bottom of the steps looking up to the beveled window at the landing, today a circle full of blue. Nothing I really wanted to ask could be put into words. Everything I knew about them was a secret. I did eventually try to write a letter, but accounts of school and clubs and friends sounded paltry and childish on the page. Instead I walked to the dry goods store one afternoon when I was thought to be at a book club meeting and brought back some small remnants that I smuggled in, folded inside my sweater. I cut them into neat squares, the way the Old One would have, and wrapped them in a package with a note saying I thought they could go into a quilt for the new baby. Father told me to tuck the parcel into the bottom of his instrument bag. Two days later he told me the gift was appreciated. Two days after that, on the first warm day of spring, I started walking in the direction of where I believed they lived, but I was afraid someone would see me and later ask Mother where I had been going. I turned and went home. In all of New Marango I seemed the only person who could not accept their exile and who questioned the justice of it.

One hot afternoon in June I sat on the front porch with a book on my lap and stared out at the rump of the bronze mastiff. Mother came to the door, and I hoped she would ask if I cared for a glass of lemonade.

"You might as well know," she said. "Edwina's had a girl."

Her manner was curt, as if I'd slighted her in some way.

"She and the child are both well, according to your father."

When I asked her what they named the baby, she said she didn't know. "What will two women do with a child?" she asked me and went back into the house. I was curious to know if the baby would be called Anna and wanted to see her and hold her and know how tiny and alive she was. Yet she seemed to exist in another world I didn't know the way to and if I were to know her, she would have to come to me.

Later I was just coming out of the kitchen with a drink, when I heard my mother on the stairs, her skirts rustling and hand sliding softly down the rail. She stopped on the third step from the bottom and arranged her reflection in the center of the mirror with the crown carving at the top. She smoothed her skirts and tugged one earring straight, moving her lips silently. I pressed closer to the kitchen door, which swayed slightly against my weight. She raised her arms to cradle an imaginary child, looking into the space where its face would be, the way I had with dolls when I was very small. When she glanced in the mirror again on her way down and noticed me deep in the reflection, she broke stride slightly, like a stream bumping over a rock. "It is impolite, Anna," she said, "not to make others aware of your presence." Then she shut the door to the parlor behind her.

That night Father called me into his office and put his arm around my shoulder. "She's come," he told me, "a beautiful little girl. When I dropped by this afternoon, Mrs. Selchie whisked the child out of the basket where she was sleeping and presented her like a princess. She is a wonderful baby, 'a bonny wee one,' as the Old One says."

"Is Ed all right?"

"She did well."

"Did she have a caul?" I asked. "The baby, I mean."

"A caul?"

"For the sight?"

"Oh, that. I don't think so. But she had all her fingers and toes."

I had expected her to have at least that. Two weeks

after her birth Father called me to the parlor and had me sit between him and the Prussian on the settee. He took my hand. "Anna, we have a wonderful surprise. Your mother and I have offered to take Edwina's baby and raise her as our own. The arrangements aren't complete, and we still have to talk out some things with Mr. Selchie, but she may come to live with us and be your sister."

"Here?"

"With us."

"Then Ed and the Old One are coming back?"

"No, Schatzie, just the baby. To be part of our family."

"Don't they want her?"

"Yes, but we do more because we're better able to take care of her."

"It's very complicated, Anna," my mother said. "Trust us that the baby will have a better home with us. The best schools possible and opportunities the Selchies couldn't dream of giving her. She is very fortunate things have worked out like this. Most children aren't so lucky."

"We wanted to know how you felt about this," Father said and patted the back of my hand.

The corners of his mouth kept turning upward in spite of his effort to look solemn, and even the Prussian seemed immensely satisfied with some wonderful thing she'd done. They had already decided, I knew, and I might as well agree. A baby to play with and teach, to take for walks and dress, one with fat dimpled hands and chubby cheeks, though I'd have preferred Edwina and the Old One come with her. But sitting between my parents, I started to be infected by whatever had come over them, the anticipation, excitement, and hope.

"I've thought about having a sister."

"We suspected you did," Mother said.

"Think of all we can give her!" Father said.

"But what's wrong with her that Ed doesn't want her?"

"It's not that, Schatzie," Father began.

"The baby does not have a father, Anna," the Prussian interrupted. "That cannot be."

I thought again of Hailus and Edwina naked in the grove, but then knew that if this baby found her father, we might lose her for ourselves.

"We must take her in," the Prussian said.

"And never tell her that she is not our own," Father said. "You must remember that, Anna, and promise on your heart that when she gets older you will never tell her she was not born to us. We never want her to think she was not loved like one of ours."

"Your father is right, Anna. It would be a great sorrow and worry for her to think that her mother gave her away."

"You'll promise, then?"

I nodded, and for the moment all the secrets and

distress surrounding this issue seemed to fall away. We could begin again.

Two days later the baby came to us. She looked old and scalded and made noises that did not sound human to me. She was swaddled tightly and, with her little head sticking up, resembled an ugly red moth emerging from a monstrous large cocoon. I felt sorry for Ed, for I imagined she was embarrassed for producing such a creature. Then Father had me sit on the davenport and held her out to me, but I did not know what to do, especially with both him and Mother hovering about and shouting at me to support her head. I was afraid I would hold her wrong and hurt her, maybe kill her: she was so small. Not at all like the babies I'd seen out on walks with their mothers or riding in their buggies. This was not what I had expected. I'd wanted a baby to sit straddle-legged on the floor and take the blocks I handed her, but not this shriveled tiny crone. I said I didn't want to touch her, but Father told me not to be foolish.

"You were just like this once," he told me.

After the first few moments that she was in my arms and did not break, I began to enjoy looking her over: the way she strained to focus on me when I spoke to her, the pulse beating at the top of her head where there didn't seem to be any bone, and the tiny hands gripping my finger for dear life.

"I'll take her now," my mother said.

"No, I want to hold her more." I turned my shoulder into the space between the Prussian and the baby. They let me feed her then, with a glass bottle full of heated milk. When I touched her lips the baby's tongue worked like a fat lazy snake's, and she rooted for the thick nipple. As much as she tried, she couldn't get her mouth around it to suit her and kept attacking and drawing away until she cried. In an instant I was as frustrated as she and started wailing for someone to take her. Neither Mother nor Father did any better, though. She fussed for hours, until finally Father got her to suck from a cloth dipped in the formula. But she could not fill herself and got the colic besides. All night the three of us wandered in and out of Mother's room, where the cradle was kept. Through the night and into the morning, we took turns rocking and walking her, the baby all the while pleading for comfort we didn't know how to give.

I finally lay down, but the baby's wail kept me awake and I listened to Father and the Prussian out in the hall.

"We'll take her to Edwina to nurse," I overheard him say.

"No, she must never see her again," Mother replied.

"But the baby's starving, Etta."

"I don't care. She'll have to learn to take a bottle, as Anna did."

The baby refused, but after a day of her squalling and mewing, of being carried all night and sleeping only for brief fits, Malina's mother, who had a two-year-old not yet weaned, came to wet-nurse. As soon as our baby was presented with a human nipple and the warmth of a soft breast, she sucked and smacked and nursed with a fury, then fell soundly asleep with the nipple still in her mouth. Mrs. Dvorak laid the child in her cradle, and we all stood in a circle around her, her tiny hands curled into fists and her mouth still dreaming of milk. So peaceful she was, it was hard to think of the last two days as more than our imagination.

"I want to name her Alice, after your grandmother, Will."

"That's a wonderful name, Etta."

"And her first name will be Rose."

"Rose?" I asked.

"It is my favorite. What I wished my father had named me," she said. "She will be Rose Alice Berter."

Father glanced at me, then quickly looked back to the baby. "That's perfect. Our little Rose."

I wondered if Ed and the Old One had called her Anna. It didn't matter, really. There couldn't be two of us in one house, and besides, what Edwina wanted didn't count anymore. I looked down at the baby sighing softly in her sleep. Rose Alice. My sister. Rose. I slid my finger under her fist, her fat dimpled hand with tiny nails and tinier white half-moons, so small as to seem unreal. Her fingers uncurled and curled, and she held on tightly with a power beyond her size. At that moment I forgot that all was not right—that Edwina was not with her and she had no father and Douglas Selchie had arranged this coming, which was not in any form the way most babies came into the lives of those who love them. But I didn't care. All that counted was Rose clinging to my finger and nursing on her dreams. Rose, sleeping in my mother's room. That's all there was.

Chapter Seven

AFTER ROSE HAD BEEN WITH us for a month, my parents again called me to the parlor. They told me that Ed could never hope to stay in New Marango and marry. She would always be considered unfit for employment in decent homes and shunned. Because of this, they told me, Douglas Selchie was moving her and the Old One with him to the Dakotas.

"It's for her own good," the Prussian told me. She rose from the sofa where she had been sitting, her back not touching the cushions.

My father stood looking out the window at nothing

but the empty lawn. "Your mother's right. Her grand-mother will take care of her."

"You understand," she said, touching my shoulder as she left the room. I felt that she had just told me in a veiled way that Edwina was dead and better off because of it.

Before my father followed her out, he sat down beside me and took my hand. "I'm sorry about this, Anna. I hoped they could stay. But your mother has a point. We cannot change the ways of the town, and it's better that Edwina find a life of her own beyond that of an outcast."

"But how do you know it will be like that?"

"You've heard me speak of Thomas Rafferty? He was born in much the same circumstances as Rose, but his mother tried to raise him by herself. They were never accepted, and he grew up mean because of it. You would not wish the same hardship on Edwina and Rose, would you?"

I could not argue against their case nor grasp what Ed and the Old One had been forced to do. Since I had never seen Edwina with her baby, Rose didn't seem to be that child, and because of that, I was not touched by Ed's loss. I missed the Selchies, of course, but as far as I knew, matters of children without fathers were always settled like this. Any other options threatened the safety of Rose's place in our family and were too dangerous to think on. I concentrated on her instead.

In quick succession Rose learned to smile, to crawl, to stand, to talk, to play, and to call us Mama, Dada, and Ah. On her first birthday, the party guests dotted the whole sweep of the lawn—women in summer voile under silk parasols, men with their shirt sleeves rolled up in the heat, and children racing after each other down the expanse. Malina and her mother worked for days preparing tiny sandwiches with the crusts cut away, melon balls in a scalloped watermelon shell, German potato salad piquant with vinegar and bacon, cold fried chicken, tart lemonade, white cake frosted in pink roses, tiny petits fours with pale green leaves, and other delicacies for the feast. Father organized the older children in games and, as a finale, sat Rose on a small wicker chair, she being the marker past which the tug-of-war contestants had to pull one another, and she clapped and shrieked in glee as the long rope of bodies tussled and fought each other before her.

Later the Prussian helped her open her gifts, stacked in a pile taller than herself. High-topped shoes of soft calf with pearl buttons. Eyelet dresses and petticoats covered with white tattoos of embroidery. Pull-toys and mechanical banks and dolls with eyes bluer than her own. Silver mugs and gold lockets with her initials engraved in tangled script. I sat cross-legged on the porch beside her and operated the mechanism on one of the banks, which caused a bear to pop out of a cast-iron tree and a hunter to shoot it. I ran my finger over a doll's small bisque teeth, like those tiny upper ones between the canines of a dog. Looking over the array of food and gifts and people, I felt the warmth of the attention lavished on Rose spill over onto me, as if I were somehow responsible for her existence.

Later Mother carried Rose around to all the guests, and I collected the gifts of jewelry in a lined mahogany case so they would not be lost in the chaos of ribbon and bright wrapping. I laid each small bracelet and necklace and ring in a separate velvet compartment, admiring and tracing my fingers around the twists of letters engraved on a locket. Then suddenly I was hit with the same dread as when I'd come upon a fledgling robin, maggoty and half decomposed at the edge of our garden. What were the proper letters to be written on Rose's things? What was her rightful name? Before Berter, should there be a *T* for Tucker or an *S* for Selchie, or only a space for what was uncertain and unknown?

I took the box inside then and laid it on the table by the front door. I watched the party, darker and crossed with lines behind the screen door, and felt the sick feeling at seeing for the first time the confusion and deceit here. My parents holding Rose, now rubbing her eyes and starting to fuss from heat and exhaustion. Rose between them like a child of their own making, and the guests, each one taking Rose's hand to kiss or hold in farewell, as though they believed she had been born a Berter. The total complicity in the lie, the seamless illusion that Rose was theirs from those same people who would not even allow Edwina to live in the same town. I could not make sense of their reasoning then, how Ed had been judged so harshly for her secret and my parents forgiven and embraced for pretending Rose was theirs, how Ed could be so shunned when the child that came from her was so cherished. I could not decode the rules for banishment and so could not hope to avoid them.

The Prussian called to me to join in telling the guests goodbye. I drifted among them like a sleeper among dream shapes and was filled with apprehension that these were creatures who were not as they seemed. I looked at their familiar pleasant faces, felt the soft cheeks of the women pressing against mine and the hands of the men clasping my shoulder like protective paws, saw their children dance in tired excitement, and was afraid because I could be blind to that meanness in them that had driven Edwina away. And fearing my blindness here, I was also afraid of what else I might not see.

That evening, after Rose had fallen into slack-mouthed sleep, the Prussian took down the baby book where she had recorded the events of Rose's life: the date of her first tooth, her weight at three months, the treatment for her croup, and the like. We pressed in a lock of Rose's soft brown hair tied with a blue ribbon, and I read from the list Lucy Minchion had scribbled during the party. The Prussian filled in the pages for Baby's First Birthday and Gifts Received, and after she was finished, she turned to the Family Tree and began writing with her strong, firm hand:

> *Rose Alice Berter*
> *Her Mother—Etta Vette Berter*
> *Her Father—Wilhelm Augustus Berter*
> *Her Sister—Anna Margaret Berter*

And all the family names back to our great-great-grandparents, each on its separate line branching down the page in geometric progression like a pyramid being built backward.

I realized as I watched my mother fill in each space how that empty page had worried me. I had expected it always to be blank or, worse, to be someday filled in with the other names. Edwina or Hailus. Selchie or Tucker. It seemed we were only borrowing Rose until her mother returned and claimed her by calling her birth name, that secret name none of us had bothered to find out but which could change her from our Rose to another.

Since she had come to us, I had not said the name "Selchie" out loud for fear of its power. I tried not even to think it, the silent sound of it echoing in my mind; yet now, after the Prussian had written "Rose Berter" officially in the book, that name also sounded unnatural and made up. I called her only Rosie, and we went on as usual.

As usual meant that when I was not occupied at school and my friends there, I helped my mother with her parties and was in charge of Rose each afternoon. I sometimes went with my father on his calls and saw to his instruments for him. I read books because I liked to and learned to embroider and tat and knit because the Prussian said every young lady must. I knew no other way, and assumed all households were like ours or should be.

I also took for granted that each month my father posted a letter to Douglas Selchie somewhere in the Dakotas. He always left it on the hall table to pick up on his way out, and I knew it was money for Rose, as if we had bought her but had not yet finished paying on our debt. Shortly after Rose's birthday party he received a letter that he carried open limp to the dinner table. It was from the Old One, letting my father know that Edwina had been institutionalized in the state asylum.

"Her grandmother says her condition had been deteriorating since they got there, until she was . . ."

He stopped.

"Well?" the Prussian said.

"Until she was wild with grief." He glanced quickly at me.

"Edwina Selchie was never sound," my mother answered. "You could never trust what she would do."

"What happened to her?" I asked.

"She had a breakdown, Anna."

I had no idea what that could mean, but he said it as if I should understand. I could only imagine her with every bone broken and was afraid for her. Yet I pushed away that vision as best I could, entangled as it was with the idea that we had made her sick by sending her away.

"There's nothing to worry about," my father went on. "She'll be fine after she has had some rest."

That made me feel better—my father would know about such things. Indeed the news that Edwina had been committed seemed reassuring for the Prussian. My mother had not left Rose for more than an hour with Mrs. Dvorak, and not at all with anyone else besides me. Now she went out occasionally and began training Malina as a mother's helper.

"I need to get out more, now that the baby is older," she told me the week after we'd heard about Ed.

But the Prussian still kept Rose close. When Rose started walking, the Prussian attached a red cord between her wrist and Rose's. Rose followed the Prussian, sometimes playing happily at her feet and other times pushing with the flat of her hand at the cord that encumbered her.

Once when the Prussian would not allow her near the set table with the damask cloth falling in a soft avalanche, Rose strained with her free hand toward it until the cord disappeared into the bracelet of fat at her wrist. She stretched between the table and the Prussian like a crucified child, taut as the cord and screaming in red rage at being kept from what she wanted.

All the while the Prussian kept telling Rose that she might as well give up. "You are not nearly as strong as your mother," she said, reeling the cord to her. When Rose lost her balance and fell, the Prussian swept her up and held her tight. "It's all right," she crooned over Rose's crying. "I have you now."

"Is she hurt?" I brushed a lock of hair off her sweaty brow.

"She'll be all right. It was for her own good."

My parents passed on no news of the Selchies after the asylum letter, and it seemed that they had died and we had taken in the orphaned Rose. Soon I began to forget about Edwina and think of my parents as the ones who had been involved in Rose's making. I never confided the details of Rose's coming to my friends, and like my parents' friends, they never mentioned the incident, though surely they knew the gossip. Because I wished to, I believed the family tree my mother had recorded in Rose's book and did not think too carefully about the past.

Then one afternoon, the summer Rose was three and shortly before I turned sixteen, when the air was too humid to move through and the clouds dropped low and black with the weight of the storm they carried, Father came home from his rounds and, without waiting to make sure I was out of listening distance, told my mother that Edwina and her grandmother were back, living in the cabin behind Lucy Minchion's house, not a mile from ours.

While the voices of my parents boiled under the floor, I stood by Rose's crib, which she had almost outgrown. She was in that most peaceful balance between wake and sleep, her fingers loosely in her mouth and her attention on nothing but the spaces dreams leave. I lifted her up and took her to my own room, locking the door and propping pillows all around to keep her safe from falling. I lay down next to her, and it seemed strangely then like the night I had slept with the Old One on the cot in the kitchen, her arm over me. The same tenseness strained the air, the same weight of sky pressed down at the moment before breaking. I felt the terrible ache of missing her and Edwina, of not having looked on their faces for more than three years, and I wondered if they had come back to take Rose.

Then, because I could make no better sense of the jumble of joy and terror inside me, I began to sing softly about the seals taking human shape. The mighty selchies from their ocean come to claim their children begot with mortals. The Great Selchie shot dead for stealing what men had decided was not his.

The next day in the kitchen, as I played with childish indulgence with ice in a bowl, making it the wide sea my seal hands swam in, my thoughts were still on the Old One and her stories, of all the days I'd spent with her, so many more than Rose had spent with us. The Prussian asked what I was doing, and in a moment of recklessness I told her.

"Thinking of seals."

"Seals?" Her hand closed over my wrist, and her ring bit against the knob of my bone.

"The Old One used to tell me stories about them, about seals who turn into humans."

"Foolishness."

"About the ones who change."

"Promise me you'll forget that woman and her stories."

I watched a drop of water speed down my hand and hang suspended until it stretched out into its fall. "Won't we see them now that they're back?"

"They made an agreement to go away and leave Rose in our care."

I shrugged. "But they came back."

She handed me a towel from the stack folded neatly in the drawer.

"What good can come of it, Anna? Would you have a lunatic around your sister? Could you trust she would not be frightened or harmed or kidnapped?"

Danger in all its shapes opened before me, and I wanted to hide Rose away.

"No," my mother said. "We will see them no more often than when they lived away. I'll make sure of that. They've signed papers, and they must live up to their word, by force if necessary."

It seemed then for that instant that my mother owned the town and commanded all who lived in it. She would never allow Rose to be taken, and for once I was glad of the Prussian's ways. Yet I knew by the hot uneasy pressure in my throat that I could not bear to think what Edwina would do now that she had come back, what she wanted from us now that she was here.

After the Prussian left me, I locked myself in the bath and ran water in the sink, cupping handful after handful to my face and wishing I could wash away the pounding in my head. I began to think of the Selchies as my enemies who had come to steal Rose, and I felt betrayed by their change from those I loved. Yet I could not get over the idea that the Old One and Edwina in the shape I used to know them still existed, separate and distinct from this sinister new form of them that I had yet to see. I could not get over my fear that I was not large enough to hold all the contradictions that seemed bent on existing simultaneously inside me, all the selves and doppelgängers multiplying and shape-shifting until I could not keep track of, make sense of, or name them.

Part Two

Chapter Eight

$\mathcal{F}$OR WEEKS I LOOKED FOR them, for glimpses as we drove to church or on our way to making calls. I ran to answer the doorbell each time it rang and watched for the mail as if they would write to warn us of their coming. I expected to see them standing together at the foot of the front lawn, Ed placid and cowlike next to the Old One in black, like a small ancient crow.

I sat on my windowsill and watched the spot at the end of the lawn where I expected their vigil, and if they had suddenly materialized out of nowhere, I would not have been at all shocked. I could feel them looking toward our house through all the trees and other houses that separated us, and I felt the very air disturbed and turbulent by their thoughts and energies pointed toward Rose.

As if she, too, expected them, the Prussian pulled the drapes on hot afternoons, saying it would help keep the house cool, and though she had done this before, she now did it more often and kept the rooms shut off even after the sun was past. We sat in humid twilight and slept away the midday heat on cotton comforters laid on the floor in front of electrical fans with black wire faces. We drifted through the early summer like fish hanging listlessly in water too deep for the light to penetrate.

But after a week I began inventing excuses to go out, which the Prussian countered with excuses for my staying in. When I asked to borrow a book from a friend, she told me to read the books in our house first. When I asked to see a friend's new puppy, she told me it was not safe to be around animals during the rabies season. When I asked to go on errands with Malina, she told me the reason we had a servant was to avoid such drudgeries. I wandered around the house, sometimes pushing my shoulder hard against the wall, or loathing the familiar wallpaper so thoroughly that I wanted to scrape it off with my nails, five parallel swaths clawed evenly across each wall.

I blamed the Prussian for my confinement, yet in a

way was glad for how it saved me. I did not know what I would say to the Old One after all this time, or how I should treat Ed. I did not even know whether to mention Rose or just pretend that she did not exist. The new configuration of relationships was so confusing, I wished we might go back to the way it had been before Hailus Tucker came to stay, with the Selchies in our employ and Rose substituting for me as the child on the Old One's lap. I even suggested this to my parents one night at dinner, explaining how Ed and the Old One were already more experienced than Malina in both house-keeping and child care.

The Prussian laid her knife across the back of her plate and raised her eyebrows.

"Will," she said.

He wiped his mouth slowly with his napkin and rearranged it neatly in his lap.

"It may seem like a simple matter, Schatzie, but there are more things at work here than you understand."

"Your father is right, Anna. Not only are the Selchies forbidden in this house, but we must not have any communication with them."

"Why?" I asked.

"It can only come to no good," she said. "What can you hope to accomplish by continually keeping open old wounds? Isn't that right, Will?"

My father hesitated. "I don't know if we should go that far, Etta."

Later, in private, he promised that he would arrange a visit with the Selchies for me, but two weeks went by and nothing more was said. Then one afternoon when Malina was in the middle of making elderberry jelly and the Prussian on her way to take a dressmaker's pattern to Lucy Minchion, Clara Cooney stopped by, the wide brim of her hat sailing in the door well before her. The Prussian pushed the pattern into my hands.

"Take this to Miss Minchion. She wants to borrow it. The girl's coming to fit her this afternoon, so be quick and then come straight home."

I flew down the driveway, feeling as if I had just been unwrapped from layers of swaddling, newly light and curiously naked. Not since the week before school was out had I been this far from home by myself, and the houses and yards I'd passed a thousand times now looked so different that I swore they had all had a gable or porch built in my absence. The air shimmered so hot and bright that the bones around my eyes ached, and I saw all things sharp in detail—grass blades between sidewalk cracks, earth balls in anthills, and the black nose of a dog standing panting and pink-tongued beside a tangle of purple snapdragons.

Even the ink stood so dark on the pattern's envelope that I felt I could read it like braille and touch the texture of the fabric on the dress pictured there. I handed the pattern to Lucy Minchion, smelling of moist powder, and she served me lemonade, which moved like a solid shape of cold into my stomach. We talked politely, the way I'd learned from the Prussian, and almost by rote, so that my mind was free to race with the excitement of being so close to the Old One's cottage, not three hundred yards away. When Lucy closed the door behind me, I leaned over the porch railing, scanned the grove of trees that bordered the yard, and watched a bird shoot across the sky. I wished the Old One to appear and imagined our conversation, easy as one we would've had before Rose was conceived. Then I scolded myself for being so childish as to play this game of pretend.

Yet as I started down the steps, the Old One did step from the grove, so like the way I had just pictured that she belonged as much to that fancy as to reality. She herself had been changed less by age than by my memory, and I was shocked by her presence, emerging as it did so sudden and autonomously from my imagination. She stopped when she saw me, raising one hand to tell me to wait, and stepped up on a stump while she scanned the windows of Lucy Minchion's house. Her skirt grazed the tips of her boots, and she appeared to be hovering there, so tiny and slight as to be able to stand on the heavy summer air.

Then she motioned, and I ran out into the yard,

turning back once to look at the house. The windows like dull glass eyes stared down, and I felt myself then a passenger pigeon caught away from cover. A thought came, born of white summer light and the weight of heat, that a hunter inside raised his gun and pinned me in the sight.

I ran to the Old One. She towed me down the path and into the green flecked with splinters of cold. Leaf edges pulled across my skin, and the trees closed over and behind until the space back into the yard shrank to a hole only a medium-sized dog could get through. When we were out of sight of the house she stopped, and I was suddenly shy of her in her black clothes and little bonnet, formal like the Prussian gone calling. She was now smaller than I, her line of sight aimed at my chin and mine directed just over the horizon of her hat. I felt as if our bodies had become confused, she now being my child size and I the adult, cow-boned next to her fragile skeleton of bird wings and air.

She grasped my forearms and held tight, working up my arms and shoulders like a buyer at an auction checking the soundness of a horse's legs. She held my face in both her hands, her palms flat against my cheeks, and I tingled. Her eyes were as green as the grove around us.

"You have grown into a fine strong woman, Anna Berter."

My tongue grew thick as a sausage, and I could only blush. She tucked a sweaty lock off my forehead, and the air dried cool on that spot.

"There weren't a day that I did not try to imagine what you looked like at the moment I was thinking on you. But all my imaginings didn't make you as fine as you are, my girl."

She put her arm around my waist and led me down the path, asking first about myself, then telling about Ed's pining.

"There weren't nothing I could do to keep her from the sickness, Anna, and there's not a thing more terrible in the world than seeing your own child slip away from you. She kept saying over and over that she could not live without seeing her babe."

"Father wrote every month."

"It's not the same, hearing about a thing and knowing it. What would you trade for that child? Not letters once a month."

We walked in silence, my heart thumping wildly with the thought that that was the trade they intended to reverse.

"But Ed's all right now?"

"Well enough, I suppose, for what she's gone through. She don't cry night and day, and now she sleeps some."

She told me that after Edwina had been released from the asylum, they left Douglas Selchie in Bismarck, sitting in the store he'd started with his blood money and the Old One swearing at him that he could not be a son of hers for what he'd done to his daughter.

"It weren't only the original sin, Anna, how he let properness and finances convince him of what they should have never. It were how he kept telling Ed to never mind about what was done with, and how he were blind to her pain, threatening to punish her if she didn't stop her keening. I told him if he could not see how this had sickened her, then he didn't need to be seeing us at all."

She left me sitting on the top step of the porch while she put her hat away. I had never been inside her house when she had lived in New Marango before, but it was a house like the others on her street. This cabin had no such resemblance, being nearer to a large chicken coop, with two windows on each wall, a door centered between those on the front, a porch circling it all, and a cupola on the roof. Grasses grew deep around the porch, and elms huddled thick around the clearing. The windows had no glass but were instead heavy boards hinged from the top and propped out from the bottom with cudgels, like wooden awnings.

The roof bowed alarmingly over the porch, lined with bottles—green and brown and clear and blue, all slick and naked without their labels—and several small clean animal skulls with flat brows and rows of tiny teeth. A kitchen table scabbing paint was pushed in one corner and loaded with ropes and tools, the rusty blade of a scythe curving out of the confusion. A brown tabby with one eye rose to a crouch, then streaked between the porch railings and off into the woods, past washtubs and boards and wringers and baskets and clothes, men's pants and women's drawers and baby kimonos waving like confused banners on rows of line.

I was taken by the fact that the Old One and Ed lived surrounded by things the Prussian would not allow in our house and, indeed, lived in a house without plumbing or electricity or straight clean walls or even a sound roof: so unbelievable that I could easily think my time with them a daydream I would have had on my walk home from Lucy Minchion's and therefore not worthy of telling the Prussian at all.

As we sat waiting for Edwina to come back from delivering packages of laundry that she did up to make her living, the Old One took my hand. Hers was still the cool dry way I remembered, half-moons rising on the nails and the wide gold ring covering almost a whole joint of her finger.

"Anna," she said, "when Ed comes, do not be fearing her."

"Fear Ed?"

"Or be taken back by what she might do. She's not the same as you'd remember. Oh, sweet child, sometimes she is, the old Ed who's wishing for a true love and singing while she works. But sometimes when we're scrubbing the clothes she'll by chance pick up a cunning little dress or a sweater small enough to fit a doll. Do you understand me, Anna, a bit of clothing the size what might fit her baby, and then for days she'll go quieter than stones.

"During the blackest night I'll take the lantern and find her in the woods, down on her hands and knees she'll be, sweeping her hand before her like that path were choked full of webs to keep her from passing. Crying, Anna, like the souls in torment."

"I thought she was well when they let her out of that place."

"The asylum?"

"My father said she would be better."

"He was telling you a hope like it were a real thing already here, child, but not one of us knows how delicate the thread holding her."

I wanted to pull my hand away then, but she kept it captured in hers.

"Do you know, Anna, her only peace is to know the child is well and daily growing."

"But Rose is fine."

"I know that, child. I've seen her, the rosy wee thing toddering after you."

I looked at her quickly.

"I watched as you took her round the yard."

"But where were you?"

"There with you but out of plain sight."

Her green eyes narrowed to bright slits, and she sat up straighter, about to say more. But just then Ed emerged from the path, her hair disheveled and the old faraway look in her eyes. She left the small cart she'd taken to tow the laundry and drifted toward me. I rose to meet her and put out my hand. She moved close, the top of my head still lower than her chin, and I smelled the acrid tang of her sweat mixed with soap and bleach and bluing and lye.

"You've come finally," she said.

I studied her for changes, expecting that what happened had left her features rearranged, but I saw none of the signs I imagined marked the insane, just Ed's broad face sprinkled with more freckles than I remembered. We stood awkward and silent until suddenly she said, "Come see my garden, Anna."

She took me around the small plot fenced off to keep the deer away and bursting with buxom tomatoes, vines curling into pumpkins, and red-gold daisies with fat brown eyes. The Old One watched us from the porch. I walked behind Ed down the rows, afraid to start a conversation that might upset her.

"It's good to be back," she said, tucking another ripe tomato among the others nestled in the hammock she'd made of her apron.

"We're glad to have you."

She looked back over her shoulder at me. "Your mother isn't glad, is she."

I didn't answer.

"I hated the Dakotas," she said suddenly and moved on. "So cold the winter storms could freeze your marrow, and dark like it was always night. I got so sad, Anna. I climbed in my bed, I did, and pulled the covers up like a squirrel sleeping through until April."

"It was colder than here?"

"And darker. Nothing to distract a person from that freezing black close around them all the time. Nothing to get your mind away from it. They took me away and wrapped me up until it turned light again, you know."

She shuddered as if the black had brushed against her there in the open sun, and I, too, felt it touch all that was near her.

"I want to go back now," she said, and I obediently followed.

The house had no walls between the rooms. The edge of the bedroom intruded into the corner of the kitchen, which ran without distinction into what must surely be the parlor and on to the pitcher and bowl that served as the bath. Bunches of flowers hung upside down to dry in the rafters, rabbit skins stretched in furry stars between the windows, and three turtle shells sat by the door. At the table in the center, the Old One labored over her writing, the way I remembered she had the morning I had needed a note to school. Edwina brought me a glass of tea sweet with mint leaves, and the Old One sealed the letter and pushed it across the table.

"Take that to your father when you go, Anna. I was on my way to him this afternoon when you came, but this will do well enough."

I folded it into my pocket, where it lay bulky against my thigh.

"How many letters does this make?" Edwina asked.

"Shush," the Old One said. "We can't do more than's been done."

"The letter's for your father," Edwina said, "to ask him if I can see my child. Maybe he'd let me if it were up to him, but he keeps telling us your mother doesn't think it's good. Good! How can it not be good for a child to see her mother?"

Her mother and her mother. Rose had too many.

Her eyes narrowed. "You are on her side, aren't you?"

"I haven't thought on it. It is confusing, and you've just come back."

"Ask her if I can see the baby. She'll listen to you."

"Just like that? What would I say?"

"I wouldn't hurt her, if that's what's troubling all of you. The last thing I would do would be to harm my baby. So will you ask her, Anna? You're my best chance."

The Old One reached across the table toward Ed. "This has not been Anna's doing, nor is it in her power to change it."

"But I don't even know how my baby looks or talks or smiles."

"But I can tell you all that."

"No words can make up for one second of looking on her." Edwina's hand fluttered like birds against glass. "I just want to touch her! Why won't you help me?"

She stood up suddenly and began walking in a wide circle. Her glance flew all around, and she kept striking the heels of her hands against her hips as she paced the room.

"I want her. I want her. They tricked me out of her, and I want to see mine what was stolen."

The Old One called to her, and when Ed would not stop, she rose, stood in her path with her arms wide to catch her, and kept repeating her name.

"Edwina Selchie, my own Edwina."

Ed stopped suddenly.

"Oh, I want so to have her dead and buried, so I can have my baby back."

"You can't be wishing such things."

"But I can't help it."

"Her dying wouldn't fix it, Ed."

"I want it anyway, that she fall down dead."

She turned, one way then another, and finally just threw herself facedown, rigid on the bed, her arms up over her head.

"I know it's not Anna's fault, but I can't forget she comes from those people I wish dead."

The Old One stood swaying slightly at the foot of the bed and made low quieting noises.

"I can't help it. I promise you I can't," Edwina cried. She curled her hands in tight fists and dug her knuckles into her skull. "I can't help anything until I see my baby."

I turned away, embarrassed by witnessing her pain as if I had stared at her naked. She seemed to be dissolving in misery and turning into some creature of amorphous shape, shining and gelatinous and unpredictable.

I wanted to throw a blanket over her and hide her transformation until she could be returned to herself. I heard the Prussian's voice telling her to stop this instant. Yet I could not be that harsh. If all she wanted was to see her baby, what harm could it do? I edged toward her. I wanted to say the matter would be settled, if only she would stop.

"Everything will turn out," I said.

Edwina didn't answer.

"I have to go now," I whispered, "but I'll come back when I can, and maybe I can bring her."

Edwina made no sign that she had heard, and I was glad that I might be able to take back my half-promise of Rose. The Old One raised her hand.

"You've not forgotten the letter, have you?"

I patted it bulging in my pocket. She nodded and returned to crooning over Ed. I walked straight across the clearing and, when I was out of sight, ran down the path in spite of the heat. My breath came in hard gasps, and bright pain throbbed in my side. From the clearing came a wail like every terrible cry chorused into one.

Sweat had rolled between my breasts and stuck my blouse like drowned skin to my back. Yet when the edge of the cry reached me, I turned cold all over and ran blindly. At the instant I broke into the yard, I collided with a man who caught me by the shoulders and whirled me around. I yelped in surprise and pushed his hands away.

"Watch it, girl," he growled. "You don't own this path."

Without breaking stride, he pushed me toward Minchion's and continued on his way. His wide brim was pulled close over his face, and he smelled of beer and smoke and old wood, like the air on warm days when the tavern door was left open to the street. I was almost home before my mind settled itself, and it came to me that for the first time I had seen up close—been touched by—Thomas Rafferty, the closest thing to the devil that we had living in New Marango. Thomas Rafferty, on his way to the Old One's clearing.

Chapter Nine

$\mathscr{I}$ SQUEEZED IN THE DOOR around Clara Cooney, taking her leave, and the Prussian enclosed her
fingers around my wrist and pulled me to her.

"Here she is finally."

Clara pinched my cheek and told me how grown up
I was. I ducked away. Feeling faint, I told them. I needed
a splash of cold water on my face after coming in from
the heat, and they believed me.

Shut in my room, I threw the note on the bed. The
paper unfolded itself slightly, as paper does when the
creases are too round and fat, and stretched out as if

begging me to straighten it the rest of the way. I turned my back and sat looking out the window. The arguments mingled and rose like babel, the more so when my own voice tried to answer each with logic and reason.

I unfolded the note, one crease and then another until I could see the top third of the writing, thick, black, and softly smudged.

"Dear Dr. Berter, I would not be bothering you again if this weren't an emergency and Ed's health going down."

I opened the next fold enough to see the lines at an angle inside the walls of the letter.

"I am hoping if she can see the child it will satisfy her and ease her restlessness, but as of now she is acting much the same as she did before we had to . . ."

The Prussian called my name from the hall as she turned the knob of the door. I wadded up the paper and pitched it under the bed before letting her in.

"I've told you not to lock this door a hundred times, Anna," she said, searching my face for what I could only guess were clues to my lies. "There's no need for locked doors in this house."

Then she asked if I was feeling better. Fine, I told her. I had walked in the sun instead of down the shady side of the street, but now I was fine. That was foolish, she said and laid her hand across my forehead, warning me of heat stroke.

"You were gone terribly long."

"Miss Minchion made lemonade and invited me to visit."

The Prussian studied my face, and I concentrated on not betraying myself.

"She is alone too much," my mother said.

"I could call on her more often," I said quickly, "if that would help."

"That would be charitable, Anna, if you really intend that as your reason."

"Maybe I could occasionally bring Rose along."

The Prussian waved her hand rapidly. "No, no; Lucy's nerves can't stand a young child around, and what if Rose broke something? I think it would be too much."

"But can I call again?"

"Possibly. After we get back."

"Back?"

"I've decided to go to the lake the day after tomorrow."

"To the lake?"

"Of course, as we do every year."

"But for how long?"

"Perhaps the rest of the summer. Your father will come up whenever his schedule permits. It is not a long drive."

After the Prussian left, I grabbed for the note, shoving it deep in my pocket, and I carried it there like some burning thing the rest of the afternoon, through dinner and the interminable time afterward when my parents sat at the table, talking. Finally the Prussian went to her room to pack, and Father retired to his office. I waited another twenty minutes before knocking at his door and closing it behind me.

He looked up in surprise. "What is it, Anna?"

I slid the note across the desk at him.

He unfolded it and sighed. "Did you read it?"

I shook my head no. Not all the way through, I hadn't.

"Of course not," he said, "but you've seen Carline Selchie?"

"Mother sent me on an errand to Lucy Minchion's, and when I started home, the Old One was just coming up the path into the yard. She asked me to visit, and we waited at the cabin until Ed came back."

"That old cabin, back there out of the way." My father pushed back his chair and stared at some spot in the air. "Lucy's grandfather built it and planted the grove when he first settled here years ago. After the big house was completed, her father, Edward, used the cabin as a retreat. He spent hours, sometimes days down there, doing God knows what. Whenever he and his wife had a squabble or he got disgusted with her foolishness, he'd disappear there, more and more frequently as the marriage went on. He forbade Lucy's mother ever to set foot down the path, and after he died she sold off the property to spite him." My father laughed with more rue than humor. "She said she wouldn't keep a rival and sold it to Thomas Rafferty, with the hope he would abuse the property as he abused everything else he got his hands on."

Thomas Rafferty again.

"Did he?"

"Abuse it? No, Thomas Rafferty always squires his land well. It is only people he treats badly."

"Is he terrible?"

"There are stories."

"About what?"

"Nothing fit for you to hear. Just a long list of tricks and lies and how he legally steals what belongs to others."

"Surely I'm old enough to know."

"Anna, there are some things so distasteful you can go your whole life without knowing. And why this sudden curiosity about Thomas Rafferty?"

I shrugged. "He was going down to the Old One's as I was coming home."

"To collect his rent, no doubt. I suppose he's overcharging the Selchies for that shack and Edwina's working herself to death to pay for it. She's charging less, you realize, to get customers. I don't know why they didn't stay where they were taken care of."

I picked up a crystal paperweight with red glass waves swirling inside and turned it back and forth as if I could move the solid sea.

"You're not paying them anymore?"

"I send money to Douglas Selchie as usual."

"But does he send it on to them?"

"How can I know that, Anna?"

"Then do you know why they came back?"

He raised one eyebrow and studied me.

"They didn't tell you?"

"The Old One said Edwina was pining." I paused. "For her baby."

"She wants to see Rose, once a week or Sundays or whatever is convenient. Your mother is against it, of course, on the grounds it will only confuse Rose, not to mention we have no idea what condition Edwina is in after her ordeal."

"And you?"

"It's not that simple, Anna, not after all this time. The Selchies are fine people, and Carline Selchie taught me what I know about delivering babies, but their presence only complicates what is already delicate. Mrs. Selchie wrote letter after letter pleading her cause, and for the first month she was back, there was hardly a patient's house I came out of that she was not waiting. Always dressed in her best black outfit, standing by the horses and running her hand along their muzzles while she talked to them. The woman is old and fragile, Anna. I could hardly believe she had the stamina to follow me and the persistence to wait."

"But what did she say?"

"She told me that she could not take Rose away from us but also that we could not change the fact that she and Ed were blood kin. She said we could change Rose's name and the house she lived in, but all else was set from before time and until after. And she said they returned because she was afraid Edwina would die from her sorrow. That's not unheard of in medical circles, Anna. People can make themselves die of grief."

Then he gave a little laugh.

"Then she cursed me. Oh, it was very polite, but she left no doubt that if I went against nature by keeping a blood kin from her, she would bring a blight of soul to afflict me. My dreams would be filled with creatures no humans should look on, she said.

"It's just her way of talking, of course, and I told her that I couldn't believe a sensible woman like herself would try to scare me. But you can see from it how much this means to her."

"Then you're going to let her see Rose?"

"Oh, Anna, on one hand I see no harm in it, at least once. But then again, your mother is right. We're not at all sure of Edwina's mental stability, and indeed Mrs. Selchie's, for that matter. And how will we explain to Rose what Edwina is to her? It was one thing after her birth to think of letting Edwina see her, but we have all gone on too long in another direction."

"Do we have to tell her anything? I never asked who the Selchies were when I was a child. They were just the people who were always here."

"I don't know, Anna. I just don't, and because of that, I'll have to think on this at more length. We have to consider first how it will affect Rose, not to mention how it has already disturbed your mother." He looked off across the room again and drummed his fingers on the chair arm.

"Well," he said finally, "I didn't mean to trouble you with that. I suppose your mind's on the trip tomorrow. I know I wish I were going right away, but until I get there, you must start teaching Rose to swim. Remember how you loved the water at that age?"

I ran my finger along the edge of his desk, where the leather top met the mahogany lip. "And Mother would carry me out too, wouldn't she? So far out the water was up to her chin."

"Your mother in water that deep? I doubt it." He watched a moth circling the lamp as if that would help him picture her carrying me.

"But I remember a time she carried me out so far the water was over my head," I said, already unsure if that had happened in reality as well as dream.

"Then you couldn't have been more than two or three. By the summer you were four I had taught you to swim."

"We were in the water far from shore."

"It's possible, but I have never seen your mother in water over her knees. She's deathly afraid of it."

"I know she doesn't care for being wet and mussed and that she thinks the bathing costumes ridiculous."

"It's more than that, Anna. She was never taught how to take care of herself in the water nor allowed near it to learn for herself. One summer when she was no older than you and at the lake with friends, they took a boat out and overturned it. She nearly drowned, though they were no more than ten feet from shore and she probably could have stood up in the water, had she but the presence of mind to try it.

"That terrified her, that and the fact her father never forgave her for endangering her life. I could not talk her out of her fear. She even objected to you learning to swim, but I insisted, the way I insist you be allowed to go with me on calls. I told her you must know to be spared the same terrible experiences she had had.

"Still, we must ask her if she truly did attempt to overcome her terror for your sake. Yes, I'll ask her. That would have been a fine thing for her to have done."

He absently ruffled the pages of the medical journal he had been reading, his face full of pride over Mother's possible triumph. I felt such tenderness for him and his protectiveness that I forgave him for keeping the secret of the Old One's notes. By then we'd traveled so far from the subject of the letter that I didn't know how to get back to it. It seemed too rude to ask him outright what the Old One's message had been, and so strange that he took my meeting with her for granted.

"Then it is all right that we go?" I said by way of asking if Edwina would survive our absence.

"Certainly, Anna, go and enjoy yourself. I will be just fine."

He bent over his reading again, my father sitting in a pool of yellow lamplight like an island in the darkened room. I stopped on my way up the stairs, my shape a dark shadow in the mirror opposite. They hadn't talked to Edwina the way I had. They didn't know how simple it would be to make her better. Surely they would approve of that.

Yet I could not stay the dread of what the Prussian would do if ever she found out, nor the sensation of Rafferty's hands on my shoulders as he waltzed me roughly about, nor the sound of Edwina's wailing. What had I begun that now I could do nothing about? To ease my conscience, I imagined all life in New Marango suspended until we returned from the lake.

The next day while the Prussian took Rose with her to finish errands, I was left to help Malina with the packing. Mother backed the auto into the street, one of the only women in town who drove, her legacy from

Hailus Tucker, and as soon as she was out of sight, I hurried to Ed, sure I could not be blamed for my mother's plans.

As I came into the clearing, I saw her sitting on the top step of the porch.

"You didn't bring her," she said accusingly.

"I couldn't."

"You promised."

"I didn't."

"You promised. I stayed up all night to finish her."

She held out a doll, the size of a year-old child, cunningly made from muslin with the suggestion of fingers and toes drawn on the mitts of its hands and feet and dressed with material I recognized as one of my old skirts. Yet the head was round and bald, the face blank and featureless, like some undeveloped embryo born without nose or mouth or eyes.

"I wanted to see her before I put in the face. I'll make it look like her, and make the hair the same color too."

I stared at the doll.

"Now I can't do it because I still don't know what she looks like."

"I'm sorry," I said. "Mother has her."

"You should have stopped her."

"We can't make her suspicious, or I'll never be able to get out."

"But you said."

She got up and stood with her back to me, rocking slightly on her heels as though she were lulling a baby to sleep.

"You have to understand, Ed. There was nothing I could do. We're leaving for the lake tomorrow, I don't know for how long, and Mother took Rose with her."

"To where? Out for more mischief?"

"What do you mean?"

But she wouldn't turn or speak. And then I was angry at her for acting like a child, not even grateful after all I'd done.

"I'll bring her when I have a chance. You know I'll keep my word."

She stopped rocking and swayed from side to side.

"Yesterday morning when I took the clean laundry to the Cooneys, their kitchen girl said they wouldn't be needing me anymore. She told me your mother had come calling and told Mrs. Cooney it wasn't right for a decent family like hers to have me in their employment. The girl said Mrs. Cooney hadn't thought of that, and that besides, she liked the way I did the laundry. But later when some other women called that your mother had talked to, Mrs. Cooney decided against me and went over to your mother's to tell her. They're trying to starve me out, they are, as good as taking bread out of my mouth."

"Oh, Ed," I cried, "you must have misunderstood!"

She turned around and looked at me solemnly, the way Rose often did. I imagined Clara Cooney's hand on my face from the day before.

"The girl spoke plainly. There's no mistake."

"My mother wouldn't do that to you."

"Why not, if it gets her what she wants?"

"She just wouldn't. It's not fair."

"Do you think this is a game, with judges making her play by the rules? My grandmother's there now, trying to talk the Cooneys back to sense."

Edwina turned away again, and I felt defensive on my mother's behalf. This was all wrong, this direction in which the conversation was sweeping us.

"Don't be difficult, Ed. We have to talk about this."

"Then what would you have me say? That your mother's a devil? If I said it, you wouldn't like to hear it."

"Because it's not true," I said.

Edwina would not answer.

"You know it's not," I said.

Still Edwina was silent.

"If you act like that, I'll never come back," I said.

"I don't care if you do, as long as I see my baby."

"Who'll bring her if I don't?" I shouted. "You have to understand that Rose is not yours."

Edwina swung around then and glared down at me, her eyes like green fire and her wild hair ablaze.

"You don't even know her name. Not her real one

that I gave her when she first came out of me. I thought about it the whole time I carried her, and when I finally decided, I knew it was the true word she should be called by."

She looked down on me triumphantly, Edwina looming three steps above.

"Esther," she said.

I could not answer.

"Esther. Not named after a silly flower, but a queen. She couldn't tell anyone who she was, either. They would have killed her for being a Jew. So she kept her secret until it was time."

She stepped forward, hugging the doll tighter. "When her enemies weakened, she told everyone, and you know that story is true, Anna, because it is in the Bible."

Edwina looked at me so intensely, unblinkingly, that I had to turn my gaze away, to stare at the tubs and at the lines crisscrossing the yard like a maze.

"Truth will out. Not only Esther, but the rest. Moses and Jacob and the others. They always tell their true names in time, and you can't stop them."

"Ed," I began.

"I trusted you to help me, Anna, and you would not."

Then she marched into the cabin and slammed the door behind her. Stunned, I stood dumbly for several minutes, then shook myself and strode across the clearing, determined never to come near her again. I was glad I was going away. My mouth was dry, and I shoved my trembling hands into my pockets, swearing I would show her she could not act like that with me. I would show her.

The words ran through my head like a chant, in rhythm with every step. Show her, show her, show her. All the way up the path and down the hedgeline of the yard, for each step square in the middle of each block of sidewalk, the words ran in my head and the air seemed stirred up around me, yet not so completely that I could close out the last vision of Edwina's face or the sound of her wounded voice. I chanted with more force and was so mesmerized I did not notice the horse and rider come up beside me and drop into a slow gait at my side, not until the bay chest of the animal and the toe of the rider's boot came even with the edge of my vision.

"The little bastard's gone visiting again, has she? Going to stir up the pot until it boils over, eh?"

Thomas Rafferty. Sitting easy in the saddle, one hand on his thigh and the other holding the reins loosely, he grinned down at me. Close up, how handsome he was. About thirty-five, with straight, even features and gray eyes ringed heavily with lashes like a woman. A suit and tie, white shirt starched and pressed. I had been taught men with bad habits looked seedy and debauched. I walked quickly, nervous about his presence and that the neighbors would see me talking with him.

"Well. Cat got your tongue? Did your mother send you to set the madwoman straight?"

The heels of his boots worked the side of the horse, which was streaked with lather and chewed at the bit, trying to set the metal more comfortably in its mouth.

"It's none of your business."

"But that's exactly what it is. When anything disturbs my renters, I lose revenue, understand? Take this horse. A gift from the drought. One of my tenants gave it and a fifth of his bean crop in trade for what he owes me, and now I have to bother with selling it or riding it to death, when I'd just as soon have the cash. See how it works? The drought caused the wheat to fail, and now I own a horse. The little bastard is calling on the Selchies, and soon I'll have an empty cabin, if your witch of a mother succeeds in ruining the laundry trade."

"Don't use bad language."

His eyes grew wide in mock surprise. "Just which word caused a young lady like you offense?" He leaned forward, as if eager for my answer.

"You know the one."

"Which one? Say it."

I bit at my lip.

"Bastard? Is that the one?"

"Don't say that."

"Bastard? A perfectly proper word, not to mention practical, describing as it does a whole tangle of seductions and missing parents and women done wrong. Why, my poor mother produced a fatherless child that she had the bad sense to keep, and to her face all of New Marango called that child bastard. It became a familiar word in our household."

"We don't use language like that in my home."

"Then how do you call each other?"

"It's none of your business."

"It was merely a rhetorical question, of sorts. The whole town knows the Berters and their daughters."

"If you know, why should I tell?"

"I can only say what we call you."

"You mean what we are named."

"Ah, the names. Rose and Anna Berter?"

"Of course."

"Those names, yes, but what are the others?"

I slowed my pace and glanced up at him, smiling in mocking amusement at his evil game of riddles. It occurred to me that he was drunk, or crazy, or dangerous like the gypsies who camped on the edge of town each fall. That he was one of those gypsies, disguised and left behind to cause trouble.

He leaned over the saddle and met my eyes evenly. "I meant the real names," he said.

"But those are," I said, unhappy with the words as soon as I'd said them.

"A spade is a spade. The leopard cannot change its spots, so why should bastards think they can by calling themselves ladies? All my life I've been a bastard, and I don't think it's fair you've gotten away with lying about it. I mean, if we don't have fathers, we bastards can at least have truth, don't you think?"

"Bastard" again, its proper definition mixed with slang and used like a weapon against me.

"I don't know what you mean," I told him.

"Do you not know the meaning of the word 'bastard'?"

"Of course I know. I am no child."

"No child of theirs, at least. They have no children."

"Who?"

"The good Doctor and Mrs. Berter. Childless. And not all their riches could bring them one of their own."

He leaned over me, his eyes merry. A dimple showed in one cheek, and his voice rang with false sorrow, as if he were reading about the little matchbox girl without believing in her plight.

"The Berters do have two children of their own."

"Two children, but neither of their own."

He watched carefully for my reaction. I tried to keep my face as placid as Rose's when she studied me, but inside, the thoughts cartwheeled and tumbled. Always before the community fiction, and now this dangerous game of puns and implications.

"Then you know nothing," I said, angry at the shrillness of my voice, "if you don't know they have two daughters."

"But I know all, and I can prove it. Just because we all pretend does not mean that we do not know. Have you not noticed, when the paper reports citizens dying of 'unknown causes,' the chances are good a farmer hung himself in the barn or an old maid drank a teacup of rat poison? 'Premature delivery'? The honeymoon came before the marriage, and the baby came too soon on the heels of the wedding. 'Not decent folk'? Not our kind, not on the surface at least. All words are in code, and we must learn to read their meanings."

"You don't know that."

"But I do know the bastard called Rose is the child of Edwina Selchie. Is there a doubt? And though she claims there is no father, the whole town guesses it was that young fox your mother was baby-sitting a few years ago, sampling the grapes in the arbor without even having to leave his own yard."

I kept walking.

"Now, you are more interesting," he went on, "more unknown, dropping out of nowhere, so to speak, as you did."

I stopped, and he reined in the bay, which stomped restlessly and tossed its head until the bridle jingled.

"All babies drop out of nowhere," I said.

"Are you such a baby that you don't know they drop out of their mothers?"

"You know what I mean."

"But you obviously *don't* know what I mean."

"Then speak plainly."

"You cannot guess what I am going to say?"

"I cannot read minds."

"Don't be coy."

"You started a story. Finish it, sir."

"Sir! How polite!"

The horse danced in a circle.

"You know the story," he said, "about the doctor and his wife taking the train to Chicago and coming back two weeks later with a month-old child. That shortest of pregnancies, like a miracle, a religious man would say. Why, the town could not stop talking about it. By the time we saw her, that bastard called Anna, the Berters were claiming to be her parents, but the mystery of her birth gave us endless material to speculate on. Was she left in a basket on a doorstop, like a little Moses? Or was she bought from a vendor on the streets? We went on for years, trying out stories to amuse ourselves, about her origins and the wonders of Chicago, where babies must grow on trees for the plucking."

Thomas Rafferty's eyes narrowed.

"You don't know, do you?"

I looked at him blankly. Know what? Then slowly the words took on substance. The bastard called Anna. He could not mean me, but what else could he mean?

"The bastards never told you, did they?"

A vein of disbelief beneath his taunting. Then he threw back his head and laughed.

"You don't know where you came from. You simply don't know."

The horse reared, and its hooves lifted slightly from the ground.

"Go ask your father to tell you. Wait until dinner, when there's only the sound of silver scraping against china, and say, 'Mommy and Daddy, dear parents, where did you find me?' Ask them that and see what happens. Then you'll have so much uproar at home you won't have time to meddle with Edwina Selchie."

I opened my mouth to speak, but no words formed.

"Poor little bastard," he said. "I almost feel sorry for you."

"You made this up," I cried out.

"No, my dear Miss Berter or whatever your name really is. The terrible thing about me is that I always tell the truth. It is my revenge on all New Marango for running my mother to ground."

He dug his heels into the horse and turned at a trot in the direction of the livery stable. Once before he turned the corner, he twisted around with one palm resting against the animal's rump. I thought I could hear him laughing even after he was out of sight.

Chapter Ten

❧

THEN IN ADDITION TO MY worry about what
Edwina would do in our absence, I carried with me to
the lake Rafferty's words, the word "bastard" shouting
above the rest. All night I had lain awake, looking for
ways to prove those words false, but the evidence countered that hope. If my parents had kept the facts of Rose's
birth from her, then of course they would not have told
the secrets of mine. Indeed, as much as my father loved
to tell of births, he did not know how much I had weighed
or if the delivery had been easy or if I had a caul. It was

as if I had been born before he knew me, which was of course Thomas Rafferty's news.

All the way to the lake I thought of this. Rose stood on the back seat and looked out at the road turning dust behind us. I sat beside her, charged with keeping her away from Mother at the wheel. The drone of the engine and the regular passing of the telephone poles put me in a doze, and I imagined the Prussian, a half-drowned sixteen-year-old with water running out of her nose. My fantasy was so real that her grown body sitting so solidly in the front seat struck me as out of place, and I imagined her adolescent self like a tiny old baby inside her.

I drew up my own knees tight and imagined the reverse, my future self at her age curled in a compartment inside me, a curious midget of a woman, perfectly proportioned yet too delicate to leave that protected place. Since I could not imagine the face of myself as older, the face of the woman remained that of a bisque doll's, and I was overcome with the strange sensation of being inside and outside myself, both the future Anna and the long ago child orphaned in Chicago. I closed my eyes and was carried through the waiting time of travel, feeling both the forward motion and forced inactivity, the contrariness of which tired me though I did not move.

And what I had both left behind and yet taken with me exhausted me further. I heard Edwina's cry and saw her turning from me, captive in the automobile that carried me from her. The Prussian sang softly to herself. Though the wind blew the words away, I recognized the tune of "Cherries Are Ripe," the song I'd taught to Hailus Tucker and the one she had often sung Rose and me to sleep on. My mother's lullaby. Not even sure she was my mother. Yet how to ask. Said silently in my mind, the words were ominous and fearful. I could not imagine finding voice for them. "Are you my mother, the first one? And if not, who was she? Why did you not tell me about her?"

I needed to know this and was mute to ask. Not even sure why it was so essential. My mother, this one before me, was all I knew of mothers. She had cared for me and was caring still. Yet there was more and I was more. What came first and what else there was to know hung unanswered, and those missing answers opened into an endless void.

Then in the repetition of telephone poles clicking past I sensed another pattern of repeating abandonment and parents vanishing. The first Anna, who died, and the father who got me and the mother who bore me. Certainly Hailus, whom we only heard about in notes on his mother's holiday cards, and Edwina, swallowed into the Dakotas. How in turn my father and the Prussian might decide to sever this fragile tie with me, as easily as they had chosen to take it on.

Then I felt sick with the heat and dust and motion of the car. Tired out with all my thinking, of not knowing enough to make an answer. What had I started? Now the Prussian carried me away, and Edwina's cry hung in the heat and wind as the miles of road ticked away beneath me, helpless and unsure.

When we arrived at the enormous white frame building that was our hotel, big and square on the flat shore of the lake, I wanted to stay on the very top floor, the fourth, in a room with a dormer window from which I imagined the other side of the lake was visible and, beyond that, New Marango—my misplaced hope that if I could see, then I could control what happened there in my absence. But the Prussian assured me that the heat of the building rose and was trapped in those attic rooms, reserved for the domestic help at the resort and the servants of those guests who had brought them. Our room was at the corner of the second floor, light and airy, with a bed for the Prussian, a daybed for myself, and a youth crib with side rails for little Rosie. Yet the view was only of the porch roof and the plot of lawn arranged with lawn chairs, a little spot of lake visible through a circular space opening among the tree branches, and the land's-end section of the dock, tied with rowboats and canoes.

After we were settled, the Prussian allowed me to go down to the lake, as long as I promised not to go onto the dock. But first she made me change from my dark blue traveling dress into a white voile with rows of tucks across the bodice and around the edge of the skirt. She said I must dress appropriately at this resort, where I might meet young people of my station, but I felt uncomfortable in an outfit so much more delicate and perfect than I felt myself to be.

I stood looking out over the gray-green water, while sweat trickled down my chest and under my breasts. The heat muffled ordinary sound, except the shouts of the bathers echoing sharp and rude, and the humid air had a substance of its own, which hung heavy in my lungs. I didn't see any of the mythical young people I should be glad to make acquaintance of, and was about to turn back to the hotel, to take a book from my suitcase and sit reading on the porch for the rest of the afternoon, when a boy fishing off the dock shouted and jumped around his line. His father, leaving his newspaper on his lawn chair, hurried to help his son, both of them leaning over the water and watching intently for the catch to break the surface.

I could see the silhouette of the man and boy, and then a turtle, legs out and neck extended from the round disk of its shell as it was pulled from the water and swung crazily, like a pendulum. It bumped once against the side of the dock and then toward the man and boy, both of whom jumped back as if it were dangerous for even their toes to be within the circle of swinging line. The man took the line from the boy and held it at arm's length, the turtle twirling like an acrobat on the hook through its mouth as it was carried to shore.

I joined the other guests gathering around the prey, the children openmouthed, some of the women covering their mouths and running off as soon as they caught a glimpse. The man held the line up so only the turtle's hindquarters touched the ground. Its long fleshy neck stretched taut to the hook, and it clawed the air it hung in. The boy stared at his catch, glancing up once at me, his eyes round and liquid as a deer's.

"A snapper," the father said. He lowered the line slightly, and the turtle's feet scrabbled at the ground.

"It's wonderful," I said, meaning the strange shape of its life, the abilities it had that I had not.

"Terrible creatures that ruin the game fish," a man next to me said. "They eat the sides right off the walleyes and muskies and feed on the bottom filth as well."

The turtle swung around his slow head, covered like his shell with amazing points, the same gray-green as the lake, transformed from waves that stayed peaked like whipped meringue. He lifted his front leg, deliberate and lumbering, and opened his mouth like a pink rose blooming against the leaves of his shell plates.

The man's foot came down suddenly against the shell, the sound of its cracking like the concussion of a gunshot. The turtle moved in slower, more deliberate motion, as if swimming through the thick air of a dream that had stopped its progress.

"You've killed it," I said and felt a hardness square in my chest, as if the man's boot had pressed there also.

"Should I throw it back so it can bite your toes off while you're swimming?"

The father's foot came down again, and a smell like sewage rose from the animal.

"Smell its dirt."

I squatted down and reached out toward the broken pieces of the shell.

"Watch your hand, girl," the man next to me said. "Two days after it's dead it can reach out and bite a man's finger off."

I stood and pulled my hands behind me. "That's impossible," I told him.

"I've seen snappers with their heads cut off crawling back toward the water, just like I've seen frying fish twitch out of the skillet and slaughtered chickens run in circles. Some life's so dirty and low that it's unnatural."

He kicked the turtle over. Its uncracked undershell lay like a tabletop, and its legs made one more slow stroke against the air. His foot came down and ruined what the first man had missed.

"Here," he said, cutting the line with a penknife and wrapping it around his fist. He carried the turtle dangling to the end of the dock, swung it over his head, and released it. The body flew in a great arc over the water and disappeared far out from the end of the dock. As the other guests returned to their previous occupations, talking all the while of the disgusting animal, I stood watching the spot where the lake had closed over it, half expecting the water to leave the entry point open like a wound. Yet the gray-green stretched unbroken, and behind me I heard the father laugh.

I returned to the room, where Mother sat by the window with Rose on her lap.

"What was the commotion out there?" she asked me.

"A man killed a turtle."

"Good," she said.

"It hadn't hurt them."

"Think of them, Anna, under the water where you can't see, their horrible mouths open. If only we could kill them all."

Then, for all my father's efforts to cure me of her fear, an ocean filled with reptiles and the stench of rot. I felt hard shells bump up against me and wide pink mouths clamp my legs, the sharp point of beaks piercing skin and muscle. I bunched my shoulders and hugged my arms tight to me.

"Are you ill?"

"No, only thinking of the turtle."

"Creatures like that don't deserve to exist."

Then Rose held up her bare foot, and our mother

returned to the game she had been playing with her, counting her toes and tickling the bottoms of her feet.

"This little pig went to market," the Prussian chanted, her head bent next to Rose's.

I wondered how a pig was killed. How long it twitched and jerked. I wondered. Then I took my book and went down to sit on the porch, dappled with the shadows of leaves, as the late afternoon breeze blew across the flatness of the lake, an opaque green floor hiding what swam below it.

The next day Mother engaged one of the hotel servants to care for Rose and chaperon me while Mother joined friends for lunch. The girl was seventeen, pretty and dark-haired, with milky skin and a cupid's-bow mouth. When the Prussian spoke to her, she lowered her eyes and mumbled "Yes, m'am" to every order as she bobbed in a half curtsy, and my mother made it clear to the girl, Edith, that she was leaving me in charge.

But as soon as the Prussian left the room, Edith lay back on the bed and pillowed her hands under her head. "Now, that's the ticket," she said. "You can't imagine how my dogs ache after standing on them all day, not to mention what happens to my back from doing up all these beds."

Then she announced that I certainly was a lucky little brat to get such a room, when all she had was a miserable

corner of the attic, hotter than hell and so cramped that
every time she sat up on her pallet she cracked her head
against the sloping walls of the dormer.

"The rich get everything," she said.

"We're not rich," I answered.

"Then I should be so poor and underprivileged," she
said, swinging her feet up on the bed before I could tell
her she would make the coverlet dirty with her shoes.
"So what do you say we do?"

Two days before I would have answered "Swim," but
now the afternoon stretched long and empty before us.

"I say we stay in here and relax," she went on. "I've
been up since four, you know, and then again, the baby
won't get dirty if we keep her inside. I've already served
breakfast for sixty and made up a dozen rooms. I don't
want more work than necessary on my afternoon off."

"Then you should have rested."

"I can't pass up the money when it's offered. My
mother would beat me; but that doesn't mean I should
do extra here."

She rolled on her side, tucked her feet up, and rested
her jaw in her cupped hand. Unlike other servants I'd
known, Edith overflowed the spot she was supposed to
occupy. I hated her then, with her heavy high-topped
shoes and striped apron and pretty face, the way she would
not listen and assumed I was her accomplice.

"C'mon, be pals," she said. "We can have an agreement. A trade. What do you really want to do that your mother can't know about? I've got some cigarettes. I'll teach you to smoke. Or later tonight you can sneak out and I'll take you with me when we go meet the boys after work. I bet she never lets you do anything like that."

"Yes, she does."

"Like what?"

"Things you wouldn't know about."

Edith whistled through her teeth. "You're a hard nut to crack." She rolled over on her back again. "How old are you?"

"Seventeen," I lied.

She arched one eyebrow and snorted. "So what do we have to do?"

"Take Rose for a walk."

"Doesn't she nap?"

"Not until later."

"Lunch?"

"We ate earlier."

"Swimming?"

"No, we can't go near the water."

"Or much of anything, as far as I can figure." She swung her feet off the bed, yawned and stretched, then sat staring at Rose, playing with blocks on the rug. "You know, the little one looks like you a bit, the shape of her eyes and chin. Quite surprising, really, and lucky. Strangers would probably never guess."

"Guess what?"

"That she don't belong to you."

"What do you mean?"

"You know, that she's your serving girl's, the one who left and's come back."

"You don't know that."

"It's what they're saying in the kitchen. We got so much time to talk while we're scrubbing pots and polishing silver that the gossiping goes on the whole long day."

"Gossip isn't true."

"Sometimes it ain't." Edith stretched one arm high and yawned wide again. "But we got some New Marango girls working the summer, who came with the same story. That's one of my personal ways to judge gossip, if two people who didn't get together tell the same story on their own, like these two did. Otherwise how do you begin to tell?"

She held her palms out flat to the ceiling. I felt hot, as I always did when caught in a lie, but also in a strange way relieved at finally finding someone to talk frankly with.

"How do those girls know?" I asked.

Edith lay back and settled in. "One of them's father knows the old grandma. Says she and the one who had the baby couldn't stand being exiled."

I got up from the chaise and walked over to look at the circle of lake through the trees. "What else?" I asked.

"There's lots of guessing who the father might be, but that's usual in cases like these. I think it was that young gentleman you had staying with you, that Harris Taylor."

"Hailus Tucker."

"That's the one, don't you think? Always around in the house together. Not even your mother could follow that girl all the time, and men are always more in mind of being romantic when they know they'll never see you again."

I sat down on the bed, with my back to Edith. "Then everyone thinks it was Hailus?"

"If they had to come to a conclusion, they'd have to stop talking and pay more attention to those pots. The cook's even betting it's your father, of all people, though I would never guess an old man like that."

I swung around suddenly and shouted at her, "He's not!" though later I could not tell if I meant not Rose's father or not an old man.

Edith sat up and leaned around to look at me. "You know it's nothing to get upset about. Why, when there's so many possibilities for a baby's father, then it's like she never did have a father at all. Mine cut out on my mother before I was born, and I'm not missing him. When I feel left out about all that, I make up what I think he'd be like."

"You don't mind that you don't see him?"

"Sure, to see if he looked like me and what he was like. But I don't know, even if he was a decent sort, if I'd want him back when I'm so used to being without."

"But what if you were like her"—I inclined my head toward Rose—"and never knew you had other parents?"

"Would they be rich, those people who adopted me?"

"I didn't think about the particulars."

"I'd want them to be really rich, not just my relatives or some old people who always wanted a kid, to do work and not for much else."

"All right. If they were rich."

"And had servants and autos and a pair of those little white lapdogs on red leashes?"

"Anything. Would you rather think you were theirs?"

She walked around the room once, running her hand along the edge of the dresser, laid out with the Prussian's toilet articles. "If I knew I wasn't theirs, it would always make me nervous that they might change their minds about wanting me and throw me out. You know, if I did something they didn't like or had to go against them in some matter."

"Your father left before you were even born. You were his and he left you," I pointed out.

"Then there must be something wrong with me. Like he knew I was faulty somewhere in myself."

She turned quickly and looked out the window, and I felt cold from her words.

"Well," she said, turning back and smiling slyly, "if you put it that way, and blood parents aren't no more dependable than the ones you pick up later, I'd for sure want to know the whole story, just because I like to know what's going on."

Edith reached out and touched me lightly on the hand. She was serious again and her voice soft. "I think what you're doing is real fine. Taking her in and treating her like your own. She won't never have to work hard or be ignorant or poor. Why, I wish in some ways that had happened to me. Think about it. Spending a month here and never having ever to change the linens or wash a dish. I'd sit myself on one of those lawn chairs I'm not allowed to touch and never move my behind for the full thirty days!"

Edith twirled about the room and then threw herself back on the bed, her arms out in abandon. She broke into laughter, shrieking and crowing as though she'd just heard the best joke.

"But then I'd have to be dressed up all the time and stay in my room and never meet the boys after midnight.

Oh, life is full of hard choices, and it's probably good I never was handed that one to make, between kissing and your mother."

She went off into another peal of laughter, rosy and bright. I sat silent, wishing to avoid seeing what she'd shown me, a glimpse of myself in her place.

"C'mon," she said, "you're all gloomy. Show me your mother's clothes. Did she bring fancy things with jet beads and heavy lace? That's what I've always wanted, a gown with bare shoulders and all covered in beads. A little bag to carry too, all beaded with black glass. Does she have one?"

"At home," I told her. "She doesn't get dressed up in evening gowns at the lake."

"Then her shoes and summer linens and white voiles."

Without waiting for me, Edith opened the closet and was running her hands down silk slips and telling me that if she had such underwear as this, she would never wear clothes to cover it up. Then she tore at her laces and kicked off her shoes, putting on the Prussian's best calfskin heels, which fit perfectly, and she lifted one foot on the dresser to see the shoe in the mirror.

"Oh, it makes my foot look so dainty and small, not like it does in these clodhopper boots."

She untied her apron and skinned off her dress, standing in her chemise before me.

"Which dress would go with these?" she said, pointing at the shoes.

Before I could answer, she whisked a pale lavender linen off the hanger and dropped it over her head. She couldn't reach the hooks and eyes down the back and so stood in front of the mirror holding the dress closed with one hand and her hair gathered into a bun with her other. I was both in fear the Prussian would walk in on us and entranced by how lovely she looked, how transformed.

"Oh, it must be her Sunday best."

"No, for regular afternoons."

"I can't imagine a dress like this for every day."

I stood next to her, our reflections side by side in the mirror. She was almost exactly the Prussian's size, yet different in her coloring and bright expression.

"Here," I said, hooking enough of the clasps that the dress stayed closed. Then I opened the dresser and took out Hailus's drop earrings from the Prussian's jewel case and gave them to Edith to hold by her face, and I took a corsage of silk violets Mother always wore pinned to that dress and attached them to the collar, afterward holding Edith's hair up for her.

We stood for the longest time, looking at her new self in the mirror. Rose sat on the edge of the bed and studied us. "I want to try on Mama's things."

"You know you can't, Rose."

"Then why does she get to?"

"It's time to put this all away," I said quickly.

"Yes," Edith said.

She was quiet as she replaced the Prussian's clothes, and spent the rest of the time carrying Rose piggyback around the grounds. We were making our second turn around the building when she finally spoke.

"I don't think that was a good idea to try those things on."

"I don't think she'll find out what we did."

"No, the woman's not a mind reader, of course. I meant it made me sad to know what I'd look like if I'd only been luckier. I just didn't realize what a terrible thing it was to see that."

I didn't have an answer, so we spent the rest of the time in almost silence. That evening the Prussian noticed the earrings out of place in her jewel box. I told her I had taken them out for Edith to admire, and she told me never to show off our belongings to servants, since it might tempt them to steal. Then she took the box and hid it under the mattress before we went down to the dining room for our evening meal.

I watched Edith serving tables across the hall, her face a passive blank as she set platters and bowls in front of people who ignored her. I wanted to wave at her and pin silk violets on her breast and give her her own beaded bag to carry. I wanted to put my arm around her and say her father had been a worthless, stupid man.

Yet I did no more for her than I had done for Edwina or myself. I finished my meal and left the dishes to be cleared. I went upstairs with the Prussian, and we all retired early, the lake a circle of black mirror hung in the branches of the trees.

Chapter Eleven

$\mathcal{F}$ATHER ARRIVED TWO DAYS LATER for a short visit and asked almost immediately if I would care to go for a swim. When I made excuses, he argued and teased then suddenly blushed, apologizing for pushing me at a time when I was "indisposed." That night when my mind was occupied with nothing more than readying myself for bed, it came to me that he must have assumed it was my time of the month. Though as a doctor he dealt with all bodily functions, I felt embarrassed that he was aware of mine. Yet I also felt a certain power over him, that what happened deep inside me was such an occasion that I required no other reason for my actions.

It seemed a trick then, the way older children at school frightened the younger ones into submission simply by being older and larger, the way I sometimes shouted "boo!" at Rose and accidentally scared her. I had intended nothing on my part, done nothing but allow what I could not stop, and indeed, in this case, my father had deferred to me on mere assumption. Yet this automatic power made me angry at my learned fear of swimming, and the next morning I asked Father if he would go into the water with me.

The light air was already burdened with humidity and buzzing gnats. Yet shots of sun bent and stretched over the water in surprising leaps, and the early quiet was like a lullaby, just my father and myself on the edge of the round green lake. I yanked at the sleeves of my blue knit suit and pulled the legs down below midthigh, as if I could stretch the material into armor to cover me against the turtles.

"Come, Anna," he said and waded out.

I stood on the edge, tapping my toes lightly against the liquid plane, and then followed, picking my way over the small stones that covered the bottom until they gave way to soft silt five feet out. In the shallows the stones and pebbles, my feet and ankles, were all pale green and slightly distorted beneath the ripples of the lake, until the water lapped the tops of my calves and the greenness became too dense to see through. I went on trust then, following my father, who whistled random snatches of song. When the water passed his chest, he pushed himself out into it, arms wide like an embrace, then stroking once, he glided farther, rolled over, and floated on his back, chin up, eyes closed, sunning himself. My foot brushed a smooth cabochon of a rock, and I yelped loudly, thinking it was the shell of a turtle. I swam then, quickly. When I reached him, my father opened one eye and said, "Your stroke is rough from lack of practice. I thought you were a whole crowd of something."

"What?"

"Something large."

"Only me."

"I see that now," he said and laughed at his joke.

I hung beside him, my hands paddling up out of the dark water into the twilight green until they broke white like fish at the surface. I lay back beside him and tested this phenomenon with my legs one at a time, watching my feet rise from the depths into green vision and back down again. I made the lowering a test of courage, to allow without flinching part of my body to disappear down into the invisible, to move my feet about in those depths. Then I floated beside my father, hearing the heat of sun and water lapping, the rasp of my breathing magnified by the lake and vibrating in my ears. Like a turtle in the turtle world, I drifted in the contentment of feeling only existence and sensation.

"Anna," my father said eventually, "I want to tell you this while we're alone. After you left, Edwina began standing in front of the house each day. She doesn't bother anything but just stands on the walk by the street.

"I went down there several times to ask if I could help, but she said she was waiting. When I asked for what, she said you would know. The night before last, her grandmother sent Thomas Rafferty to pick up drops for Ed's insomnia."

He stroked his arms back and forth, holding himself upright in the same spot. I was afraid he was about to tell me she had blamed her bad spell on me.

"The clinical term for this is melancholia," he went on, "and while I don't want to alarm you, you need to know how potentially serious Edwina's condition is. We talked about arranging visits between her and Rose, and at first I considered that, but now I must tell you I could not professionally condone it. I want you to know so you will not blame me, Anna. I would do anything for the Selchies, as long as I felt it was for their good. But Edwina must be kept away from any reminder of what has happened, lest it upset her more, and above all we must protect Rose. Do you understand me, Anna?"

"Is that why we came here on such a long visit?"

It seemed safe to ask, so far from shore and drifting on the water, where the Prussian was afraid to come.

"In part, I suppose. But aren't you glad of this luxury? Almost a whole summer to yourself?"

"Of course, but I worry about how sick Edwina seems."

"Anna." He moved closer to me, and I watched his green hands coming up through the water and back down. "You are so tenderhearted toward those you love, but you cannot worry about what you have no control over. You cannot do anything for Edwina Selchie—her problem is clinical—and your concern for her becomes a hindrance to you. I promise if there's anything to be done, I will see to it. You'll trust me to do that, won't you, Anna?"

I had the feeling that he would have liked to put his hand on mine, but our hands were stroking through the water, keeping us afloat and moving always in opposite directions.

"Yes," I said.

My father smiled. I smiled back, glad of his reassurance but in part to avoid looking at his green body fading and disappearing into the murk.

"Don't mention this to your mother. It would just upset her."

"No, of course."

Then he lay back, his toes and knees breaking the surface, and paddled in toward shore a bit.

"What a lovely summer day," he said and then floated in silence.

As I swam slowly in an arc around him, I tried to distinguish if any of the women sitting out on the resort's lawn was the Prussian watching us, but all the women looked remarkably alike from the water. I kicked down, and a strand of lake grass curved by my ankle like a long strand of woman's hair. I could not help crying out, but my father did not notice. All was quiet save for the distant calls of early bathers coming out to wade into the shallows and the chur of an auto pulling up the drive to the hotel. All silent except the guilty pounding in my chest that I had done Edwina harm and now could do no more to save her. I lay back, felt the sun bake my skin and lap my chin. Only the water's strange roaring like the ocean sounding in my ears. I closed my eyes and wished never to go back to shore, where all things seemed beyond my power. Here, to stay here, the water holding me up, with nothing required but that I let it.

FATHER LEFT THAT AFTERNOON, and the next ten days stretched lazily toward August, detached from schedule and responsibility, so much so that dressing for luncheon seemed taxing and not worth the effort. Better the days with no form other than what we gave them by stringing together in different combinations the hours of reading, walking, swimming, or sitting empty on the porch with nothing on our minds. Yet in those vacant moments Rose, as Esther, would come to me, and I would invent how her life would've been with the Selchies, her running free like a cub or sleeping like a kitten in the Old One's lap.

I also imagined the serving girl Edith as my older sister and wondered how with the Prussian for her mother she would have been different from herself. Sometimes I even pretended that Edith's missing father was also mine. Then, unsure of where all that was taking me, I sat on a porch step in the sun, my face raised and my eyes closed like a basking turtle's, trying hard to fall into the emptiness of a turtle's mind. One evening the Prussian sent me to find a toy of Rose's left on the lawn, and I met Edith walking with a boy, his arm around her shoulder and her arm about his waist. They leaned into one another, and though I had expected them to pull away, as Hailus had with Ed when I came upon them, Edith and her friend touched like cats rubbing.

"Come with us, Anna," Edith said. "We'll find a friend of Jack's to walk with you, the night's so perfect."

I said the Prussian expected me, and then fled back to the room. While she readied Rose for bed, I sat by the window and looked out over the dark, wondering about Edith and Jack circling the lake, their skin as hot and laughter as bright as the turtles were cold and silent, yet no less frightening in their way, like feral cats grown large as people, wild and comfortable in the night.

I wanted to go with them, I wanted to stay in. I went to sleep thinking on how it would be to walk with a boy in the cool velvet black, to feel his solidness next to me, only the sounds of cicadas and lake water rustling. The inside of my mouth tingled, and I felt tender all over. I thought of climbing out on the roof and shinnying down the porch post to meet them after the Prussian fell asleep. I told myself I would actually go out with Edith before we left and, as I lay awake and restless, invented a dozen versions of that night to come.

In the morning the Prussian received a telegram from Father, saying her second cousin had died of the tetanus in Cedar Rapids. He was only 37 and had left three small children and a wife not known for her capabilities. We packed quickly and left that afternoon for Mother to get to New Marango and go on with Father to the funeral. Just before our departure, I ran back to the kitchen, that area forbidden to guests, and found Edith with the other girls, polishing coffeepots and serving trays at the end of a long counter.

"Will you be here next summer?" I asked.

"If I'm not married or working at a factory."

"We could write."

"I'm not so good at that," she said, all the while

wiping at a three-tiered dish, her rag blackened with tarnish. "Go on now. I won't forget you."

At the door, I glanced back at her profile framed by the window, her strong straight features clear and beautiful against the light. She stopped for a second, looked after me, and smiled, green and lovely as a strand of water grass in a clear-water lake, for one moment at rest and removed from all the forces of work and hardship that drove her. The last image I might ever have, the last I might ever know of her.

On the way home the Prussian drove faster than usual and drummed on the steering wheel with her fingers. "He was so young," she kept saying. Five years younger than herself. Then, several miles later: "I've told you about being careful with rusty metal, and I hope this convinces you. Children will never believe their parents."

She also told me she and Father would probably stay a few days after the burial to get the family affairs in order, and she would ask Mrs. Dvorak to stay with us at night. Otherwise Rose and I would be alone with Malina during the day, and she depended on me to be in charge.

"I regret leaving you alone, Anna," she said, "but it can't be helped. You'll have to take my place with Rose."

"Will you be bringing them back? His children, I mean."

"Why, of course not. They must stay with their mother."

I didn't ask any more questions but was caught up with the possibilities, whole days without the Prussian and the chance to see Edwina if I wished. But that was too much to think of at first, with my mother right there beside me. Instead, flying past cornfields down the road to New Marango, I thought about her cousin, whom I had never met. His death was a faraway and unreal thing but in a way, I began to realize, something to be grateful for in that it would give me the opportunity to go to the clearing. The car carried me toward home and the Old One and Edwina. Their words shouted at me and their faces grew large until they reached from earth to sky. We drove toward them, and they opened to receive me, carrying my sister Rose.

Chapter Twelve

ℐ WAITED FOR AN HOUR after my parents' train was scheduled to leave, in case they might come back for some forgotten thing. Then down the drive and down the block, my heart thumping and temples tight. Down the street to the Old One and Edwina. Rose kept wanting to stop and look at flowers growing on fences or cats sleeping on porches. I yanked her after me.

"I'm thirsty, Anna," she complained.

"Hurry. I'm taking you to get a drink."

She trotted after me, her small legs working to keep up. "How much longer, Anna? This walk is too long."

I picked her up piggyback then, and her fingers dug into my neck. At the edge of Minchion's yard, I ran. Like a thief, a kidnapper. The thick summer growth crowded the path, and I ran down the green length of it, down the slight incline and into the space of the clearing. The Old One turned and Edwina raised her head, like deer startled from grazing.

"Ah, Anna, you have brought us a gift," the Old One called.

I slid Rose from my back, and she hung back behind my skirts. The Old One knelt in front of her and held out her hand the way you would for a cat to sniff. "Don't be strange with us, child."

Rose grabbed bigger handfuls of my skirts and swung out around my legs to look at her.

"Are you thirsty after your long walk?"

Rose nodded.

"Then would you drink some lemonade we've made pink with cherry juice?"

"It's pink?"

"Like the sky at sunup. Is that the kind you'd like?"

Rose nodded.

"Then come with me."

I nudged Rose to her, she put her hand in the Old One's, and they went up the cabin steps, the Old One pointing out everything they passed, the turtle shells and rabbit skins, and Rose beginning to chatter, the way I remembered myself with the Old One, the memory warm and also jealous.

Edwina dropped a wet sheet back into the washtub as if it had burned her. "Oh, Anna, I hadn't imagined she would look like that, so beautiful and small I am afraid to touch her."

"She won't break," I said, thinking of Ed broken in the asylum. "Come see her."

The Old One sat on the porch in the rocker, Rose perched straight-backed on her lap, the toes of the Old One's black boots poking from under her skirt like the rumps of two sleeping kittens.

"Look, Anna." Rose held her cup up suddenly, and some of the lemonade spilled. She looked frightened, but the Old One mopped Rose's dress with the edge of her apron.

"There, I filled it too full for you, didn't I? Weren't a soul who could lift that without spilling." She patted Rose's arm. "See what a lovely child she is, Ed?"

Ed stood stock-still at the foot of the steps.

"You're prettier than I've seen in all my days, on this or that side of the ocean," the Old One said, "with eyes the color of spring sky."

She ran her finger lightly in a circle around Rose's eye.

"And cherry cheeks and a button nose."

She touched Rose's cheek and nose and cheek with the tip of her finger.

"And pearl teeth."

She tapped her lips.

"Let me see your pretty teeth now, child."

Rose opened her mouth like a bird for feeding.

"Oh, such lovely teeth!"

Rose smiled and took another drink, looking up at the Old One over the edge of her cup and licking her upper lip when she was through. "Can I see the turtles again?"

"Ed, get the shells for her to look at."

Ed did not move, and Rose watched her quizzically.

"I petted the rabbits, Anna."

"Their skins, child, that's all that's left of them."

"Where are the rest?"

"Gone in our stomachs. But they left their skins to remind us of the beautiful dinner they were and how they gave their meat to give us life."

"Will they come back for their skins?"

"Perhaps, child. Some night when all New Marango is sleeping so deep there are no dreamers. It has to be that dead still before they'll think of returning, you know. Then they'll steal their skins back and take the babies they left, out in their field nests, to a place where humans will not trap or hurt them."

"Then the turtles will get their shells?"

"Get them for her, Ed. Go on now."

Edwina walked up the steps sideways so her skirt would not brush the rocker in passing. Rose pointed and asked about each thing she saw, and the Old One named them for her—ginger tom and trumpet vine and chippie sparrow. I straddled the railing and watched them like watching myself through time, though they sat on this porch instead of in my mother's kitchen. I remembered how the Old One's hands felt solid and yet like moths that danced tingling over my skin. I saw how Rose fit in the place I had outgrown and how I had grown larger than the one whose lap I would sit in. The times in the kitchen seemed both far away and as close as the baby that I could reach out and touch. I was she and I was not.

Then the Old One had me get Rose a fresh oatmeal cookie, cooling on the table inside. Edwina stood watching through the window, the turtle shells held loosely in her hands.

"Go on out, Ed," I told her. "Don't ruin this."

"I can't, Anna, I just can't."

"This is what you wanted. What's wrong with you?" I hated my petulant voice, how it ruined the perfect mood I'd hoped for, and so I said more kindly, "Come out with me and see her."

She nodded her head so slightly I could hardly tell

she'd moved. While Rose ate the cookie with relish, nibbling around some of the raisins and spitting out others like bad-tasting rocks, Ed moved to the doorway, stone-still as though her movement would cause Rose to fly away forever.

"She is sturdy, Ed," the Old One said.

Edwina dropped the shells at the Old One's feet with a clatter and moved off the porch to watch Rose through the bars of the railing.

"Who's that?" Rose asked.

"Why, my granddaughter, child."

"Where's her mother?"

"Dead. Gone when that one was born."

Rose held her cup in her lap and studied Edwina up and down. "Did she leave her skin too? Like the rabbits?"

"No, child."

"Then she's never coming back to get it," Rose said emphatically and looked over the side of the rocker at the shells.

"Come, Ed, take her from me. My legs can't stand the weight."

"Don't disturb her," she said. "I don't want to disturb her."

"She knows only what's here, not what's come before."

"Will she cry, Anna?" Ed looked up at me.

"She is more likely to laugh or be intent. When she is investigating some new thing or learning a new toy or game, she puckers up her brow and purses her lips and talks a blue streak to herself. We can't understand her, of course, because sometimes she makes up her own words for things or mispronounces others, but she seems to make sense to herself. She sings that way too; every time she's left alone in her bed before naps or at night, she makes up songs. They don't seem to have words at all, just sounds that amuse her. She can go on for half an hour sometimes, or she'll laugh suddenly and we wonder what she's seen that's so amusing."

The Old One lifted Rose, stretched her legs, and resettled her on her lap.

"When I came here not much older than you, Anna Berter, I had a brogue and a burr so thick that when I ordered meat the butcher looked at me like I were speaking Chinese or black African. It's true. To get a simple pork chop I had to be writing notes to that man who spoke English the same as me, and it got so that when I came in his shop he began talking slow and loud, making me feel I were dull-witted or deaf or both at once. And I'll tell you that there were more than a few times that I wanted to stand crying in front of that meat counter because I could not do the simple thing of making my needs known."

Rose looked around at her in fascination and reached

up to touch her cheek. The Old One took her hand and kissed it, then blew out a great breath.

"I go on so over a man ten years in his grave. It's my own fault for still wishing a rock under his back as he's lying there for all eternity."

Then she asked me to take Rose from her, since her old legs truly could not stand the weight any longer, and I set Rose in front of the turtle shells.

The Old One rubbed her hip. "She is like you, Ed. Not in the way she looks, but in her singing and talking. In her own world she carries with her."

"She won't be big, then?"

"No, and not as small as me. I can feel it in her bones."

"And will she be smart?"

"She is already."

"She knows the names of animals we've taught her, and she likes to look at books and have me tell her the stories," I said.

"Already?" Edwina moved closer and settled crouching at the foot of the steps.

"Show her the doll," the Old One said.

"It's still not done. The face, I mean."

"The child won't care. Show her."

Edwina returned in a second, her hand cupped protectively about the blank sphere of head.

Rose rested the turtle shell in her lap and pointed with one finger, dirty and sticky.

"A baby?"

"You can't touch her until you've washed," I said.

"Until she's done," Edwina said.

"The baby has no face, Anna," Rose said.

"I'll do it soon," Edwina said, "now that I know."

"We'll come back tomorrow and see her," I said.

"Tomorrow? That soon?"

"Every day, for the next few days."

"Does no one know that you are here?" the Old One asked.

Her eyes narrowed, and I explained.

"Be wary, Anna Berter."

"It's all right," I said, and at that moment it seemed certain my parents would never know I'd been there. Rose patted the doll's head and asked her name.

"Esther," Ed answered, for the first time smiling and not shying away. "I named her Esther."

"I don't know anyone named that." Rose leaned against Edwina's shoulder and put her hand to her mother's face, the way the Old One had done to her.

"We have to go soon, for today," I said.

"Come with me for a moment, then," Edwina said to Rose. "We'll put the doll away."

I sat with the Old One on the porch and listened to

a dove cry. After a few moments, I said, "It's gone well, hasn't it?"

"The best it can after long parting."

I got up to check on Ed and Rose. They stood by an open cupboard, Ed bending over Rose with a scissors and clipping her hair at the scalp.

"I needed a lock," Edwina said. "Something of her to keep."

Something for the Prussian to miss, I thought.

"It's for the doll," Rose said. "She's bald and needs hair, Anna."

"Oh, Ed, you've ruined her hair."

"It'll grow back," Edwina said. "I needed it for the doll to have something of hers."

I picked the stubble at the crown of Rose's head. All New Marango would notice; women in their kitchens and men in the fields would hear the click of the scissors, so loud it stopped children at play. I had to leave immediately, as if my quickness of departure would cancel out all signs of my visit.

"We must hurry. We'll stay longer tomorrow," I lied, already in dread of returning.

When we came out on the porch, the Old One asked, "What has happened, Anna?"

"I just want to get home before Malina becomes suspicious, that's all."

"She said I can have the doll in a few days," Rose said, pointing at Ed.

"Then give us all a kiss to hold until you're back," the Old One said, and Rose held out her arms.

When I picked up Rose to leave, the Old One laid her hands on Rose's head and mine. Her old face seemed carved of pale stone, but her lips as they curved in were the softest pink, textured and fresh like petals. She pressed her hand and recited strange sounds, no clearer to me than Rose's jabbering but quick and flowing like water, her voice constant like steady wind. I recognized the old Gaelic from the songs she used to sing, the language she told me her mother spoke at home when she was a child. Then she finished. She closed her eyes for a moment, her lips still moving silently, and I held very still.

"There," she said and lifted her hands.

As she did, I felt released from the force that had held me motionless, surprised at the weight of her touch, which I noticed only in its absence.

"The old words have the power, they do, and all my people what came before were speaking them with me."

She smiled and brushed her hands together, like one who had just finished a heavy task.

"Was it a prayer?" I asked.

"A warning, for all those you would meet on your

travels. That none would harm a hair on your head and no robbers would think to touch what was yours."

She cupped Rose's face in her hand. "Tell your father the baby might be coming down with the pinkeye. Do you not see it?"

I peered closely.

"Here, child, in this eye. The thread of pink coming from this corner."

She traced the air over Rose's eye, and finally I saw the pale filaments in the pure white, as if they had appeared while I was looking for them.

"It's needing some boric acid in an eyewash, but your father will know that."

I nodded. As I turned to leave I leaned back to impulsively kiss her cheek, but missed and touched air instead. I stopped in front of Edwina, shifting Rose so she could lift her from my arms. Instead she held her hand just barely touching Rose's hair, the kind of touch that presses no heavier than breeze on ruffled leaves, and then quickly she took her hand away like one caught reaching for what she had been forbidden.

"Thank you, Anna, for bringing her."

"It's all right," I answered.

"Come again."

"I will," I said, almost bobbing in a curtsy.

"I want to kiss the doll goodbye, Anna," Rose said.

"Not now; she needs a face to kiss," I said, but Ed

had already run into the cabin to get it. Rose pressed her face against the doll's with such force that she would have crushed noses with a real child.

"See how she loves it, Ed," the Old One said.

"I'll finish it for her."

"For next time." I pulled the doll away from Rose. She reached for it and howled.

Ed's smile evaporated, and she looked ready herself to cry.

"Take the doll out of sight for now," the Old One said. "Children forget what they were wanting when they cease to see it."

Edwina fled into the cabin, and I danced in a circle with Rose, hoping to bounce her bad humor out of her. "Are you coming, Ed?" I called.

"Take her back now. I don't want her to cry again."

"It wasn't you that caused it."

"Take her anyway."

Then I went back through the tunnel of trees, thinking all the while that I did not know if this was what the arrangement was meant to be. Like a rat, I scurried across yards, and I stopped before I got home to warn Rose not to tell Malina where we'd been, even though I could not imagine Malina finding the words to ask.

But later the sensation of the Old One's hand laid on my head like a cap returned. I felt her touch from the end of each strand of hair, down each shaft and into my scalp, spread out along the bone of my skull and the length of each nerve connecting in tributaries down to my toes and out to my fingers. The lightest touch and yet the most substantial, coming from inside myself as well as out. Her hand like a cap, like a caul taken off at birth and put on again. Then the slithering and crawling inside my chest returned. What if the Prussian found out?

When Malina came to stand stupidly silent and wait for the dinner orders, I told her curtly that I could not stand how she went about the house like a dumb cow. I told her she had to start acting like a person with backbone. She stood with her head down and did not answer. Later I burned with shame at how my words must have struck her, but I was too embarrassed to apologize. Yet another part of me wanted to chase after and corner her, to shout and berate her silence until she turned on me and fought me off, until she came after me and stopped me from my viciousness.

Chapter Thirteen

$\mathcal{F}$ FIGURED THREE DAYS IN the clearing at the very least, one each for travel to Cedar Rapids, the funeral, and travel back. Then extra days, I didn't know how many, for the Prussian to set affairs in order while she was there. On the first day I sent Malina to shops she liked for things we didn't need and carried Rose piggyback down the path to the clearing that held cool air like a cellar, down into its greenness. The Old One stood, her arms wide to embrace us, and Ed waited by the laundry tubs, pushing her sweaty hair off her forehead with the back of her arm and watching.

"Is the doll finished?"

Rose pointed toward Ed.

"No, child. She's putting each hair in separate and making it enough clothes for a princess."

By that afternoon I had become sufficiently brave to stay for lunch and to lay Rose on quilts spread under a tree for her nap. Holding the half-bald doll, she slept away the afternoon, her sweet face flushed with sleep and summer, her mouth sometimes working as if she were talking in her dreams. The Old One pulled her rocker across the clearing and sat piecing quilt patches. I rested in the earthen sling between two roots, my back against the trunk, while Edwina worked on a pair of felt boots for the doll's winter outfit. We spent the afternoon in a room with sky for ceiling and ground for floor, the wall of vegetation wrapping us and always filled with movement of breeze, the light shifting and changing through the switching leaves, dropping mottled patterns on the earth. We talked when we liked and were quiet when we had nothing to say. Sometimes Edwina hummed softly at her work or Rose sighed. After a while I said that I would like to sleep outdoors all summer.

"Bugs would eat you alive, chiggers and mosquitoes," Edwina said, "and there would be bats to get tangled in your hair so you couldn't get them out."

"When have you seen a bat so clumsy to run into a human?" the Old One demanded.

"My father told me not to go out at night, or the bats would get me."

"That were foolishness he invented, girl, to keep you close and save himself from having to watch you. If he would have had half the brain of a bat in regards to you I would have been pleased, though as his mother I took him the way he came."

She held up two patches, deciding between them.

"He told me that to scare me into behaving?" Ed asked.

"Behaving the way he wanted. Why, when I was no bigger than this sleeping child, my own mother told me goblins would chew my foot off if I disobeyed her, and for the longest time I'd lie awake until I dropped off from exhaustion, afraid to my bones that the goblins had a different idea of good from me."

Ed moved close to Rose and held her hand just over Rose's shoulder. "If she were mine to care for, I'd be so gentle that she'd never fear me or what's around her."

Rose opened her eyes halfway and stared out of focus at the air before her.

"Ed," the Old One said, "get a cup of milk from the crock for the child. More lemonade will be too acid on her stomach."

She went off to the cabin, and the Old One followed her with her eyes.

"What do you see, Anna, when you study Ed?"

"Just Ed," I answered.

"No strangeness hovering?"

"A little nervous, but all right."

"She won't take the drops your father left her, not unless I fight with her about them. It's no shame, I said, to lean on a stick when your foot's been bruised. That Cooney woman takes them, and Lucy Minchion too."

"She seems fine when we are here."

"Until next week, when you are not."

"We'll come whenever we can," I promised.

"I'm beginning to fear that no matter how often that is, it will not be enough."

I could barely bring myself to say the words. "Do you want Rose back after all?"

The creak of her rocker was the only sound.

"That's not a question that has an answer, girl, nor a solution, either. There are some things what can't be fixed but only lived with as best we can."

She slowed her rocking and sat with her feet in a splash of sunlight and a line of shadow cutting black across her lap.

TWO DAYS LATER I HELPED Edwina start her washing. She had so much more than we had on a normal washday at home that I was sure she had exaggerated or even lied about the Prussian ruining her business. She had given Rose little turtles she had made out of walnut shells and wire and cloth to play with, then pumped the water and poured it into the kettle already heating over the fire. In the freshness of the bleachy soapy smell I watched Ed sort out the clothing on a clean tarp laid over the packed earth. By person, by color, by fabric. The empty clothes, husks without corn, hulls without wheat.

A blue-flowered dress I recognized as Mrs. Rothermich's and a lace-trimmed shirtwaist I knew was Mrs. Boschert's, and the rest of their families' things. At first I was embarrassed by their underwear, but then it gave me great glee to see how broad across the beam their drawers were, how I could twirl around and watch them billow with air, each leg filling out like sausage casing. Then Ed told me I was ruining her system for keeping the clothing straight, and I laid them out like drying pelts.

"Next week when your parents are back," Edwina began, "how will you get out to see us?"

"I won't be able to every day, but there will be times."

"When school starts, you'll be in class all day."

"I'll come after."

"Not in winter you won't. It'll get dark early, and cold like in Dakota. I can't stand that, not on top of being kept from her."

"But you'll see her, Ed." I paced around in a circle, my arms over my chest. "Things will turn up, like this week."

"You'll have me waiting on the dead, will you? Hoping some other relative of yours will pass on so I can see my baby? If I could wish them dead, you'd be an orphan inside of a month."

"Come on, Edwina, don't be like that. Let's go play with Rose."

"I can't. I have to finish this before I lose the customers I have left."

She looked helplessly around her at the piles of sheets and towels and linens.

I didn't know how to help Edwina. I could not make my parents disappear for her sake nor did I want to. Yet I could see how she became more at ease and full of life with Rose. After Ed had hung two kettlefuls of clothes to dry, she showed her the ruffled bonnet she was making, and Rose made her try it on the doll, still with no face but almost a full head of hair.

"What else will you make her?" Rose said.

"What else do you want?" Ed asked.

"To take her home."

"The doll lives here," I told her.

Rose scowled and hugged the baby tighter. "I want to keep her."

The Old One brought out lunch and, for lack of a

bib, tied a towel around Rose's neck. But Rose refused to eat the beans and the square of fatback pork set before her. The Old One buttered the biggest piece of corn bread and handed it to her instead. "It is all we have, child, though I know it's not what you're used to."

Before I left that afternoon, I told Edwina not to worry. "Tomorrow at the very least, and then we'll worry about the rest later."

But when I returned home, Malina handed me a telegram:

HOME TOMORROW MORNING STOP HAVE JIM COONEY AT DEPOT 10:30 STOP ALL IS WELL STOP.

Right after breakfast the next morning I hurried to tell Edwina. She sat on the porch holding the doll, finished, on her lap. From across the clearing I thought at first it was a live child, so to proportion had she made it. But drawing close, I saw the painted features like Rose's but stiff and frozen, blue eyes open, like a corpse, and the lock of her real hair woven into the yarn.

When I told Ed about the change in plans, her fingers dug deep into the breast of the doll and her voice began to rise.

"I told you, Anna, but you would not listen. Now I'll never see her, except from a distance, and I'll never touch her or play with her or watch her sleep. I cannot stand how cruel that is. I just cannot stand it."

She shook the doll with great violence, its head snapping to and fro. I repeated all I had told her the day before, how we would visit somehow, though we could not say when. But the space left by the Prussian's absence was already filling with her presence. The train at that moment was carrying her to us, and she was again taking up the room I had found to move around in. I said words to Edwina that I no longer believed, and I left her sitting alone on the steps in the clearing, the blankly staring doll on her lap.

I hurried back toward my house, again wishing that the speed of my departure would erase the fact of my having been there. Already I was nervous that somehow the train had traveled faster than possible and the Prussian would greet me at our door, demanding to know where I had been so early. But I had time to tie up Rose's hair over the cut stubble, and my parents came as they had promised, driving up to the house at a little past eleven. Jim Cooney, Clara Cooney's slow-witted brother who did odd jobs around town, carried in their bags, and Malina took them upstairs. I greeted the Prussian and hoped that I appeared to have been waiting the entire three days for her return.

Mother said the brother of her cousin's widow had agreed to set the estate in order, so there was no reason after all for her and Father to stay. She asked if anything important had happened while she was away, and I told her nothing out of the ordinary, except Rose was coming down with pinkeye. By noon Edwina was standing at the foot of the lot, staring patiently at the house but going on her way by one. Neither of my parents commented on her, and the Prussian told me Rose's eyes were fine.

Around three Mother sent Malina on errands, and I went along, afraid to be too near my parents while I was so full of secrets. As we left the butcher's, Thomas Rafferty came up behind us, slid his arm through the handle of the basket I was carrying, and said, "Let me help you."

I could not very well yank the basket back from him and make a scene. He was tall and well-built. He took Malina's packages from her also, reminding me so much of Hailus that I thought he was after her the way Hailus had been after Ed. I couldn't imagine Malina with a man, struck dumb as she was by life in general, or a man like Rafferty wanting to seduce a rock of a girl like her, but I imagined the plain orneriness of it, to cause trouble where no one thought defenses would be needed.

So he walked along with us, commenting on the weather and on passersby in a voice false with mocking, or whistling softly under his breath, until he said out of nowhere, "You know your mother's gotten rid of all but two of Edwina Selchie's clients. She doesn't have enough work to make a living now."

"You don't know that."

"I know everything, Miss Anna. I make it my business to. The poor little mice are so intimidated by that kaiser mother of yours that they've capitulated. Now that she's back, I imagine she'll dispose of the two who are still left sleeping on clean sheets."

I stared straight at the sidewalk in front of me as if it would disappear if I took my eyes off it.

"I doubt whether their brains can handle the intricacies of Mrs. Berter's ethics, but you don't have to understand her to want to obey her, as you well know."

He moved nearer, and our shoulders brushed.

"All her artillery aimed at Edwina Selchie. 'Who breaks a butterfly upon the wheel?' But it's done now, though it's not right what's happening to her, and worse yet that no one's stepped forward to help her."

"You could. Father says you always get your way in cheating farmers out of their land."

"I never cheat but only receive what has not been taken care of. Besides, your mother and land are two different propositions entirely. If I would defend the Selchies, can't you hear her? If a devil like me is for them, then the rest of New Marango must be against. Oh, no, I'll not play her game."

"Then you could at least charge them less rent."

"And just how much am I charging now? What figure lies in the ledgers that you've been privy to?"

"Father told me it was an outrageous amount."

"And how does he know?"

"He knows what kind of man you are, and from that he can guess."

"Ah, Miss Berter, do you not see how the game works here in New Marango? The gentleman Tucker is accused of getting a child and sent home with a box lunch and a kiss from your mother. I collect rent on my own land, and suddenly I'm an evil Shylock."

"Then how much do you charge?"

"Seven shirts and fourteen socks a week, the shirts ironed and the socks folded. It is robbery to ask that much, but Mrs. Selchie insisted they pay their way, and so in return I bring them food as often as they will believe I have that many leftovers from my plate."

I was embarrassed and angry that the argument held no weight.

"Cat's got your tongue again. Well, nonetheless, the mill's set in motion and the grain will be ground, poor fool. The best I can hope for, now that my rent and laundry are on their way to being lost, is a good entertainment. Those fine ladies with their proper banners flying, out for the kill."

We came to the curb, and he handed our packages back to Malina.

"You know," he said, taking my arm and sliding the basket over it, "the good doctor doesn't know what his wife is up to, but if a person were worried about Edwina Selchie, that person might tell him what's about."

Thomas Rafferty winked at me, his eyes deep dawn gray, and turned back the way he had come. He whistled a jig, and though I wouldn't turn around to see, I imagined him dancing away from me.

"Liar," I said.

Malina's face screwed up in concentration, and her mouth labored over a word that would not be born. I looked away in discomfort at her effort.

"No," she said finally, her lips twisting in search of the next sounds. "He's not."

I did not ask how she knew, though I guessed it was serving girl gossip. I did not want to put her through the torture of trying to explain so complicated a piece of information, and we walked in silence the rest of the way home, the handle of the basket leaving a red mark on my arm.

That night after standing a long time in the hall, so quiet I could hear my mother turning the pages of her book in the parlor and my father's pen scrawling across a ledger in his office, I sat down across the desk from him. He looked up occasionally from his work to smile at me. I wanted him to say, "Anna, we need to straighten out all the confusion."

Then he would tell me the story of Chicago and the good reason—for there must be one—why he had not told me before. He would say the Prussian had changed her mind about having the Selchies come back to work for us. He would put everything right, and I wanted so badly that he do this that I kept repeating the words in my mind: *Save me, Father.*

But this time was no different, and finally I asked, instead of all that I had been thinking, "How was the funeral?"

He looked up absently as if trying to remember which one. "Oh, yes. The widow held up well. She was not nearly as bereaved as your mother had predicted."

"And the Selchies?"

"I've told the druggist to have the boy deliver medication whenever needs be." He pulled his reading glasses down on his nose and looked over them at me. "I'm sure they'll be all right, if nothing happens to agitate Edwina further."

I wanted to confess that I was the catalyst of her upset and ask him then to help, the way Rafferty told me I must, but he pushed the glasses back up and entered a number in the ledger.

"I should hire an accountant to do this. Or maybe you'd like to take over?"

"I don't care for numbers."

"Just like your mother. My last hope is Rose."

I wondered if I truly was like my mother. Like the Prussian or like that mother before her. I didn't feel like anyone but my own self, foreign and strange and disconnected from all others. Like no one and from no one. I did not know how to ask him about any of this.

"I'm going up to bed now," I told him.

"Dream with the angels, Schatzie."

And so there was silence, as there had been so many times before, and the whisperings of night voices that could not find tongues to speak in light. I lay awake again until after my parents had gone to bed and listened in the air to all that had not been said.

Chapter Fourteen

*T*HE NEXT MORNING AT BREAKFAST, the conversation went on too long between my parents, and I watched Rose arranging her glass and spoon in a line with her plate. I knew she was doing what I used to as a child to pass the long mealtimes, when I imagined the cloth as snow, the teapot as a church, and the flatware as distant silver rivers, quiet and perfect in the cold. Rose, left to her own devices, wandered in her mind and returned to that place where she would go. During a lull in the conversation she suddenly asked, "How do they get their skins off?"

We all turned to her.

"Who?" my father asked.

"The rabbits who lost their skins."

"Rabbits?"

"The ones those people ate."

"On one of our walks while you were gone," I said quickly, "we stopped once to look at a hutch."

"Where was this, Anna?" the Prussian asked.

"Over past Clark Street, I don't remember exactly which block."

"Then what's this about skins?"

"They had some of those too."

"Pelts?" my father asked. "They skin them off, Rosie."

"How?" Rose asked.

"Don't tell her such things, Will."

"If she's seen the rabbits and the pelts, she should know how one became the other." He turned toward Rose. "They slit the skin around the neck and paws and make a long incision down the belly, then the pelt slides right off."

"Then how do they get them back on later?"

"Who?"

"The rabbits."

"They can't do that, Rose," the Prussian interrupted.

"The lady said they did."

"What lady?"

"The one who gave me lemonade. She said the rabbits come back at night to get their skins."

"Who was this, Anna?"

"The woman who owned the hutch. It was warm out, and she brought us a drink."

"You know better than to accept anything from a stranger. And what is all this about the rabbits?"

"Rose has it confused. The woman was telling us about raising them, and Rose must have heard her wrong."

"No, Anna, she said they come back at night."

"You heard it wrong, Rosie. I was there."

Rose looked at me for the longest time, her face placid, her eyes still. I was taken by how during those becalmed moments she was like Edwina, detached from all around her, and I was disturbed by how I had missed that resemblance, looked at Rose and not seen Edwina in her.

Then Father left us to see to his first patient, and the Prussian called Rose to her.

"Sit in my lap, Rose," she said, lifting her up. "You know that when animals are butchered, they never come back."

Rose sat silent.

"They are gone forever, and you never see them again." The Prussian untied the ribbon I had hastily put in Rose's hair. Then her fingers probed the stubble where

Ed had cut the lock, pushing the longer strands away. "Oh, Anna, how can I trust you to watch her if you let things like this happen? Go on to Malina now, Rose. Anna and I have to talk."

The Prussian gave a last nudge at the stubble with her thumb, and Rose looked at me over her shoulder as she went to the kitchen. The Prussian and I sat silently until the door finished swinging back and forth.

"Now, Anna, just what went on?"

"Not what Rose says. You know how children get things confused. Who would tell her a silly notion like that about the pelts?"

"And her hair?"

"It was my mistake. She reached too quickly for my sewing scissors. It all happened in an instant, and I couldn't stop her in time. I put them up after that, where she couldn't reach them, as you always do."

She hesitated a moment, and I saw I had touched her vanity.

"Then what about this woman? Who was she?"

I shrugged. "I don't really know if she was the owner of the house or merely a servant. She was older but not old, heavyset, with brunette hair, and she had a wen the size of a pea on the end of her chin. I don't remember ever seeing her before, but when we stopped, she came over from where she was hanging out clothes and was quite pleasant."

I made up more of the story, and the woman with the rabbits became real. I could clearly see her small house under a large elm, a fence tangled over with sweet peas, her brown forearms and rolled-up sleeves. The Prussian concentrated on a spot of vacant air halfway across the room, and I knew she was seeing her own image of my story, a similar but slightly different stranger and yard and house and hutch.

Even I had begun to believe in this place, it was so clear the way the sun dappled through the elm leaves and the rabbit twitched its nose. That scene began its own life, separate from the afternoon in the Old One's clearing with Rose on her lap, and was clearer than what had happened, so easy was it to control the exactness of detail and know the intentions of all those involved. So easy to end the story neatly.

I went on, saying what I knew the Prussian would want to hear, and, in a faint, guilty way, was aware I was tricking myself in some way similar to how I was deceiving my mother. For me the story seemed so safe. The woman at the hutch wanted nothing of ours nor wished us harm.

"But you realize you were wrong to allow Rose there, even though nothing serious came of it."

"Oh, yes! It was stupid of me."

"Still, her hair is ruined, you know." She folded her napkin and slipped the silver ring over it. "It'll take months to grow out, not to mention how badly she could have cut herself."

"I'm sorry."

"Never do this again."

"Never. May I be excused now?"

"You'll promise?"

"Yes, of course."

"You are excused."

Excused. I went to my room and went over and over the reasons that excused me from my lie. But they all came down to this: I could not tell her the truth. The whole truth was impossible, and part of the truth was still a lie. And once I had begun to lie, other lies fell out in an endless chain, though they all came from that one point, from the Prussian, who would not listen to what she didn't want to hear and who forbade anything she disagreed with.

I could have nothing inside me that was not hers, approved and visible. Yet she was wrong about Ed and Rose and myself, and I did not know where to put all the facts and truths and images I knew that the Prussian would not admit into existence. What I wanted of my own, what I thought when I wasn't interfered with, what I would do without restriction.

To take Rose to Ed and stop her screaming.

To please the Old One.

To move freely like a selchie diving down the fathoms and having the whole wide ocean to swim in.

What harm in any of that?

But when I went to the window, Edwina was standing at the bottom of the lawn, staring up at the house with bovine patience, her arms loose as if she had nowhere else to go ever in her life, the way Father said she came while we were at the lake. I had been the one to start this, to promise I would bring Rose again, and now I did not know how to keep my promise.

I yearned to ask the Old One what to do, or even Rafferty. But all morning the Prussian busied herself putting away the travel things, and I could not walk down the steps that I did not meet her coming up. No chance to get away. At lunch Father looked at Rose curiously, then reached over to hold her face in his hand and turn it toward a certain light.

"Pinkeye. How did I miss that yesterday?"

The Prussian glanced at me but did not tell him I had warned her. After lunch she went with him into the office to hold Rose while he gave her an eyewash, and from upstairs I heard her screaming. I knew what the Prussian was saying to her through it all. "Hold still and stop screaming. It is all for your own good." As she would tell Edwina. Stop screaming. This is for your own good. To withhold the secrets of our births, to keep us close forever. For our own good. All our good. As if the Prussian were privy to the scheme of the universe.

The Prussian went through all the rooms and adjusted figurines on tables and straightened pictures as though the household had tilted out of balance in her absence. Finally at four she left for the post office to mail a letter to her cousin's widow, and she mentioned she had some other stops to make. I could not calculate how long she would be out, but as soon as the auto was out of sight, I ran for the clearing.

It was deserted, the door left open and no laundry on the lines. I walked through the empty cabin, trailing my hand along the bed quilt and rough wood table, over the pelts hung on the wall and the blue enamel pot on the stove, as if by touching their things I could tell where they had gone. Without Ed and the Old One there, it was a curious, broken-down place where life had little softness or beauty or comfort. I wanted them badly then, to fill the emptiness and speak words the Prussian would not say. It was so easy to forget why I thought her wrong when she was the only one to listen to.

I could not find pencil and paper to leave a note. Instead I took a stick and scratched ANNA in the dirt in front of the steps, wide letters that reached across their width. Then, so Ed would not become upset, I added "no Rose now" and "later" beneath my name before turning back toward the long path. I ran then, until I got a stitch in my side looking for Rafferty, who perversely was nowhere to be found. People passed me on the street. They waved and made me afraid they would later tell my mother where they had seen me, and I worried how long it had taken me to go and return. What had seemed so important to find out? I could only promise the unknown and the uncertain, which was worse than no promise at all. Nothing the Old One could say would change that.

What had I wanted, then? My feet hit the sidewalk in rhythm with my breathing, and all around, the late bright sun threw hard shadows on all the streets and houses of New Marango. The empty clearing had left me with immeasurable sadness, and I knew then I did not want to be without the Selchies near. I had gone in truth to look into their faces and feel the Old One's hand soft and strong against my cheek. Her absence made me want to cry with loss, and I could not bear to think my mother might drive them away again. I had accepted that once, thinking it was in trade for Rose, but it was always for the Prussian and her peace of mind. I could not stand that. Then I turned into my drive and saw the automobile. The Prussian had returned before me, and all my sorrow turned to fear.

Chapter Fifteen

ALL WAS QUIET IN THE house except for the ticking of the mantel clock. In the parlor the Prussian sat with neither reading nor sewing to occupy her. She watched the door as I came through, and I felt the warmth of fear spread throughout me.

"Where have you been, Anna?"

"For a walk."

"And where did you walk?"

"Nowhere in particular. A few blocks that way and then around. I really didn't keep track."

"Is that your usual way?"

"I have no way."

"I saw Lucy Minchion downtown. She says she's seen you cut through her yard and go down the path behind her house. She saw you once alone and twice with Rose, and since Lucy is not in the habit of sitting by her window, I can imagine there were other times she missed."

I stood not letting my eyes waver from her eyes watching me with cold passion, her hands folded in her lap. I could neither explain all the complex reasons I had gone against her nor believe she would listen. I could only keep my gaze locked with hers to prove I could stand to face her, triumphant as she was at having caught me.

"You will not disobey me, Anna Berter. As long as you live in my house and eat at my table, you are subject to my will, and you will not go where I have forbidden you."

She tapped her finger in time with her words and I wanted to clap my hand over her mouth and hold her still. But she went on, swearing that she would not have her family endangered by exposure to those people, protesting that they had filled my head with nonsense and made me believe that I could do as I wished, just as they went about at whim as if there were no order in the world.

I had no way to reason against her argument, which had no reason in it. We were beyond words, and all was condensed in the feeling that she was a weight bearing down on me and I was the counterweight resisting, that we had left our bodies and become masses of force with no more visibility than the air but with the strength of storms wishing to occupy the same sector of the sky. I felt her pushing against me and myself pushing back until the immense tension between us threatened to explode the very room into nothingness.

And as I held steady with all my might, I wanted her to suddenly embrace me and say, "Oh, Anna, we must stop what we have started here," so I could cling to her until the maelstrom around us settled back into calm. But I did not believe she would do this of her own accord, and I was afraid to ask for tenderness, which she would see as weakness to break through. Instead I called up feelings so solid and hard they were like rock around me, and the mantel clock ticked off the minutes until she spoke.

"Have you nothing to say about all this?"

"I cannot say anything to you," I replied.

"I will not leave you alone with Rose again. You will have no chance to leave here with her."

I shrugged as if that were nothing to me.

"You will accompany me everywhere so I may keep my eye on you."

"Is that all?"

"All, except for the fact that you have betrayed me

and broken your trust with your own mother. I am hurt, Anna, that you would treat me so, and I cannot estimate how long it will take before you will be able to win back my approval."

I wanted her words to echo back to her in my own voice: "You have betrayed me and broken trust." By keeping the secret of my birth. By treating the Selchies in ways you would have punished me for doing. By not being as good and strong as I always believed you to be.

I shrugged again and said I was sorry in a tone no one would take as genuine, then I asked to leave the room. She raised her eyebrows and nodded, but before I reached the door, she addressed my back. "You will understand my position as you get older, Anna, and someday you will know that I am right."

I stopped for a moment and swore to myself that her prophecy would never come true. I closed myself in my room and came down only for dinner. The Prussian was polite but curt, the way she always was when one of us had displeased her. I caught my father giving me furtive looks, but he never later asked my version of what had happened. The next day and for what seemed a hundred days after, Rose and I went with the Prussian on her calls and errands, to meetings and lectures, like unborn circus twins attached to each other and to her. Always with her, waiting for her to be ready to come or ready to go. For two weeks that seemed like two ages I yearned for school to start, if only to escape contact so claustrophobic that I felt us like livestock wedged in our slaughter pens with no room left to stand or breathe.

I amused Rose during the interminable afternoons and watched the Prussian with her public face, this charming woman so different from the tyrant in our home. She guided conversations, produced plans, assigned jobs, and sent off her friends, happy to do her bidding. I was leery of being seduced by her, so full of graceful power, and I wanted to warn the ones who paid her court that she was not as she seemed. But no one would believe me that the Prussian I would tell them about was the same as the one before them.

Then on one afternoon that began like all the others, the Prussian stopped for a fitting of a toast-colored linen that was the envy of the other women in the crowded shop. But when we came out of the dressmaker's, the Old One was waiting on the sidewalk, her old black dress and bonnet gray with age, her gnarled walking stick planted square in front of her.

"Etta Berter," she said, her green eyes sharp, "how can your heart be so hardened that it is empty of mercy?"

The Prussian paused for a moment and then turned as though the Old One were not there. The women crowded about the shop windows, a passerby slowed his pace, and a couple driving a farm wagon turned around in their seat to watch. I stopped, Rose's hand in mine, and was embarrassed for my mother that all of them would soon know the business of our family.

"Stop, Etta Berter," the Old One cried. "I will follow you until you listen, so 'tis best you hear me now."

The Prussian turned. "This is not the place for this, Mrs. Selchie. Make an appointment to see me when we can discuss this in private."

"When you carried your spite to the other women of this town, you brought your hatred into the open, and here we'll finish it, in plain sight." The Old One clasped her hands more firmly around her stick. "Did you think I'd stay silent while you poisoned their minds against my granddaughter? When you steal a person's work, Etta Berter, you steal not only the bread from her mouth but her spirit too. It is worse than thieving, though you touch not money or possessions."

"I said this is not the place, Mrs. Selchie. I'm on my way with the girls to another shop."

"I have made it the place, and here I'll ask you to undo the mischief you've set loose on Edwina. She is a fragile thing, and there is no reason for you to set more on her load than she can carry. 'Tis bad enough that she cannot see her babe, but to take the last of her work is the devil's own plan."

"How can I take work from anyone not in my employ?" The Prussian pressed one palm flat against her chest.

"I'll not waste breath telling you what you know from doing. But I'll warn you to set it right or suffer in your soul for it."

"I don't know what you're talking about." Her eyes were wide in mock bafflement. "You stop me on a public street in front of my own daughters and accuse me of God knows what." She took a step forward. "What did you say? Of poisoning your granddaughter, when I've had no dealings with her? Surely, Mrs. Selchie, you cannot expect me to stand for such outrage."

Several more people had stopped on their way down the street, and from the corner of my eye I could see the women in the dress shop nodding in agreement.

"I'm astounded also," she went on, "that a good Christian woman like yourself would bring false witness against her neighbor and flaunt the breaking of a commandment. Why, I cannot imagine what is on your mind."

The Prussian kept her eyes on the Old One, not breaking the mood of injured outrage that she had set and fully expecting, I am sure, the Old One to avert her own eyes. Yet the Old One stood as if she would hold that spot until time ended. She took a deep exasperated breath.

"If we found you with your hands around a dead man's throat, you'd claim to heaven you didn't know how the corpse came to be that way."

The Old One shook her head and pointed at Rose and me.

"For the sake of your daughters, Etta Berter, I'll tell what you are pure blind ignorant of. The closer you try to hold them to you, the further they will fly away; the more you close them in darkness, the harder they will struggle to the light: For in that cave of yourself is all you would not have them know, yet to that is where you press their faces."

I felt suddenly naked and lifted Rose into my arms for cover. The Prussian glanced at her audience in the window. "Now you're telling nonsense riddles, and I worry for your sanity."

"You can mock, but that won't change a word of what I'm saying. Contraries hold truths in their folds and turnings, and I tell you that trusting in their sense is the beginning of our wisdom." The Old One stepped closer. "If you will not hear me for your own sake, then listen for the good of your daughters, else you lose what you would most like to keep. It is the truth that will out and the secrets that will tell."

The Prussian stood shaking her head slowly and making soft noises, the way she would before the most pathetic of cases. "It is small wonder that the granddaughter has trouble keeping her wits about her. Come, Anna, and bring Rose. We're late for our next appointment."

The Prussian wheeled and turned down the street, and I wanted to speak to the women in the Old One's defense.

"Go, Anna," the Old One said. "You'll help nothing by staying here."

As I passed her, the Old One caught my arm and laid her hand on Rose's head. The Prussian turned at that moment to see if we were following.

"Do not touch my daughter!"

The Old One held her hand on Rose. "She were born with my touch upon her, and there is nothing that will erase the mark.

"Keep her safe, Anna," she said as she turned away, using the walking stick to pole her along the sidewalk as if it were a river. In the silence her words hung like visible text for all to read, and it seemed that since she had spoken the prophecy to all, it was now bound to come true.

"Hurry, Anna," my mother called. "I told you we're late for our appointment."

I knew there was none, but I hurried toward her to get out of the sight of the women in the shop and those lingering on the street. She held her arms out like a herder shooing geese toward home. "Get in the automobile, Anna. I have one more stop, but you and Rose wait here."

I got in the front and closed my eyes. The sun had been too bright, the meeting with the Old One too intense. I wanted to shut out all of it and recline into the blackness I had made, but I kept seeing pieces and snatches, revolving and changing. The Old One's face like an ancient angel's, the Prussian's superior smile, and Edwina breaking apart into crushed bits of sorrow. Always Edwina, and Rose evaporating with her.

"Exhausted, are we? And you didn't even do any of the sparring," the voice said.

I opened my eyes. Rafferty was at the window, not a foot from my face, his arms crossed on the door and his weight forward, the way he would stand at a bar. Rafferty grinning, his teeth even and white, his hat tilted back on his head, and his shirt collar open in the heat. I leaned away from him.

"Leave us alone."

"Ah, the Berter family motto, dismissing all until they are the only ones left in the world. If only you could have it so."

"Get away from the automobile, then. It's ours." I sat up straight and looked out the windshield.

"If your mother had her way, the whole damn town and every public thoroughfare would be hers." Rafferty shifted his weight but did not remove his arm. "She would've scared almost anyone but Carline Selchie off of

Main Street this afternoon, but the old girl stood her ground. I like that in a woman, a sure claim on what is her own and a healthy respect for what isn't."

"This isn't your business."

"What happens in the street belongs to us all, and thank goodness. Why, the last excitement we had to save us from boredom was when Jim Cooney fell off that roof and we had three days to speculate on whether he'd die. Just shows humans are a crooked lot who would just as soon eat each other as sneeze."

I glanced at him, his mouth twisted in its usual wry grin but with something tired and melancholy about his eyes.

"Cat got your tongue?" he asked.

Rose climbed over the back of the seat and crawled in my lap. "Hello," she said.

"Now here's a sweet, friendly child." He held out his palm, and Rose placed her hand on it. "It's no wonder why Edwina Selchie mourns her loss and becomes unbalanced in her absence."

"It hasn't been that long since she's seen her," I snapped.

"But every minute turns into a lifetime for a mother who never knows if she will see her daughter again. Think about it. If your sister were lost, every second of her absence would be agony. It's uncertainty that changes the game and makes it dangerous. I'll wager your kaiser of a mother can't stand a gamble. Better to put poor Edwina Selchie in her grave than be unsure of what she's going to do."

"You talk as if my mother were a murderess."

"The good Mrs. Berter? The first lady of New Marango?"

"Stop this in front of my sister."

"She's too young to understand, but you're not. If someone runs another to ground by taking all that person cares about, why, we might as well bury what's left, you know. Not enough, at least, to count as human."

"Stop." I felt trapped, with him against the door and Rose on my lap. I rubbed my free hand up over my face and held it tight against my temple, but he went on.

"So. Are you going to let her do this?"

I turned to him sharply. "Let her? Do what?"

"Take Edwina's work. Keep her from seeing her child."

"But what have I to do with it? I tried. I did my best to help, but what can you expect now?"

"You know there's more. You tried, up to a point, but that's no excuse. You didn't speak with your father, I'll wager."

I looked out the windshield again.

"And if you can't find the courage to talk to him, then it's a safe bet you've not tried to approach the empress herself, have you? Just think. If she knew you knew, if her own daughter came to her and said, 'Madam, I cannot tolerate what you've done. I'm taking my sister calling, whether you like it or not.' Just like that."

He snapped his fingers.

"What do you think would happen, Anna Berter, if you stopped tiptoeing around the woman and just defied her? Oh, it's a gem of a scene to speculate on. And what have you got to lose? What else could she do? Lock you in the mansion? At least you'd have your whole self intact."

I hugged Rose to me and tried to shut out his words.

"You hear me, don't you?" he said and leaned in the window, closer. "You know you haven't done all you could. Wait just a while longer and it'll be too late. Then what will happen cannot be your fault. It's the way your mother does it. She never dirties her hands, not directly, and then none of it is ever her fault. Well, you didn't come from her and you don't look like her, but it's all the same anyway. The leopard has passed on her spots."

Rafferty reached in and gave Rose a soft pat on her cheek. "Take care, little one, living in a den of panthers as you do."

He walked off abruptly then, leaving only the heaviness of his words and warning.

"I want to go home, Anna," Rose said.

"We will, as soon as Mother gets here."

It could not have been more than ten minutes later

that the Prussian returned. Her face was composed, and she went on about the slowness of the clerk, who could not count out her change correctly. I tried closing my eyes again, but never without the thought that when I opened them Rafferty's face would be before mine, his gray eyes accusing. I watched the Prussian as she drove along: her straight nose and finely molded chin, her high cheekbones and delicate brow. I ran my finger down the center of my face, dragging the skin over the bone and knowing my profile was so different from hers, yet wondering if somehow inside it was identical.

"Let me tell your father about this afternoon, Anna. I want to explain it in my own way."

I wondered if she would really tell him at all, or, if she did, how the story would change and the Old One be transformed. Whatever the variation, I knew the Prussian would become the victim, unjustly attacked. Then we turned onto our street and I saw Edwina standing on the walk at the foot of the lawn with her feet wide apart and her body swaying slightly. Her arms cradled each other, and her lips moved, I could not tell whether in conversation or in song. But she stood rocking herself and speaking to the empty air, swaying and singing to the wind.

"Keep your eyes straight ahead as we pass," the Prussian warned me.

But Rose pointed and stared.

"Look, Anna."

"Yes, Rose."

"I want to play with her again."

"Another day."

"Tell her never, Anna. Never."

I laid my face against Rose's hair and hugged her to me. Edwina glanced toward the car as we passed but took no more notice than if she had been blind. Her eyes were fixed on a point above us, and her vision was filled with what we could not see.

"Tell her, Anna," the Prussian repeated.

"Never," I answered. "Never."

Part Three

Chapter Sixteen

$\mathcal{E}$DWINA BEGAN TO APPEAR LIKE thunderheads at the base of the lawn. More frequently she came, the vigils longer and each time more agitated as she paced and turned and veered. I passed by the windows often to look for her, sometimes stopping to watch if she was there.

"Do not go out there, Anna. I forbid it," the Prussian said each time she caught me.

"I would only talk with her."

"There is nothing you can say that would do her any good."

After three days of this, my father said at dinner he would like me to go with him on calls the next day. The Prussian laid her fork at the back of her plate with a click and folded her hands in her lap.

"No, Etta, we don't know how long it will take to settle all this. You cannot keep her in indefinitely."

The next morning I dressed in a long, loose smock to cover one of my older dresses and carried my father's leather satchel of instruments and medications out to the buggy the stableboy had waiting. My mother, as was her habit when I accompanied my father, did not come down but took a breakfast tray in her room, and I knew that for the next few days she would be taciturn and curt as our punishment. But as always on days when I left with him, I looked over my shoulder at her window as we went down the drive, hoping to see her standing there, and always the empty window both disappointed me and justified my leaving.

"Your mother has not broken custom, has she?" my father asked.

"Of course not." I leaned back in the seat, happy to see sky and be out of the prisoning house.

"Do not blame her. The leopard cannot change his spots."

I turned to him sharply, wondering at how he had quoted Rafferty. "Why did you say that?"

"What?"

"About the leopard."

"It seems to fit her."

"But why a leopard?"

"I'm only quoting. Shakespeare, I believe, though I cannot tell you which play."

I stared at the rhythmic movement of the horses' haunches, shocked by the thought that Rafferty read Shakespeare or did anything that was at all decent. Then after too long a silence, long enough that we had passed the city limits and were trotting down a road that seemed to run through the middle of an endless field, my father said, "I know she is difficult and unyielding sometimes, but she has her reasons, and we must let her have her way."

Then he was quiet again, as if that statement was all he could bring himself to say about her and that it in itself explained everything.

"She's against the Selchies," I said.

"She merely wants what's best for all in the long run. Especially Rose. She's so concerned this will confuse and harm her."

"She doesn't even want me to come with you on calls. She never does."

He let out a deep sigh. "There are some things we cannot help, Anna. You have two parents and a right to both their influences. If I didn't insist you come with me sometimes, I would feel that I was not doing my duty by you. I'm sorry she takes it so badly, but she is more yielding in this matter than in others. She does seem to have found her solution in ignoring us, and we must let her handle this in the way it suits her."

The contradiction lay like some awkward thing on the seat between us. To give in and go against. To comply and defy. I could not tell how he knew when to use one over the other, or if he gauged his rebellions only on personal desire. But as we moved down the avenue of corn, the wide summer sky above us, there was the opportunity to talk about her, out alone where no one could possibly interrupt us or overhear. He had said she had her reasons, and I wanted him to tell those secrets he was privy to. I wanted to understand what dark things had happened that excused all she did to us and those around us.

But I was afraid of those things as much as I was curious. I sensed they had not been told because my mother was protecting me from their horrifying shapes. Hailus had told some of her secrets, and I could not quit thinking of the unborn calf caught in its mother's womb, nor of my grandmother's frozen corpse.

The untold possibilities were monstrous. Of baby-stealers and hypocrites. Of those who drove the innocent from our town and kept the rules only when it suited them. Of liars and deceivers. I could not bring myself to ask my father for fear of what he could tell me, and we drove down the lane in silence.

We stopped first at an old farmer's to check his gout. Then we went down the road and followed a thin, tired woman into the kitchen, where her six children, all infected with ringworm, were waiting for us. The two youngest cried without stop, and the four oldest stared at us sullenly as if we were there to cheat them. They were all dirty and beaten-looking, and while Father cleaned each sore, he asked them if there had been enough to eat and if they listened well to their mother and obeyed her. As he and I rinsed out the basin at the pump, he told me in a lowered voice that their father could not be depended upon and this was the result.

"A new baby every other year and nothing much else. The pack of them would be better off in the orphanage. But now the best for last," he told me as we swung toward the Hannach place, the farm of a young couple he always talked about fondly. "Now you'll get to meet them."

Mary Hannach answered the door for us, so great with child she looked deformed, and I imagined the fetus was trying to stand up inside her. She led us into the parlor, where her husband Paul's bed was set up to take advantage of the cooler air and save her from running up and down the stairs to nurse him. His leg was propped on a mound of pillows and his back against a mountain more.

"Mary's having her pains," he announced cheerfully.

"It's nothing yet, I told you." She leaned against the doorjamb and put her hand flat against her swollen belly.

"How frequent are they?" my father asked.

"On the half hour," Paul Hannach answered. "You got here with no time to spare, Dr. Berter."

"Time to look at your leg first."

"He's been in awful pain," Mary told us.

"Not bad enough to send for you."

Father folded back the covers propped over the leg and gently unwrapped the packing until a great green and purple knot showed. Deformed and disgusting, but I assumed that was what a broken leg should look like and so betrayed no emotion in front of the patient, as my father had instructed me.

He glanced up at me quickly, then at Paul. "The leg's not healing, and it must be straightened, Paul, or it will never be any good to you. You waited too long to have it set in the first place."

"Then we'll do it after the baby's delivered."

"The baby's in no rush," Mary said. "Do it now so you'll have some chance of laying in the winter wheat."

Then she turned quickly and left the room. I followed Father into the kitchen to scrub our hands, trying all the while to look professional and calm, the way I imagined I should.

"Anna, I hadn't planned for you to see this," he said.

"I could use you to help with the anesthesia, but perhaps you should wait in the buggy until I'm done."

"But I can help you," I said. "There will be no blood."

"All right then, but do not be brave. If you feel faint, leave the room."

Then he explained the procedure and what he required and told me he trusted that I had a calm head. I assisted him in laying out his necessities and then sprinkled ether on a gauze pad, being careful not to breathe any of the fumes and happy in a way that Paul Hannach's misfortune had given me the chance to do something important with my father. Then Father nodded, and I held the gauze over the man's face, lifting it to lean close enough to smell the pipe tobacco on his breath and call his name so loudly he would have jumped if he weren't unconscious. I kept his limp hand in mine, and whenever I felt it stirring I laid the gauze back over his face, careful to give him just enough so he and the pain were both too bleary to get their hands tightly on each other. Father twisted the leg, and I heard the snap of bone and groaning of muscle. Paul Hannach cried out from the pit of the ether. Then Father rewrapped the leg tightly and strung it securely in place, while I wiped the sweat from both his brow and the patient's. In the hall we found Mary, white as death.

"Is it done?" she asked.

"Take her upstairs, Anna, while I scrub my hands."

I put my arm around the swelling that had been her waist, and she fell softly against me. "I didn't mean to have it now. I told him the pains were further apart so he wouldn't worry. I tried to wait until his leg was fixed."

"Shush," I told her. "Everything will be fine."

But her skin was clammy and pale. Her palm pressed at the baby with every pain, as if she were trying to push it out of her. I tried not to look at her as I got her undressed and unwrapped the binding around her middle, but I could not escape seeing the white expanse of her backside and the blood smeared down her legs. As I pulled her nightgown down over her head, her waters broke and soaked my skirt with warmth.

"Father tells all his patients not to bind themselves," I said, mopping up the lake of fluids with her petticoat.

"The baby was so heavy. I was afraid it would fall out through my skin." Surprised by the pain, she gave a short quick cry. "Oh, help me. I was so afraid I would be alone with only him when the child came."

"How long has the labor been?"

"Before dawn."

"And how frequent the pains?"

"They are falling on top of one another." Her fingers dug into my arm, and great beads of sweat broke out on her forehead. "Help me. I am going to die."

And I was afraid she was. Her false calm of an hour

before had been ripped apart by the creature inside her, trying to get out. She twisted and arched her back against it, as if she were being eaten alive from the inside. My reason told me this attack was not as sudden as it seemed, and Mary Hannach had both lied about her pain and intensified it with her fear. Yet somehow what I knew about that lie was not as strong as the sight of her bent double before me.

I lowered her onto the bed and tried to hold her down. I wondered if the child inside her would kill her the way the Prussian had done her mother. At that moment it seemed that bringing life to light meant death for the bringer and all parents were in danger from their children, and in her screaming that truth became stronger than all I knew of live babies and living mothers.

I laid my palm flat against her forehead and my hand against her thigh. I pressed down with all my weight, pushed her deeper into the mattress to hold her still with force past reason, and between the pains she was quiet. But the space between them was nothing, and in my holding I became the Prussian of the dream I'd had when I was twelve, holding myself struggling under the lake and making me fear water.

I was still Anna Berter keeping Mary Hannach still. But also I became Etta Vette proving her power over her child, pushing her under to prove what could happen if she didn't obey, and still again I was the child begging for air and pleading to be held above the lapping waves.

I warned Mary Hannach to be still, not only for her own good but so as not to frighten me and disprove the lie of an orderly and controllable world. And inside myself I just as loudly cried for air and my right to be disorderly in the blood and slime of birth. As I was horrified over her transformation, I understood and sympathized with the baby inside her fighting for air, a baby old enough to breathe on its own being drowned inside the lake of its mother. I decided if I must pick between them, I wanted the child to live.

Then Father came in from scrubbing and took his place at the foot of the bed.

"It's crowned," he said.

I leaned over to look between her legs but in the blood could not tell baby from mother.

"What is wrong?" Mary tried to sit, and I held her down.

"The baby's head is showing," I told her.

"Mary," my father said, "I'm going to send Anna to fetch old Mrs. Selchie to help us. She's close down the road and has delivered many babies in her time."

I tried to question him with my eyes. He wiped the pudendum with a sheet and, parting the folds of skin there, pointed at a curve inside, the tiny arc of an ear. The baby's head was slightly turned.

"First babies take forever to be born, Mary. I'm sending for Mrs. Selchie to spell me during the wait and help with knowledge Anna doesn't have yet. Go on now, Anna. Hurry."

I stopped to check on Paul Hannach, who dozed in a morphine haze, then gathered the bays' reins, wishing all the while Father had let me stay with Mary Hannach, since I'd no more experience driving horses than I'd had birthing babies. The team took off at a run over the rough ruts of the farm road, the carriage bouncing as if it weighed nothing, and I clinging to the slender reins, like to the strings of an enormous kite. The momentary weightlessness as I flew off the seat, the low scuttle of clouds racing over my head, the rasp and foam of the horses' breathing: I had the thought that none of what took place in the farmhouse had been real. No leg broken or woman being torn or baby dying in its borning. In my mother's house all was clean and predictable; this was what happened when I went out. Then a wheel hit a rock in the road, and I flew again into the air with such force that I feared being thrown over the horses' haunches and dragged beneath their hooves. I caught myself on the rail but not before a long look down between the horses at the road blurring away. I braced my legs and reined in, yelling loudly at the horses to stop. They slowed, bumping shoulders as they changed stride, and looked back at me with white lunatic eyes.

I left the team in Lucy Minchion's drive, raced down

the path to the cabin, and pulled the Old One from her quilting.

"It's not Ed something's happened to?"

No, I told her, but I couldn't explain what the emergency was, only my father's words and the glimpse of an ear. "The baby is caddywampus, she is"—the Old One raised her voice over the clatter of the horses—"and her head stuck sideways. If we try to turn it, the neck may break. If we wait for her to turn herself, the mother may die. Now the day becomes a contest to avoid taking either of those choices."

The wagon jolted us against each other and the dust rose behind. We turned in the Hannachs' lane, and she was up the stairs to Mary, the day becoming long and the night endless. At first I busied myself by checking on Mr. Hannach and fixing nourishment for my father and the Old One. I was hurt that she had no glance or touch for me and felt useless doing nothing while they worked. I dozed on the couch and walked out to the barn. A small herd of Guernseys, their udders full and swollen, shoved themselves against the corner of the fence. I had no idea how to unknot the crowd of them and relieve their suffering and so stood helpless until a neighbor, who had heard their lowing, came to milk them. I threw scratch to the chickens in the yard and fed Paul Hannach spoonfuls of clear broth before Father gave him more morphine, as much for worry as for pain. At dark the kerosene lamps threw dancing shadows on the wall, and overhead Mary Hannach screamed and cried, making me wonder if the voices I imagined as a child in my own upstairs were the true cries of mothers and babies who had died in births before mine.

Then Jim Cooney came to fetch Father. There had been some sort of terrible accident at the grain elevator, staying open late to take in the bean harvest, but Jim could explain it no better than I could the baby's distress. As best we could figure, a farmer had caught his arm in an auger and lost his hand. Father drove off with Jim, leaving the bays for me. The Old One waited by the bed where Mary Hannach was tied with soft sheets. She showed me how to change the pads and judge the flow of blood, how to count the pulse in Mary's wrist and whisk the bottle of ether under her nose to keep her in the nowhere place from pain, how to lay my head on her belly and listen for the baby and slide my fingers around the tiny crown of skull.

"Keep the watch, Anna, while I close my eyes, but first wash your hands so you don't kill her with dirt."

I watched her leave, like a stranger, so businesslike and intent. She and my father had worked over Mary with barely a glance at me or word of reassurance. Now I sat close by the bed, feeling deserted and betrayed, afraid if I stopped checking for signs, both Mary and her baby would die and it would be my fault. The fourth time I counted the thumps in Mary's wrist, the numbers came different and erratic, the blood heavier between her legs, and I ran to the top of the steps and screamed for help.

I don't remember the Old One coming up. She was suddenly just there and pulling me with her to the room, checking the pulses and blood. Out of a bag like Father's satchel she lifted long metal tongs with flat iron pads on the ends and leaned over the end of the bed, wiping her hands on her apron like a blacksmith.

"Hold her legs open and don't let her move."

"What is it you're doing?"

"Taking the baby with forceps. Pushing her back and pulling her out straight."

"You'll break its neck. You said yourself."

I held Mary's knees close together.

"They're both dying. We have to help them."

"You can't break its neck."

"What's come over you, Anna?" She stepped closer and peered at me in the twitching lamplight. "I'm not here to kill the poor thing but to try to save it. Do you think me a monster who would break a poor child's neck for no reason?"

"But to save the mother is a reason."

I wanted the baby to live. Not Mary Hannach screaming and bleeding, with her naked legs spread apart, but the innocent baby. The Old One stepped toward me, waving the amazing iron tongs as if she would put my head between them. She swept them in a wide arc in front of her so I was forced to duck and back away from the bed. "You don't know a thing about this. Now help or be gone."

I was stung by her anger.

"You told me yourself there would be a choice. You've picked the mother."

And strangely I seemed to be arguing two things at once, the choice between the life of this mother and child, the choice between Edwina and Rose. She loved the mothers before their children and would look out for their welfare first.

"I've told you I'm trying not to have to make the choice. But yes, if it comes, I'll take the mother. Do you think this wrinkled little creature will nurse a crippled father or run an Iowa farm or keep the lot from starving and freezing in the coming winter? Survive first, Anna Berter, then worry about the niceties." She swung at me again with the forceps. "Now help, or the baby will suffocate before a forceps ever touches her. I promise if there's a way to keep them both alive, I'll do it."

I held the knees open, leaning across her body and finally straddling her for balance. The Old One with one quick stroke split the skin in the episiotomy and sopped the wound with gauze. The rich, ripe smell of blood and fluids filled the room, and the Old One angled the metal up into the woman's body, crooning all the while to them both. "Now turn, my wee one. Don't be afraid of this world. Push her out to me, Mary, and I'll catch her."

She regrasped the handles, more firmly, and tugged so that I was sure she was crushing the baby's skull and it would finally come out in pieces of bone and bits of brain. Beads of sweat rose on her brow and lip, her pupils dilated in concentration, and her face flushed ruddy with the effort. The Old One, so frail I was afraid that she would break in the struggle, and beneath me the woman's body, worn out from her thrashing, wet blood her only sign of life. Then the Old One grunted and twisted the tongs delicately to the right, slowly eased back, ever so slowly, and the baby's head slid out like an elongated egg.

Its face was covered in blood and what seemed like cottage cheese. It was blue-lipped and blue-veined through translucent skin, wizened and tiny like a shrunken, dried-up dwarf. Its head was uneven and dented on the sides, discolored blotches starting to rise and spread in purple seepage. The narrow hips and slimy cord were covered all over with quantities of the shiny juice of slugs. The Old One dropped the forceps and reached in to disengage an ugly little foot. Quickly she stuck her finger in its mouth and down its throat, turning and cleaning, then she laid it across her lap, letting the deformed head dangle, the snot and juice stream out of its nose and mouth as she rubbed it briskly with a rough towel. It lay still and blue, deepening to purple.

"Pack that cotton batting between her legs as tightly as you can, then cover and lay over her."

I stared dumbly at Mary Hannach, stretched like a corpse before me.

"Feel how cold her skin. It's shock. Save her with your warmth, and keep your knee wedged against the batting."

I lay over the woman I would have killed. My cheek pressed next to hers, and I kept my face down so as not to have to look at her pallor or at the blank eyes rolled back in her head. I rubbed her arms briskly and prayed that she would not die beneath me. All the while I heard the Old One working over the baby, the sound of her hands hitting flat against its back, the friction of the towel against skin, and the Old One's breath blowing into its mouth. Then a sound like the faint mew of kittens in a faraway night room, the weak cry of Mary Hannach's daughter finally suckling the air.

The Old One unbuttoned her dress and chemise. She carried the baby against her old breasts and covered over with the rough bloody towel. "Here is the living child you wanted, Anna Berter. For the time being, at any rate."

She sat on the side of the bed and leaned toward me,

lifting the towel's corner to show me the battered ancient face, still pale and choking on the bubbles at its lips and gluey with the stuff of birth, but now more rose than bruise colored and making small movements and soft sounds.

"Keep over her," the Old One said.

She went back to the business of the baby, and I brushed my lips against Mary Hannach's ear. "It is a girl, live born," I whispered, then pressed my leg more firmly against the batting, already soaked with blood, and willed the flow to stop.

Then I wondered if my grandfather had lain over the other Anna in the same way while she died in the blizzard, and if he tucked their baby between them and prayed both should live even as one turned to ice. The strange reversal of images struck me then as I hunched over Mary Hannach, as if it were the other Anna I warmed, though she had died more than forty years before at my own mother's birth. It was as if I were trying to change the Prussian through time, to make her softer and less like the blizzard she had been born in.

Chapter Seventeen

THOUGH MY FATHER HAD BEEN all night with the man whose hand was mangled in the auger, he insisted on returning to check on us the next morning. Mother almost convinced him he was too exhausted to travel back to the delivery, which undoubtedly, she said, Mrs. Selchie had handled well. But this was one of those times Father would not defer, and he slept in the back seat of the car while Mother drove.

They found the four of us asleep in a row in the bloody bed and Paul Hannach downstairs, bellowing fit to be tied because of the pain in his leg and the fear that the silence upstairs meant all were dead. The Old One held the baby swollen-faced and rainbow-colored between her and the mother, while I lay on the opposite side, my leg and arm still curled around Mary Hannach for warmth, us and the whole room looking as if a deer had been butchered and dressed there the night before.

Father examined the baby, so weak from the delivery he could not say whether she would live or not; the Prussian cradled her, gently washed the crusted blood, and wrapped her tightly in a blanket. She stood rocking slightly on her heels and looked raptly at the child's bruised face as though it were the most beautiful in creation, her own eyes gone soft as she held the baby close, the small bundle almost disappeared in her arms wrapped around it. Suddenly she looked up at me. "I will show her to the father," she announced. "He is anxious to see her."

Then she wheeled and carried the child out, her manner businesslike, her step forceful, the moment gone from the room and forever transformed in my mind. She had looked with love on another woman's child, as she did with Rose. If the evidence held true, I did not have to be hers to be loved.

Then I rubbed the back of my hand, rusted with dried blood, and wondered if she saved her soft, fierce love only for the helpless and needy. Father returned with a basin of warm water and fresh dressings. "You did well, Anna," he whispered. "Mrs. Selchie told me."

"Will they live?" I asked.

"We can't know yet. I've asked the women from town to come here in shifts." He wrung out the cloth and wiped Mary Hannach's face, gently tucking her hair behind her ears.

"I had no idea it would be like this."

"Don't be frightened, Anna. Few births are this terrible." He laughed. "Rose, for instance, slipped out like a seed from a squirter."

"And how was my birth?" I asked, my voice so tight I was afraid it would betray me.

His hands went still, poised while he decided which part of Mary Hannach's body to wipe next, then continued moving between the water and the blood. "You were a fine, healthy girl."

"But the birth itself?"

"I wasn't at your delivery."

"Then the Old One?"

"No. She had retired a few years before you were born. I remember she said she'd become too old for picking up in the middle of the night to catch souls dropping into the world. But she delivered Rose before I could get there and tied the cord."

Mary Hannach's eyes fluttered, then flew open wide.

"The baby," she cried out and struggled to sit.

My father stroked her hair back off her forehead. "She is downstairs, meeting her father. We'll bring her to you for nursing if you're up to it." He turned. "Anna, call your mother for me."

The stairs were so steep I seemed suspended above her. "Mother?" I said.

She appeared in the lower hall, holding the baby close in a shaft of light boring in from outside.

"Mrs. Hannach is awake now."

She tucked the baby closer and cradled its head against the side of her throat. "She is so perfect and sweet, Anna. I hate to give her up."

I imagined being the child's source of life, and I felt myself grow powerful and enormous. I imagined being a baby, its head in rest against a mother's shoulder, its tiny feet curled up between the swell of breasts and covered over with warm hands. When the Prussian passed, I flattened against the wall, though she didn't seem to notice me, she was so happy with the child. I went down to the backyard then, thinking that Father had avoided answering my question, and while I knew all of this birth, I knew nothing of my own.

The Old One sat on a bench under a mulberry tree and studied the sky. The leaves shook, and the windmill by the trough in the cattle yard rattled. I sat beside her, closed my eyes, and moments of the birth replayed themselves vivid red against the black of my shut sight. To someday have another life inside me, to have once been that life inside another. So closely entwined by the cord between them that the death of one could cause the death of the other, and all things depended on both surviving. I tried to make sense of what I had just witnessed and understand why women would have no peace until they had put themselves through that ordeal, why I was drawn by it even as I was repulsed. I tried to picture myself as the baby and, in trying to remember my birth, remember the face of the mother.

Finally the Old One spoke. "I'm sorry for shouting at you, my girl, but there was no time to waste on debating in there."

"I know," I said, still feeling her words like a slap.

"Did your father say the babe would be all right?"

"He cannot tell yet."

"With such a delivery and the child still alive: it is a good sign if she has made it this far. And you, girl, making it through the whole ordeal with not a whimper."

I looked down at the toes of my shoes, covered with dust from the yard. "I didn't do much."

"To stay in that room was enough, and to do what I told you, more."

I shrugged.

"It's true, Anna. Don't be putting this aside like it were nothing. The birth of any child marks the helpers with its blood, and there's not one babe I helped deliver that I don't feel a tie to. But to stand steady through a battle like that makes a bond no human can break, one that binds us to her like her own godparents."

"Like her mothers?" I said, suddenly giddy with exhaustion and the idea she had proposed.

"Whether you see a body to death or to life, it is all part of the same thing, and that person whose soul you've touched naked, then that person is yours. You must mourn them or love them."

I glanced at her.

"Just what I said," she went on. "If you have held a life in your hands, then that life is yours for safekeeping, and you join a line of succession. If the ones before you fail, then it becomes your turn to take on that soul, as I did for Ed when her parents could not, through death or coldheartedness."

The thought came to me suddenly. "As we did for Rose for different reasons."

"Yes, child, though the way was forced. But still, as strong as blood ties it is, and lasting till the grave, Anna. It was intended that everyone should heed these bonds and the whole world be woven over so tight with a net of them that not a single soul should slip past into nothingness."

She laid her hand over mine, her fingernails stained brown and the crevices of her hands filled with the blood of the mother. "I was your caretaker too, child. Your parents gave you over to me, and I would fight for you the way I would for my own kin. Nothing what happens between your mother and Edwina can change the way I love you, no matter how it may seem different at times."

She looked at me, her old green eyes bright in spite of her tiredness, and I felt the bonds of the net then, held fiercely tight by the Old One. How underneath all I feared and avoided and fought there was the solidness of her, the security of her presence. And yet I felt other places where the net was cut and open and vulnerable. Holes through which strangers had escaped, if Rafferty was right. Places where I could not trust the Prussian to hold me to her or my father to tell me true. Ties that might be broken by Edwina in wild thrashing.

Then the Old One sighed. "We suffer most when the net will not hold, and I'll tell you, Anna, for all my spite against Douglas Selchie, I am hurt to the quick that he could not love his daughter enough to help her and that I could not love him enough to forgive."

We sat quietly amid the rustle and cluck of the chickens, and my mind moved slowly in my exhaustion. I stared stupidly at the cows switching their tails by the fence and thought of the recent times when I had failed her and Ed, when I was relieved by their absence or mine, when circumstance saved me from having to decide to stand by them.

"I'm sorry," I said.

"Why, what for, Anna?"

I could not say the words out loud. For being weak. For not loving enough to claim her and Edwina openly before my parents.

"It's all right, child. You do your best as you see it before you." She patted my hand again. "Let's go to the pump and clean ourselves, the worst of it at least."

Unlike my mother, no admission of past wrong demanded, but simply the Old One and I going on together to what we must do next. The pump stood on a platform in the middle of the yard, and I worked the handle while she squatted by the spout. At first no water came, and then suddenly a great burst, blurry-clear like ice but moving in a silver torrent. The Old One held her hands under it, and the blood washed off in rusty rivers. She rubbed at her fingers until the nails were white as moons and scooped handfuls to her face. She held her cupped palms out to me.

"See the sunlight in the water? The fire of it?"

It danced in spikes and glints, then ran between her fingers.

"When the moon rides over the ocean around my islands, it leaves itself in the water like this, only that water and light spread out as far as your eyes can take you. Gleaming shafts changing shape with the tides coming in to shore, going deeper down as the water rises to its crest. Like seeing the soul of each wave glowing and moving inside it, it is. When I lived on my island, I'd stand half the night on the shore to see the moon's fullness change to fit the water and ride its heart."

Then suddenly she shook her hands, and drops flew. "Now you, child."

Again the pump gave up nothing but the iron smell of blood, the metal of the pump, then came the cold touch of the spring water, which washed off in pale pink-brown rivulets. I scrubbed my hands together and ran water up my arms. I cupped handfuls to my face and held the water there as long as I could. The Old One held out the edge of her petticoat, which she had dried her hands on.

"Here, child. It's the best towel we have."

Her petticoat was rough and, I realized, made of feed sacking. I stood close to her and dried my hands and arms, clean and flushed from the spring water, our hips and shoulders touching.

"Who delivered me?" I asked before this moment alone with her could be over.

"Who's to know that, child?"

"Someone must."

"If it were ever known, then the name were lost to all but its bearer." She went back to the pump to fill a bucket to take inside.

"But why don't we know?"

The Old One slowed the motion of the pump until the water came in gulps and spasms.

"What are you asking me, Anna?"

"I want to know about when I was born. The time, the place, the circumstances."

"I know so little, child."

"But I know less."

"I know it were a double birth, once to life and then to them."

"Tell me."

"Of the first I know nothing. Of the second I know this: that they left for two weeks. Of that I am certain, for your father asked me to watch over two of his patients who were with child and lived close by. Before the women could deliver, your parents were back with you, a wee thing barely a month old, that your father carried around like Mary Queen of Scots."

"You were there?"

"As extra help at your christening, to take the women's coats and gentlemen's hats to an upstairs room. Your father brought you to me. To show you off, for certain, but also to put his mind at peace. He undressed you in the middle of all those ladies' coats with not a thought that you might wet them, and he had me examine your limbs and back, all the while asking, 'Do her bones seem strong?' 'Is her spine straight?' As if a doctor couldn't tell!

But he seemed to need my word before he could believe the health he'd seen in you were not a product of his joy.

"I told him I'd not seen a sturdier child, and he picked you up naked and held you high. A flying baby, you were. He said they'd put you in a basket for the trip and he watched you sleep on the Wabash all the way home. Then he told me, Anna, that he'd not had a happier day on this earth than the one when you came to him and that all his days after would be changed for the better because of that."

I thought on this secret she had told me, filled not with horror, as the ones I'd learned before, but with love and wonder. Had they kept the good secrets as well as the bad?

"Then you know for certain I was not born here?"

"Yes, child."

"And that my parents are not my parents?"

"That is another thing, child, depending how you mean the words."

My father came to the back door of the house and shouted to us that Mother was making us a breakfast. He started across the porch and down the steps.

"Did you never know?" she whispered.

Father came close, and the Old One asked loudly if I was finished with the water. I nodded no at her, answering the question before the last.

"She's got bacon started," Father said.

I looked at him blankly, so far removed were his words from my thoughts.

"The baby is nursing, weakly of course."

"That is a good thing, if she's not lost the will to suck." The Old One lifted the full bucket. "The floor needs a good scrubbing before the blood soaks into the boards. I'll just do that before I eat."

My father took the water from her. "You've done your job for the day. Save this for the women coming to help."

He guided us into the kitchen, where the Prussian was spooning up a bowl of oatmeal for Paul Hannach.

"Take this to him, Anna."

"Should I feed him?"

"Not unless he's broken his arm as well as his leg." She turned to the Old One, standing by the woodbin. "And what can I get for you, Mrs. Selchie? Eggs cooked any way you like. Oatmeal. Bacon. Toast."

Father held out the chair at the table. The Old One hesitated and then sat, not touching the chair back, and with her feet crossed at the ankles and swinging in the air. "A bit of it all, then, with one egg scrambled, if you please."

When I returned, the Prussian set my plate before me and then busied herself at the range.

"Do you think milktoast again for Mrs. Hannach at lunch, Will?"

"Then later the broth of a beef and vegetable soup strained through a piece of clean muslin," the Old One said. "I can start the pot if the ingredients be around here."

"That will be too much for her stomach," my mother said.

"Not for a mother we would fill full of milk."

"She will be sick." My mother banged the skillet loudly but as if by accident against the edge of the range.

The Old One held her palms with fingers spread across her breasts. "You don't know since they are fallen now, but the time was that the cry of my babe would start them to overflowing so the front of my dress were wet with milk before I could lift him to them. I know the mother must eat richly for the child to suck her cream."

"We are not discussing dairy herds."

The Old One folded her hands in her lap. "But still, a woman on thin gruel will make mother's milk like water and give her babe a famine."

My father said he would see to Mary Hannach's diet and leave instructions for those who would cook for her. He went on talking brightly until my mother finally sat down at the table with her plate, and we ate in silence. Before I left, I went up to see Mary Hannach sleeping with her child, so battered and dented and bruised that I was more repulsed than moved by her small body, even as I admired her survival.

Mary woke while I was standing over her, smiled weakly, and adjusted the child in her arms.

"Isn't she beautiful?"

I said yes, of course, as she was, in the terrible way snapping turtles and other strange species are handsome in their gruesomeness.

"We will call her Anna Selchie after her deliverers. Anna Selchie Hannach, if it is all right with you."

"Thank you," I said, though that seemed the wrong response and the names confused me. For a moment I wondered if I had become a Selchie or the baby a Selchie daughter. I expected a kind of family resemblance, though that thought reversed itself and I had the tired idea that I must look like the baby in some way. It was too much to figure the connection between this child and myself. The exhaustion of the night suddenly caught up with me, and I wanted to go home and sleep.

On the way home the Prussian did not speak about the delivery or the Old One, only to say she had warned my father about something like this, though I was not sure what "this" referred to. I suspected she meant the ordeal of the birth, the bloody physical things laid out for me to see, or perhaps the Old One in her mastery of what my mother would not touch. I slept all that afternoon without dreaming, and for dinner my mother ordered Malina to make one of her watery soups, as though the Prussian would feed me on the diet the Old One had condemned. I thought of it as prison gruel, but even it could not stop the feeling of pride about myself. My very bones felt denser and stronger since the day before, and I stood taller than the house.

Chapter Eighteen

$\mathscr{E}$DWINA CAME AGAIN THE NEXT day and the
two after that. Several times the Prussian sent Malina
down to tell her to move along, but Edwina ignored her,
as everyone had always done, and Malina returned to the
house stuttering too hard to explain. Mother sent the
stableboy, the gardener, and the milkman to give Ed
warning to leave, even as she ordered me to stay inside
with Rose. But Edwina never acknowledged them in any
way, and only when she was ready each day did she disappear, as silently as she had come.

I longed to show her my allegiance, but instead I

stayed inside. For three days the words of the Old One chased me.

"You do your best as you see it before you."

She believed that of me, and yet I did prove her wrong by staying by my window.

The gauze of the window curtain I looked through was white and blurry-soft, like a summer blizzard. Beyond that the green and August-hot yard, and beyond that Edwina pacing the edge of sea grass she could not swim across without drowning. Twice I put my hand on the brass doorknob, which reflected my fingers as misshapen gnarls, and felt the smooth curve of metal. Twice I failed to turn it, and each failure convinced me I was a lie and a disgrace to that Anna whom the Old One loved.

Then because I could not stand to feel inside myself that twisted and cronish blackness that I was sure not even the Old One could forgive me for, I took a deep breath and with the opening sweep of door felt the earth falling away beneath me. I ran down the lawn, spiked with solid rays of sun and filled with thick yellow air. The house grew smaller behind me, and the walk rose up to meet me. "Edwina, Edwina," I called, and she turned, massive and vacant. I touched her lightly on the arm and thought strangely of tagging home. She looked down on me.

"Where is she?"

Then I fell into the space opening around her. Always

she would ask me this when I had gone through so much to help her, and from the house the Prussian shouted, "Anna!"

"Ed," I began.

"You said you'd bring her. You promised."

"I can't."

She gave one terrible look, then gazed over my head to the house where Rose was. She would not answer or acknowledge me, and all the time the Prussian shouted, "Anna!" I walked back up the slope, and the ground pitched and yawed until my head swam with dizziness.

The Prussian locked the door behind me and stormed into my father's office. I sat down on the hall steps and closed my eyes. The strangeness of it all, Edwina and the Prussian, Rose's double mothers. Like living in a mirror where the reflection refused to mimic the shape before it.

The Prussian demanded that my father stop Edwina. He argued that she was doing no harm, just standing on the walk, not even on our lawn. But Mother insisted. "Anna is being corrupted, sir. We will lose them."

I ran up to my room and from behind the center crack of the pulled drapes I watched him approach Edwina, lay his hand on her shoulder, and try to guide her away. She stood still as if she could not see or hear or feel him, as if there were nothing that could intrude upon her senses but the sight or sound or touch of Rose, hidden somewhere in the house she stared at.

He stood with his hands in his pockets, talking in bursts until he gave up in the face of her silence, standing there with her and shifting his weight, and then trying again to speak with her. When he returned to the house I heard him tell Mother that it was a crime to disturb her.

"What harm can it cause, Etta? She is a wounded simple creature who has lost touch with her mind, and if it gives her solace to stand out there, what harm will it cause us?"

"What harm, indeed," my mother answered, "to have an unstable woman constantly lingering on our walk and dreaming up God knows what mischief against our children. To have our children influenced against me. I want you to call the chief of police and have him come remove her."

My father argued a while longer, but in the end she had her way. Edwina might not now be doing a thing by standing there, my mother said, but it was the terrible tension of not knowing what horrors she was capable of when we had not an ounce of control over her. I watched the two officers who came, how they took her by the elbow and tried to guide her away, how she ignored them like invisible vapor. My father came out on the porch, and they walked up to meet with him. They agreed they did not know what to do, but the Prussian came to the door and insisted they had better see about "that matter," for the safety of her children. This time when Edwina ignored them, they took her between them and tried forcibly to remove her.

I watched from behind my window screen, the confrontation muffled across the expanse of lawn yet sounding loud in my ears like forbidden words I could not help hearing. They took her arms and she whirled suddenly, the two men holding on like grooms to a horse that refused to be saddled. When she threw one to the ground, the other yanked both her arms behind her, but Edwina bent double and pulled him up on her back until his feet flew off the ground and he rode her. By that time the first man had regained his balance and ran at her full force. She fell and they pinned her. She tried to bite one, and he held her face in the dirt, her legs kicking furiously, her petticoats like a sea of whitecaps. I was sick then at the violence done to her. I was ashamed this treatment had been ordered by my mother.

They took her to a cell. There was no law as yet against displeasing my mother, and so they charged Edwina with loitering and disturbing the peace, though no witness could deny that all had been peaceful until the authorities arrived. They really did mean my mother's peace of mind after all, and of disturbing that Edwina was indeed guilty. My father went to the jail and calmed her with an injection, not trusting the drops he had previously prescribed for her.

We waited dinner for him. When he finally arrived he told us how it had been and then fell silent. The only sound was that of our knives cutting across the face of our plates and Rose singing her made-up songs as Malina got her ready for bed upstairs. Then suddenly the front door shook with pounding, a stick hitting against the wood until the glass rattled, and the Old One's voice called my mother's name.

"I'll go," my father said, holding his hand out flat before us.

But when he opened the door I heard the Old One clear and firm. "No, Will Berter, it is your wife I would speak to."

The Prussian lifted a forkful of food to her lips, then paused and said, "I had better see to this."

I waited until she had left the room and then stood in the doorway to the parlor, where I had a clear view across the room and into the hall, the backs of my parents silhouetted against the dusk outside. I could hear only snatches of what my mother said, her voice traveling away from me, but it was what I had heard before about what was best and reasonable and practical. Then the Old One answered, at first her voice interrupting and in counterpoint with my mother's and finally ringing out over the silence it had won.

"It is unnatural what you do, and wicked, the same as if you had put your hands around her throat to choke her. My own Edwina's spirit is dying, I am sure of it, and you must show her the mercy that will save her."

I moved closer to the window then. The Old One stood on the dusky porch, the black of her dress blending with the mottled shadows and becoming part of them. She leaned on a walking staff and pointed her white hand at my mother.

"Give her mercy, Etta Berter, or have her soul upon your hands."

"Carline," my father said, "that is enough now."

"This is not your business," she told him and turned back to the Prussian. "If you do not stop now, you will kill more than you intended and bring blackness onto your own house."

She moved back into the fast-coming dark of the yard, her hand still raised, and began to sing an eerie single line of music. She was the Old One I knew so well, and she was a stranger. I thought that she was crazy and I was afraid she was not. I tried to dismiss this as a performance to frighten my mother, even as the edge of each note touched like a blade against my skin and made the hair rise on my arms.

Then her singing ceased, and she dropped her arm. She stood still as stone, and the yard filled with the cry and echo of cicadas and katydids, while none from our house offered a reply. Only the light from the dining room spilled out into the room behind me, and the steps glowed from Rose's light upstairs. The yard turned that deepest dark, past dusk but before moon and star rise, which our eyes cannot see through. It was several minutes before I realized the Old One had left the spot where she'd been standing and that my parents and I stared at nothing.

Then they came in from the hall, and my father flicked on the bright ceiling fixture.

"Turn that off, Will," my mother said. "A lamp will do."

There was no question of returning to finish our meal, the first time I remember such negligence. I stayed leaning against the windowsill, and my father came to look over my shoulder as if he could still see the Old One standing on our lawn.

"Etta." He cleared his throat.

"I don't want to discuss this, Will, but perhaps this proves to you that your leniency has gone too far."

She sat in the pool of light from the small table lamp, which caught the chestnut in her hair and threw deep shadows under her eyes. She tapped her palms smartly against the chair arms. "You must do something about this. I don't believe I can sleep knowing those two are after my children."

My father laid his hands on my shoulders. "Leave us now, Anna; your mother and I have something to discuss."

"If Ed could see Rose, she'd stop this," I said.

The Prussian turned her face sharply from me, and my father said, "Not now."

I went to my room and first tried to listen and then tried to read. I turned off my light and could not sleep. The room itself was stuffy, and the sheets and pillows seemed to creep out of place and rearrange themselves after I had put them where I was comfortable. All around, the threat of the Old One seemed to shimmer, as if her words and song hung in faint but unmistakable vibration in the air.

Long after I should have been asleep and beyond the hour when my parents came upstairs, I was surrounded by the darkness the Old One had predicted, an eternal wakeful night filled with Edwina's crying and the Old One's warnings. I heard the church clock strike two and then the half hour after. I heard one of my parents going downstairs to the kitchen and then the other in the hall. I heard doors close, and water in the bathroom, and doors close again. I myself could not sleep, and by three it did seem that on the heels of the Old One's visit we had lost our power to close our eyes and see nothing, to stop the crowd of night figures from moving constantly in our minds.

Finally I went out of my room and stood in the doorway of Rose's nursery. The moon was only a sliver at the horizon line, and in the dimness I mistook a shadow for her sleeping shape. Then my eyes adjusted, and I realized she was huddled near the footboard. I sat next to her, and she climbed into my lap.

"I hear things, Anna."

"Everyone's restless tonight."

"But something's outside."

"It's nothing, just your imagination."

She tightened herself into a smaller ball and scooted closer to me. "I'm scared."

"Shush, there's nothing here."

I wanted to go back to bed.

"Pretend to sleep," I told her. "If you close your eyes, nothing can see you." I laid her down. "I'm positive this will work," I said quickly.

She pulled her knees up against her, her fists to her chin, and closed her eyes so tightly that her face was distorted.

"That's good. Now you sleep."

I went back to my room and closed my window—Rose's fear had made me nervous. The lawn was dark and empty, but if I stared at one spot for long enough I began to imagine it moved. Soon all the shrubs were animals shifting slightly on their haunches and waiting for a chance to run from the shadows alive around them. Outside, cicadas creaked and sawed, and from down the hall I heard my mother call out sharply, as though someone had surprised her in her sleep. Around the time the air turned soupy gray with dawn, I dozed off and swam with my dreams at the surface of my sleep.

Chapter Nineteen

$\mathcal{D}$URING THE NEXT TWO DAYS, whenever I asked either of my parents how Edwina was, they told me she was resting and things were being seen to. They didn't give me much opportunity to ask, always hurrying past me as if eternally late for an appointment, but finally on the third evening they were both home to supper.

"But what's to happen to her?" I asked.

"You don't have to bother yourself with that, Anna," my father said.

"But I want to know what's going to happen to her."

"The final arrangements were being completed when

I left, and by now she's on her way to where she'll be taken care of."

"What does that mean?"

"There are places, homes, that take care of people."

"Asylums?"

"No, I said 'homes,' Anna."

"Don't persist in bothering your father. He's very tired after his efforts on the Selchies' behalf."

"But I want to know, and about the Old One too."

"I'm sure she'll go wherever Edwina does. That's always been the case," the Prussian said.

"To a 'home'?" I asked.

"She'll go along to see that Edwina is taken care of. What more can you ask?"

"Where are these places? Is there one near here?"

My father was bending forward slightly as he lifted his fork to his mouth. He glanced at my mother and returned the fork to the plate.

"They will go to Des Moines, Anna. A city like that has many facilities. The largest state institutions, in fact. It was a terrible choice, but Edwina was out of control," he said. "Understand, Anna, it was out of our hands. We had to do something for Rose's safety."

"It was best for all concerned," the Prussian added.

I didn't believe them. Surely there must have been another way. I watched the looks between them, the wordless signals. My father closed his eyes for a moment and shook his head, two little nods, and my mother nodded back. In that moment all contracts were broken.

If they deceived, then I was no longer bound to obey. If they ceased to be good and perfect, then I ceased to owe them what I had promised when I thought they were. All things were now possible, and no boundaries existed. I excused myself before dessert and went outside, hugging my arms against the cool air that had broken the heat. I planned to walk to the foot of the lawn and back to work off my anger, but I kept going.

I walked with force to increase that sensation of being connected to the ground when all else seemed to be exploding and flying off; walking away from the house that seemed filled with tangled, knotted things and out into the expanse of lawn, uncluttered and open to the air. By the time I cut across Lucy Minchion's yard, it was beginning to grow dusk and I could see her sitting in the lighted dining room having her meal, not watching out the window at all. At the threshold of the empty cottage, a cat whose color I could not distinguish in the shadows jumped off the table and ran past me out the door, its fur brushing my leg so softly I was hardly sure I'd been touched, but all the way back up the path, phantom voices and rustlings chased behind me. I wanted to find Rafferty, but before now I was always the one to be found, and when I tried to think where he lived, I could not recall that anyone had ever pointed out his house or referred to its location.

I walked past the saloon, where men were wrapped in yellow light that spilled in diluted stripes across my feet. I went past the stores closed for the night, my reflection wavy in their dark windows like a snake curling by, past the livery stable, where two grooms sat swinging their heels against hay bales outside. Through the windows of houses I saw families going about the business of their evenings; at the hotel, the clerk reading his paper at the lobby desk and two guests standing at the windows of their rooms above. I stopped in the middle of the street I was crossing and was struck by how much can be seen by those in the dark looking into the light.

But I was also tired from walking and worried what my parents would do when they missed me. I turned to go back, cutting over two blocks to pass the police station on my way, though I was uncertain what I intended to do there. Certainly not go in, but be near the last place Edwina had been in New Marango, where her presence still lingered. I stood in the shadow of an elm across the street and watched for the longest time, with no nerve to go closer and ask the sergeant at the desk where they'd taken her. I had the thought I might be able to catch her. But so many streets they could have gone down, and I could never know which one. It was dark now. I thought of not going back, but I had no place to go other than home. Two blocks later I saw the top arc of the full moon curve over the trees. I passed the Meyer house, and a figure white with moonlight called to me from a wooden bench under the elms. "Out late tonight, aren't we?"

Rafferty's voice. I stopped, curiously appalled that he would be sitting on someone else's property.

"Do you know where Edwina Selchie has gone?" I asked.

"More clearly than she knows. Come sit and I'll tell you." He patted the bench.

"I can't."

"Afraid of trespassing?"

I didn't answer, so afraid was I of the man I'd been looking for.

"The day rules don't apply at night. Or any rules, for that matter, if they get in your mother's way. Come on, don't be stupid."

I set my foot gingerly on the lawn, half expecting lights to come on or dogs to run out or my foot to sink in the grass as if it were water. Rafferty draped his arm over the bench behind me.

"Did you see them?" I asked.

"Old Mrs. Selchie, I did. After moonrise, they're taking Edwina to the state asylum. She'll be gone before anyone notices. Then they'll lock her up, and if her grandmother kicks up too much of a fuss, they'll do the same to her."

"But why?"

"Because the two of them are crazy, that's why."

"But they're not."

"What are you saying? One's mewing around your house looking for a baby that's not hers anymore, and the other's accosting your fine mother in the streets. This town can tolerate all manner of private insanity but not that done in plain daylight."

"But it's not crazy."

"The attendants have the paper that swears Edwina Selchie is no longer herself. And if the old girl causes a ruckus, they've been promised one for her too. Official papers have the power to change a person from one thing to another."

My thoughts were too much in turmoil to connect all the information. Rafferty leaned close to me, his arm brushing my shoulder. I sat stock-still, smelling not beer or liquor, as I had expected, but cloves and cinnamon.

"Come, woman, is your mind so slow as that?" His features were barely discernible in the dark, just a faint outline of nose and lips and chin, the eyes concealed in the shadow of his hat brim. "You know who signs the official documents. The birth and death certificates, the autopsies and quarantines, the commitment papers for the insane and weak-minded. How many doctors do we have around here that the answer is so confusing?"

"No," I said flatly and leaned away from him.

"No, what?" His breath was soft against my ear, but hot like fire. He leaned closer, and though he didn't touch me, I felt his presence like a weight.

"No, that can't be. You made this up," I insisted.

"I never have to invent what's stranger than my mind can dream. It is only my job to report what happens before anyone can change the truth."

He slid his hand under my chin and turned my face to him. I trembled, though his hand was warm and dry and sure, like the Old One's and my father's.

"No tricks now," Rafferty said. "You know clearly what I've told you. The good doctor has committed Edwina Selchie, and it's too late to undo what has been done. You might have stopped it if you had gone to him earlier. If you had kept telling him that you knew, he might have been shamed into stopping before it came to this, so out of hand that even he's afraid for his family."

He took his hand away, and I clenched my teeth to stop their chatter.

"He said she was already gone."

"To shut you up and make you believe it was done with."

"But she's here?"

"In the basement of the jail, in a room where they keep the few women they get. Sometime tonight they'll take her away, and then that is the last of it."

"Can I see her?"

"The lady's not having visitors, the sergeant informed me. You might catch a glimpse when they bring her out. The only thing I'll promise is that she'll not look as crazed as they would have us believe."

"But if she's still here, why is it too late?"

"Do you think your father will arrive at the last minute and tell them he's made a small miscalculation concerning her sanity? You've been reading too many badly written books, my darling. No, the plan is too perfect. With one signature he's returned his household to safety and pacified his monster of a wife without having to even look at the victim. He'll toss and turn in a guilty bed for a few months, but eventually tonight will get lost in a host of good deeds, and after a year it will seem as if he dreamed this. He'll stop buttering his toast one morning and look up. 'Etta, my dear,' he'll say, 'I had the strangest nightmare.' Then that will be that. He'll begin remembering that the Selchies begged him to take the baby, and before she's grown, he'll believe he conceived her."

"I won't listen to this." I stood up to leave.

"You never had to. Most people don't hear as much as you."

"Are you going to help her?" I could not see him, only sense him behind me.

"I'm going to sit right here until it's over. The last thing I want is a clear image of Edwina Selchie being dragged away, crying and bleating for her baby."

I wanted to stay still with him until it was over.

"Why don't you try to stop them?" I asked.

"It's not my business."

"Then why is it mine?"

"It isn't. You didn't choose to make it that."

"I did. I told you."

"If a man fell down and cut off his leg, Anna Berter, you'd feed him chicken soup for his cold and then wonder why he bled to death."

"What?" I wheeled around, but his face was indistinct in shadow.

"All right, you did try in your little way. Two sandbags to stop the river. A cup of grain to feed the herd. I don't know why I expected more. It's against my rules to expect anything at all, but I was hoping, for the Selchies' sake, that you'd be different."

"Why me?"

"A test. Of nature over nurture. I needed to know."

"But I took Rose when I could, and I explained when I couldn't. I had to go against my parents, and you don't know what that cost me."

He pulled me down roughly next to him. The brim

of his hat grazed my forehead, and his bones of his hand angled hard against mine.

"Listen to me, girl. Whatever you did cost you no more than a few pennies. You still have your life and your home and your family and your 'sister.' You lost nothing but the worry that Edwina Selchie would disrupt what needed disrupting."

I tried to twist away from him, but he held on.

"Not yet. Let me finish. For all that, the waters will close over her head as if she'd never been here, and you'll learn nothing for it. You'll go through your life believing you were Joan of Arc and an act of bravery consists of refusing to eat dessert. You'll think there was nothing more you could've done, not for her or for yourself, and you'll be wrong. Hear me? Wrong. I want you to remember that as you turn into such a perfect copy of your mother that we won't be able to tell you apart. You'll do that without a whimper. At least Edwina Selchie has the heart to struggle. Now get home, and don't come looking for me again. The game has gone sour."

He shoved me away and turned his shoulder to me. I stood trying to think of a response that would put him in his place, but no words came. Instead I turned abruptly and walked across the yard and down the street, conscious that I was going too quickly to give the impression our conversation had not affected me. When I came within sight of my house, I stopped. The downstairs lights shone like yellow eyes over the black sea of the yard.

No tricks, Rafferty had said. No excuses that what had been done was best for all concerned. My father had signed the papers that committed Edwina. The thought leapt at me with the force of an animal, and I swayed at the impact. I stood where Edwina had held her vigil and hugged myself as she had. Before me was the house my parents and sister lived in, and I could no longer go inside. Hot tears caught behind my eyes, not only of sorrow but also of rage. As if my good parents had died and been replaced by thieves who stole their children by any method from women who had no defense against them.

I stood on the walk before my house, as though on the rim of ocean looking out onto the land. A water creature yearning to peel back her fur and find a human shape inside. Like those in the house and not like them. A single line from the Old One's song repeated itself inside me:

"Though they will kill both my young son and me."

Kill what is not like them and destroy what is different, even her who would be wrapped dry and warm in another skin and live with them who looked so beautiful from this distance, in the warmth of their yellow lights. Already I missed them, and I wanted their embrace and welcome. I did not understand how, if they loved part of me so well, they could want to destroy the rest.

I wanted to come inside the house and be done with this terrible business of matching children to mothers and sorting out their love. Yet I saw my parents' faces twisted and grotesque and myself turning into their crooked shape. I did not belong here, though I wished with all my heart that I did. I turned back the way I'd come, cutting over two blocks to avoid Rafferty, and going down the street past the jail. The sergeant still sat at his desk, but two other officers collected papers and coats and coffee. By the side curb, Jim Cooney adjusted the harness on his team, hitched to a lorry, while the horses stomped and shifted and shook their reins. Before my mind made sense of the fact that of course they had waited for moonrise, the side door opened and one officer led Edwina out, her hands cuffed behind her. She stood quietly in the middle of the side yard, her back toward me, and the Old One followed. At first I could not understand her, but I moved closer and listened more carefully. She argued that they had no right to take her granddaughter and told them steadily and low how they would not do this if their mothers or sisters or daughters were standing in Edwina's place.

The officers ignored her while they loaded their things and what must have been Edwina's, folded inside a quilt. The Old One kept up her plea, hobbling from one man to another and getting in the way of their work.

"She is bound by the medicine that keeps her quiet.

You've not seen her fuss for three days and nights. Must you keep her chains on too?"

The younger one finally went to Ed and unlocked her manacles. The Old One thanked him, but he passed her without a word. Then she and the men got into a terrible row when she insisted they load her carpetbag and they insisted she was not allowed to ride along.

"Then how am I to get where you're taking her? And how can she be a prisoner when she has committed no crime?"

This confounded them, and the argument rose in crescendo. I hurried across the squares of light falling on the lawn and stood in the shadows against the corner of the building. The older officer swore the Old One could not come, while the officer who had unlocked Edwina said it could do no harm. Simpleminded Jim Cooney complained the lorry was loaded lopsided and began pulling bags from its rear. Edwina suddenly swung around as if she knew I watched her. Her face was tired and puffy, like that of a sleeper awakened early, and she held her hands in back like they were still in cuffs. I don't believe she recognized me at first, but then a shadow passed over her expression and she took a step toward me. I held up my hand. "Stop," I whispered silently.

She looked at me quizzically. Then she blinked and rubbed her hands over her face, her eyes brighter now. She rushed at me and laid her hands on my shoulders.

"I knew you'd bring her, Anna, and not let me go alone."

I pushed at her, trying to get her from me, the great weight and solidness of Edwina coming on like a boulder rolling with such force I could not stop it. I backed away, whispering so the sergeant in the window would not find us out.

"It's too late, Ed. Go back where you belong. She's home asleep."

"Then I will come with you. Just this once it would cause no harm to pick her up and wake her, would it, Anna, for only a moment? Just a moment, Anna, so I can see her with her eyes open."

I kept backing away, stumbling over the flat beaten earth of the station yard until we were at the side opposite from the lorry, the building between us. A saying of the Prussian's ran crazily through my mind. "Do you think I have eyes in the back of my head?"

And Ed's fingers plucking at my shoulders as she danced me backward, and the soft green look of her eyes, seeing only Rose sleeping in my house. Her coming at me, saying, "I only wanted to see her, and then they hurt me. It will be so long until they let me come back, please let me see her."

When I heard the shouting and knew they missed her, I wished for a moment that they would take her off me, pull her fingers from where they snatched at my dress, and give me room to breathe. I wanted to be out from under the arc of her body, like the wall of a cave curving over me, away from her pleas, which were impossible to answer and harder still to ignore. I wanted them to stop this.

My hands locked around her wrists. I had but to hold tight and shout. Yet I could not stand the thought of Edwina being carried off or locked up or dying. I could not stand to be my parents' accomplice. I pulled her toward the back of the lot, black with shadows.

"Run, Edwina," I told her, "and hide so they cannot find you. Don't go to the cottage; they'll look there. But get away and hide."

The men stopped as they came around the side of the building. Like a deer, Ed stopped, too, and then tensed. "Run, Ed," I said again and tried to pull her away from them. But I stumbled backward over a root and fell, and still unsure, Edwina stood looking down at me.

"Edwina, hurry," I said slowly and clearly, "or you'll never see Esther again."

I used her name for Rose so there would be no confusion, the lie the only way I could think to move her. I didn't know where she could run or how that would help but to give us time to plan, and I said again, "You'll never see your baby Esther again if they catch you. Run, Ed. Go now."

In that moment her sleepy expression took on fear

and she passed over me, her long skirts brushing the length of my body, away into the hedges that bordered the yard. The men's shouts rang out like hunting dogs circling and calling to one another. From around the building the sergeant shouted at the Old One that she must come inside, and one of Jim Cooney's horses whinnied low and long. I closed my eyes and would have stayed in that dark moment forever while all around me whirled in the chaos my family had set loose.

I imagined Edwina running north until the men collapsed behind her and the land changed into hills and then the high waves of Canadian mountains, all the world turned white with winter and Edwina safe behind the miles of snow. But then I saw her cold and dead like the Prussian's mother, and again, I saw her stealing Rose. All the terrible possibilities unfolded in quick succession, piling up faster than my mind could dismiss them as silly. I told myself to think clearly. Of course the officers would catch Edwina and bring her back. Of course.

I pushed myself off the ground, the dust soft talc like the Prussian's face powder against my hands, and I ran toward my house, sure Edwina had gone there to find Rose and so afraid of what I had done. Afraid they would catch her, afraid they would not. Afraid, afraid. The word sounded with every step. My breath like a winter draft in my raw throat and a stitch in my side I pressed at with the heel of my hand. I ran through the night toward Rose, and she was all I could think of. Halfway down the block, the Old One and the sergeant shouted at me to stop. "Anna," she called, but I was no longer that Anna, and I ran into the night.

Chapter Twenty

THE DOWNSTAIRS LIGHTS OF MY house blazed, but except for the bang of the screen door behind me, all else was quiet, and I was reassured that if Edwina had not come directly here, then she might not come at all. The urgency to see Rose subsided, and I slumped against the wall to catch my breath. My mother stopped halfway down the steps, the light hitting only her white silk stockings and black-strapped heels.

"Anna, where have you been?"

She laid her hand on the banister, and her rings flashed diamond-gold.

"Don't ever leave like that again." She called up the stairwell, "Will, she's just come in." Another step down. The loops of pearls at her throat glowed white like strings of tiny eggs. "Just what did you think you were doing, running out of this house?"

Then my father stood behind her, his hands on her shoulders. "Yes, yes, tell her, Anna, what has happened."

How to tell them all I knew.

"Edwina's escaped, and they cannot catch her."

I would tell them no more; there was no use. They finally left me alone, my father going to telephone the police and my mother hurrying from door to window, checking the locks. I sat by Rose's bed, and she slept with her hands entwined and held closely to her, one leg pulled up tight to her chest and the other stretched out into a bar of moonlight. A lovely child, as all children are lovely, but not the loveliest of them all. Not the brightest nor the kindest nor the most exceptional in any way. Yet my parents would kill for her and Edwina die without her, their very existence somehow tied up with hers, and for all of us who loved her she had become what we craved to possess. The Rose of Sharon, Queen Esther herself, so precious that we were afraid to share her.

I tried to nudge my finger into her fist to have her wrap her fingers around mine as she did when she was a baby. But she pulled her hands more tightly to her and stirred in her sleep. Rose, her own self. I lay down beside her on the narrow youth bed, put my arm over her, and swore that to her I would give all that had not been given to me, all the stories and secrets, so she would see clearly what was hidden, what swam under the water and flew through the dark and where the clear boundaries of her own self ran, not tangled with any others.

Her hair smelled sweet of chamomile rinse, and I held her. Except for our breathing, the night was strangely still, broken by neither the calls of men nor my parents moving about in the rooms below. I wondered why Edwina had not come, as I had feared, and I began to hope that it was because she had indeed escaped out of the land where I was responsible for her.

A tale to go to sleep on in a place where I could not tell who was to be trusted, whether I was saving Edwina from my parents or if they were protecting me from her. Even love at that moment was confused and changeable, churned together with the rest and stirred in whirlpools that sucked and turned too quickly for me to separate one feeling from another. I curled tighter against Rose, and when I fell asleep exhausted, the last thing I saw was the blue-white moonlight filling the room like water.

When I woke, I did not know where I was nor whether the sound outside was animal or wind, then clearly I recognized Edwina. I stood at the window, unsure that I was not watching myself in a dream, but for the floor cold against my feet and the glass like ice under my fingers. Edwina's figure ran white across the lawn. At first I thought the howl she made was only wordless pain. But when I laid my ear flat to the glass, vibrating like the ocean heard in shells, I heard Edwina calling "Esther," each syllable lasting an ageless time. She suddenly ran back in the direction from which she had started, stopped, and called. Again, stopping and calling and running to each window, looking for the one that I would open to let her in.

She disappeared around the side of the house and then reappeared from the other direction. She stood looking all around her, at the sky filled with moon and the edge of the yard deep in shadow, at the house before her and the garden behind, then she rushed at the back door and threw her whole body full force against the ungiving wood, again, again, in constant pulses, until I felt the tremors down my spine.

As I watched her I thought, what madness. Then, also what courage to shed all restraints and cautions in the pursuit of her child. Such free passion was beyond my ken, and seeing it now I thought it terrifying and animal and pure, a beauty to be desired as much as to be feared.

Edwina stood dazed before the solid door, then she turned in circles, ran to the woodpile, and circled it. She stopped before the ax left leaning against the block, then went on toward the stable, the blade bumping and dragging behind her on the ground. I thought she was going to destroy the horses, hacking into their soft necks until she had ruined all their beauty. I ran into the hall and shouted to my parents, but when I returned to the window, Edwina stood in the center of the yard, staring up at the house again.

By then Rose had begun to cry the soft, confused cry of a child who cannot find her way out of sleep, and the Prussian was at our door.

"What is it, Anna?"

"Nothing. It's alright now."

I looked back out, laying my hand flat against the glass, the closest I could come to touching Edwina.

"Come away from the window now. Do not let her see you." She tucked Rose's covers in more tightly around her. "Has she stirred? I gave her a sleeping compound earlier but was unsure of the dosage."

"You drugged her?"

"I do not want her to know any of what goes on this night. Your father has called for help. You stay here until this is over."

"What are you going to do with Edwina?"

"Have her taken to where she was intended to go in the first place."

"The asylum was your idea, wasn't it?"

Before shutting the door, she stopped. "We heard you

were at the station. If you had let us handle the problem, none of this would have happened."

Then she was gone as quickly as she had appeared, turning the key in the lock and dragging the hall table in front of the door. I pounded on the window frame until the sash unstuck and opened, but Ed was not in sight. An unseasonably cold wind blew, and I shivered at the thought that somehow she could be carried invisibly into the room on its back. And so I closed the window and lay down with my arm over Rose. Edwina called again, and her voice rang bright through the stillness. The room filled with her presence, and I felt that no matter what the Prussian did to keep her out this night, she would find a way in and be there with us ever after, unseen and secret, whispering to our dreams and trailing her fingers over our faces as we slept.

Yet at the same time and now closer again, the part of Edwina crazy with the loss of her child shouted at us.

"I want her."

Glass shattered like winter ice exploding in too much cold.

"She is mine."

Like bells breaking and ringing at once.

"I want to touch her."

The steady stroke of the ax handle stove through the windows, one, two, three. The crash and bright tinkle of glass popping and flying, then the dull thud of blade buried into wood, a breath of silence, and Edwina's sobs like sad screams.

"Give her to me."

The ax hit wood in rhythm with her cries, and I counted to seven between each stroke. Edwina breaking open the Prussian's house, cracking it like an egg for frying. I sat up against the headboard and pulled Rose between my legs. Again the blade against wood, seven counts, and the blade again, as if she would open the walls and set the ax in the skulls of all who had kept her from her child.

My parents' footsteps sounded down the hall. "You can't go out there," I heard the Prussian tell my father. "She will kill you." His reply was lost down the stairs, and Rose stirred in her unnatural sleep.

"Shush, Rosie. It is only the wind crying."

Edwina's howling and the sound of her beating ax carried on the air and surrounded the house. It became the demand of all mothers calling for their children, and when it stopped it was replaced with running and my father's voice shouting, "Where are you? Let us help you."

I carried Rose to the window, her head drowsy on my shoulder. The lawn was white in the moonlight like hoarfrost, and my father ran across it, past the arbor and garden and down toward the stable. Edwina was far in front of him, her skirts flying like the wings of a white moth and her arms held out in front. I half expected her to lift off the ground and rise over the wall of trees, but she merely disappeared into the darkness there, and he after her. Downstairs, the commotion of the police arriving and the Prussian's voice mixing with the voices of the men. I sat on the windowsill and watched until my father came out of the grove again, alone, and I held Rose on my lap facing the space that had last held her mother, too late for Edwina to see her.

Half a dozen men spread out across the yard and disappeared in different directions, and I sat in the high window and listened to their calls. If they did not catch Edwina this night, they would when she came back, as I was sure she would, like some wild thing to salt. And next time they would be waiting like hunters in a blind. It would go on until they had her, and I winced at knowing that no matter how hard she struggled, her end would be the same.

I laid Rose down and tried the door, though I knew it was locked. Then I could not stand to be in that room and took a cushion from the chair and a blanket from the closet. I climbed out the window and over to the roof of the back porch and made a bed for myself in that open place. The roof was hard, and cold autumn in the air, yet I could not go back. I lay flat, with my hands crossed on my chest and my face upturned.

The moon moved past what was left of its sky, and

I stared at the vague gray shapes across its face like birth-marks, the light so luminous that I felt myself breaking with its beauty. I measured its movement by the distance between it and the tree line, the moon in its calm slow loop around us, steady in its path in spite of the dark scurrying below, changing in itself and yet constant in its journey. I wanted to lift into its orbit and be in time with its traveling. I held up my open hand, and the moon rode in my palm. I felt it, smooth and clear, and begged to be pulled along.

Now calmer, I tried to make sense of what had happened and was again bombarded with stray pieces of fear and love mixed so together I could not tell them apart. The hard roof and the cold made me strangely aware of the boundaries of my body, of its shape and line where it touched and gave against the hardness, how it remembered the shape it could return to. I felt where the world ended and Anna began, the entire continuousness of my skin, denseness of bone and strength of muscle. Yet with that separateness also came an absence that opened into the void of endless dark beyond the moon.

I dozed, and on waking at first dawn, I sat and looked out over the horizon. Edwina was hidden somewhere there, though I could not see through trees and barns and houses to where she was. When the first man returned from the hunt, walking slowly across the backyard, I wrapped the blanket like a cape and called to him, small from where I sat and foreshortened by the angle of my vision. He looked up, startled.

"Did you find Edwina Selchie?"

He held up his hands. "Not a trace."

I stood and waited for him to approach.

"Then tell my mother to let me out of here now. I cannot stand to be locked up any longer." I stepped closer to the edge.

"Stand back!" he shouted and held out his arms to catch me.

"Get me out, then." I took a step closer, and he wavered to adjust for the angle of my body's fall.

"Please, girl, sit down until we get a ladder."

Suddenly it all seemed so silly, this man afraid I would fall. More ridiculous, yet, for him to be afraid when I had never done anything in my life that was at all dangerous, not even when I thought I had. Rafferty was right: all my small braveries were just that. I looked down at this little man, and immensely indignant at him who would hunt a woman like a dog, I held the blanket up like wings.

"Get my mother now, or I jump."

He took off toward the front door then, and I could hear his banging and shouting. I laughed at spooking away one of Edwina's pursuers, then was infinitely sad that I could not've done that seriously when it counted. I dropped my arms at my sides and wondered where she was and what would happen. Behind me I heard the scraping of the table being moved from the door. At the edge of my sight, the red rim of the sun burned pink at the horizon.

Chapter Twenty-one

$\mathcal{F}$ROM THE TOP OF THE stairs I heard Mother give Malina directions to prepare a large breakfast. Two men stood awkwardly in the hall before the door, their hats in their hands, and one said to the other, "That's fair payment for a night's work, a maid serving us breakfast in the grand dining room."

"Your wife'll say you're putting on airs."

"Better hold off using the dogs, so we can last this out until dinner." He nudged the other in the ribs, and they both laughed low and looked all around them like children told to stand still and not touch.

Then two more arrived, stamping the mud off their boots before Mother let them in and guided them all to the dining room for coffee while the bacon was cooking. Their voices first were hushed, but the conversation soon gained volume. One suggested Edwina might have concealed herself inside one of the bundles of drying corn shocks that dotted the newly harvested fields.

"Then if that's the case, it'll take us until Doomsday to search cornfields as far as the eye can see."

"No sense wasting our time on that. If we wait right here, she'll show up eventually."

Then my mother's voice and the clatter of dishes interrupted. I sat on the floor, with my back against the wall. I imagined Edwina being driven through ever smaller pens to the final chute, so narrow she could not turn around to escape going through to the black final doorway. It was neither fair nor right, but I didn't know how to save her from what now seemed inevitable, her destiny more terrible because it had not always been so.

Then knocking at the door soon turned to pounding. Footsteps, and Malina talking excitedly in Czech, a man's voice deep and commanding. They have found her, I thought, and leaned over the railing to see. He looked up, a farmer I recognized as one of my father's patients, his eyes seemingly almost white-blue against the deep tan of his face. He held Edwina in his arms, hanging limp the way no living woman could, one arm bent back as if it grew from her shoulder, the other swinging loose. A thick stripe of dirt ran up her full skirts over a blur of petticoat, and a purple-black bruise covered the whole back of her hand.

How clearly I saw it all in an instant! Then he swung around to protect me from what was already pressed into my memory.

"Get out of here and do not look," he shouted. And then, to the men gathering at the door: "Where is the doctor? Find him for me, quick."

They argued where my father had last been seen and blocked each other at the door. Malina knelt shrieking near the stairs with her fists dug against her face, and I was afraid she would be trampled. But the Prussian yanked her up and pushed her back into the kitchen, then sent the men on their way. Before she closed the office door on the farmer with his burden, she glanced up at me.

"Take care of Rose until this is over. Do not let her see, Anna. Promise me you won't."

Before I could answer, she disappeared down the hall to the kitchen, and I could hear her on the telephone making calls and asking for my father over Malina's slow, steady moaning. I closed the door to Rose's room, left her sleeping, and crept down the steps to stand in front of my father's office door. As I pushed my hands flat and hard against the wood, the latch turned and the farmer peered out, his eyes so pale blue they seemed covered with white cataracts.

"Go away," he said.

"I want to know."

"Just go away. It is too late," he said and closed the door.

Inside, Edwina was dead. The words rang distinctly in my mind. It was not possible that this had happened, not in this house so protected, and yet Edwina was dead. I laid my hands flat against the door, hoping the solidness of the wood would convince me of her death. I said out loud in a whisper, "Edwina is dead," yet her death stood like something outside myself, too big to put my arms around and hold, though I knew I must hold it and look in its face and come to know each detail as if I were looking in a mirror.

I went out then and stood at the foot of the lawn with the thought that distance could help me comprehend the totality of the fact. Edwina was dead. How could she be? People who had heard about the accident stopped to get more recent news, and I told them to wait for my father. Soon he returned, riding with two men from the search party in a wagon from the feed store, and then came more townsfolk, the police lorry with the Old One, and finally the coroner's hearse. Those people there only to gossip and gawk moved off the drive to let this last go by to the door and left their horses chewing and stomping the perfect grass of the lawn. Before I was halfway to the house I could hear from inside the Old One's crying like a low-pitched wail. The farmer with the blue-white eyes sat on the top step of the porch and rubbed his hand back and forth across his forehead.

"I couldn't rein them in in time," he said.

Another man clapped him on the back. "You couldn't help it, Ray. Don't blame yourself."

"She wasn't right," said still another, leaning against a porch pillar. "The doc told me she hadn't been herself for quite a while. You know how women get after babies sometimes."

I started up the stairs around them, and the one near the pillar told me I'd better wait until my parents told me it was all right to go in. I asked them what had happened. They said the man named Ray had been driving out to his fields to load silage and had seen Edwina standing at the side of the road. He wondered what she was doing there, so early and so far from town. It was unusual to see a woman out by the fields alone, especially one on foot. But he had the horses whipped up to a fairly smart pace and so just raised his hand in greeting.

"I should've stopped, I know it."

But he was in a hurry, he said again. More concerned with filling his silo than solving riddles of women alongside the road. Nothing was further from his mind than that she would rush in front of the team. When she darted

out and turned square to meet them, he couldn't rein the
horses in. At the last second she looked up and put out
her hand as if to touch their muzzles. Then she was gone.

The man saw the white blur of her petticoats and a
gray swirl of dress down between the backs of the team.
Before he could even get the horses to break stride, the
back wheel ran up over her and dropped off her body with
a jolt that nearly knocked him from his seat. In all that,
he kept saying, he remembered so clearly her skirts flying
up between the horses like flags, and I pictured her in
death as only the gray and white of winter clouds som-
ersaulting under horses' hooves.

Then the coroner arrived and asked the farmer if there
had been anything about her—a look on her face, the
condition of her clothes or hair—that gave notice that
she was hysterical or deranged. Quite the contrary, the
man answered. When she had glanced up at the horses,
she had the still look of a woman watching out her front
window at an empty street. She had taken no more note
of them than that. And I could picture Edwina becalmed,
that distant look she'd get when she was watching what
the rest of us could not see.

"I'd do anything to have her living again," the farmer
said. "I truly would."

"In ways it was a mercy," the coroner said, sitting
down next to him on the step and folding a cigarette paper

into a roll. "There was no kind of life left to her, out at that cabin with the old woman."

"Nothing nobody can do to stop something like that," another added.

I backed away from them then and started around the house to go in the kitchen, breaking off a twig of cedar from the bushes as I went. Malina was sitting on the back steps, hugging her knees and swaying. She looked up at me and tried to speak, but her words caught in stutter, the sound of *d* stuck and repeated. Inside, men milled around the kitchen, still littered with the deserted breakfast, cold toast and congealing yellows of eggs in grease. Under the noise from the hallway they talked low about where the accident had happened, checking landmarks and mileage from town as if locating the exact spot made some difference, and reassuring each other that Ed wasn't "right" and there was nothing the farmer could have done.

I threaded my way around them toward the hall and listened to the babble and commotion on the other side. Edwina was dead, and with just a push, the door would swing wide enough for me to see. How would she look? Had death changed her into a shape so strange I would not be able to see Edwina in it?

I did not want to look, and yet to know how she looked was irresistible. I slipped into the hallway and moved around a knot of men talking, and from behind them could see into my father's office, the full view bisected by the half-closed door. Just one end of his leather couch showed, Edwina's bare white feet sticking out from under her skirts like narrow gray-white fish.

I could not take my eyes off them. I moved closer. Her feet gray-white as moon blemishes, and I imagined her hair changed into the same bright ashy color, drained in death of all its fire, and her face now framed with an unruly aura of glow.

From within the office, the Old One's keening rose over the hushed voices of the men like the high thin wailing of winter wind that forces its way through eaves cracks and fills a house with drafts. For a moment it silenced us all as it rose shrilly and then broke off suddenly. In that moment of quiet I heard Rose call from the top of the steps.

"Anna, come get me."

She sat on the top step, her bare feet peeking out beneath her nightgown.

"Anna, what are all these people doing? I'm hungry."

I went up and sat beside her and pulled her onto my lap. "It's all right, Rosie. I'll get you breakfast in a minute."

Then the office door swung wide, and two men tried to maneuver a long brown wicker basket through the doorway. The man in the rear lost his grip as his hand scraped the doorjamb, the basket tilted, and the lid swung open. Edwina's body was covered in winding sheets, and senselessly I thought of tablecloths and fields of snow, of piles of laundry and pillows on an unmade bed. The other man grabbed at the lid and swore at the first to be more careful.

Then my father followed the Old One out into the hall, his fingers cuffing her wrist as though he expected that she would spring away. She stopped and pointed at the basket being carried down the steps.

"Tell them to be careful. I'll have nothing more be happening to her."

"They will take care; it is their job."

"They almost rolled her out—I saw it with my own eyes."

"It was an accident and won't happen again."

"No accident, none of this. You've killed her."

"Don't do this to yourself, Carline. We've been over how it happened, and the man could do nothing to stop it."

She shook his hands off and turned to him.

"Not him that killed her, but your wife, and you in her bidding. Stealing her babe and calling her wicked! Even in death she will have no peace."

Father reached toward her, but she reared back. "Do not touch me."

The men shifted restlessly and stood back for the

Prussian to come through the path they had made for her. "What is the problem here?" she asked.

The Old One whirled around, and her face changed at the sight of the Prussian. In that moment I was afraid of Carline Selchie, so ancient and black and angry.

"You, Etta Berter, have killed my own Edwina, the same as if you had crushed her under your heel, and I curse you on the grave that is not strong enough to hold her troubled soul."

Her voice rang clear and loud, and even the low humming talk of the crowd was shocked into stillness. The Prussian looked around her, but the eyes of the men were averted and they stood crowded back against the wall. "Mrs. Selchie," she began.

"There is no more to talk of, save what I have to tell you."

The Old One stepped closer to the Prussian.

"I curse you with the gift of sight."

She lowered her voice, though every word carried clearly.

"That you may see the true shape of your every deed and hidden thought with the brightness of the present moment.

"I forbid shadows or night to cover over you but send lidless eyes that cannot close.

"Your soul will fill with what you would forget, and

in that sea you will swim until you make straight what you have turned crooked, Etta Berter."

She took another step, and the men shifted back to leave space about her. She stood so close her skirt and bodice buttons brushed against those of the Prussian.

"Look to your children." The Old One pointed to the top of the stairs, where I sat with Rose, my arm tight around her. "By hook and by crook they are Selchie children in their hearts and souls, and with that same sight they will see how they are not yours. For all your power over them, they will see what you have done and refuse to be like you.

"Anna knows the secrets you have kept from her. She knows her many mothers, and in time Rose will know her own true count. I have made it so, and it must happen."

Then the Old One turned and hobbled to the foot of the steps. "Do you hear me, Anna? Know that you can ever hear me, if you listen, and I will tell you what is written in the dark and upon the water. And I charge you with telling Rose the stories what I will not be here to tell myself. Do you understand me, child?"

It seemed the world had stopped turning. I nodded yes, the movement of my head so slight I suspected I had only thought the word yes. Yes, though I could not have said at that moment exactly what I had agreed to do nor swear that I wished to do it. The Old One nodded in return, her old green eyes the color of waves carrying me out to sea and back to shore, forever rocking me between the two and so strong I had not the power to resist the rocking.

"Then it is sealed between us," she said, and held her arms up, palms to us, Rose and myself.

She chanted words I could not understand but which were terrible and familiar and made the hairs rise on the back of my arms. She turned in slow circles three times, and the words spread over the house, in each crack and niche, over the walls and across the floors, like air and dust and pollen, to wherever her breath would blow them.

Several of the men ducked back from the doors, and my father moved to the Prussian's side and put his arm around her. But no one spoke, save Rose, who rested her head against my shoulder and softly hummed while the Old One's words ran out over the rest of us like water, fitting themselves around us, touching everywhere and moving on. Then she ceased and dropped her arms, the air still trembling with her voice.

"Remember, Anna, what must be saved for telling."

Without a look to anyone else, she turned then and was gone, down the drive in the direction the hearse had gone. It was several seconds after the screen door had slammed that the men began to mutter and shift, and my mother put her fingers to her lips. "Oh, dear," she said, "I'm so sorry you had to see that. How distressing for her!"

Talking low and nodding her head in false, studied regret, she ushered the man closest to her to the door, and in time the rest followed. An hour later, when the last of the people lingering outside the house had left, my father announced abruptly that he was going out and the Prussian would be in her room and wished not to be disturbed.

"Anna," he said, holding the door half-open before him. "Anna?" When I did not answer, he let the door fall shut and sat down beside me on the hall steps. "I am sorry that Edwina is dead." He cleared his throat. "I am so sorry. It was all wrong, from the beginning, so confused." He moved to lay his hand on mine, and I stood quickly, regretting immediately that I had ducked away. "Yes," he said, "yes, I do understand. Maybe you will want to talk about it later."

He left, and I sat back down on the bottom step and watched Rosie walk curiously around. She stood at the door to the kitchen, where Malina had been stirred to clean up the remains of the breakfast. Then she went to the door of the parlor, where the glazier was replacing the shattered windows, and on to the door of the empty office, trying to reconstruct the events of the day and the night before.

"How did the windows get broken, Anna? Was it the animals?"

I began thinking of stories, of how the glass shattered by itself or how a bat or owl or night hawk had become confused and flew against it. But the Old One's words rose up like gorge in my throat, and I felt her waiting for me to tell Rose what no one else would tell her. I knew the words. "Your mother Edwina came to claim you, and in her fierceness, she would have broken down these walls to get you."

Instead I said, "Ed, the woman with the doll."

"But why did she break our windows?" Rose asked.

"She was sad, and that was all she could do."

I asked Rose quickly then if she would like to walk down to see the horses, and we set out past the arbor and gardens to the stable, filled with the sweet aroma of hay and feed and dung. Balancing Rose on the rail in front of me, I looked into the box stalls, at the animals' hooves half-buried in their bedding, the fine delicate legs and the outline of slender bones. Occasionally one horse lifted its leg and set it down again solidly amid the rustling of the straw. They shifted against the sides of the stalls and swished their tails and turned to look at me with passive brown eyes. They were so beautiful, my father's horses, beautiful and strong, their bay coats rich and burnished. I tried to imagine them like the farmer's team, pounding over me, hooves like anvils and legs like pistons, their force too powerful to resist.

I thought of a body breaking under them, a leg snapping and ribs crushed, but the sensation seemed beyond me. Still I shuddered and felt my teeth on edge as if they had been filed. The horses so beautiful. One raised its soft muzzle to me and nickered, brushing its velvet lips across my fingers. Edwina had always hated to be near them. With so many ways to die, why had she chosen horses?

I drifted numb through the day like that, caught up with trying to answer all I could not know, to figure in hindsight what I could have changed to stop this death. Though I busied myself with these puzzles, at the edge of my mind hovered the grief over Ed's dying, which I could not quite take to myself yet. I could not believe I would never again see her nor that it had been her body wrapped in the sheets and carried out. I knew it, of course I knew it, but I could not believe. And deeper in the darkness of feeling about her, I feared she was not dead at all, but here with us. I did not look at Rose but that I expected Edwina to be beside her, nor put my arms around her but that I expected to embrace Edwina also. I did not know what she would look like, whether transparent or vaporous or solid, whether like Edwina in life or Edwina in death. But I felt her presence around us, not threatening or loving, but there with us, eternal and enormous and patiently waiting for what I did not know.

I could see her, yet not see her, just beyond the spectrum of visible light. Like catching a moving shape at the corner of my vision that was not there when I turned to look. Like sensing but not seeing trees standing solid and hidden in the fog.

Then I began to fear that the Old One's curse had come to me as well as to my mother and I would see beyond what I was meant to, into the secrets of the living and the life of the dead. I would know all that happened and still not be able to change its happening, nor explain to others how I knew what I knew.

I told myself the Old One had wished my mother not harm but sight. I was being childish. A curse was no more than a bad wish against another, with no more power than a breeze. If wishes were horses, then beggars would ride, the Prussian always told me, and the Old One could no more curse than she could bless. I was worrying myself over nonsense.

Yet at supper even Rose seemed to sense that she should not chatter on about the strange commotion in the house that morning. My parents kept up an uncharacteristic stream of commentary, Father repeating every word of conversation with his patients that day and my mother describing every bill and where she'd filed it. After Malina came to take Rose for bed, Father and the Prussian fell into uncomfortable silence. After some time, Father said the Presbyterian minister had offered a plot in their cemetery for Ed.

"I've told the sexton and undertaker to bill us for any other expenses."

"The burial is tomorrow? I would like to attend."

"I don't know, Anna," Father said.

"I would like to," I said.

"Think about it, Anna," the Prussian told me. "It will only upset you."

She folded her napkin in a precise square, rolled it tightly, and slipped it through the silver holder. As if we were not discussing a burial and Edwina were not dead.

"Of course it will upset me. How can we help being upset?" I said.

Then her meaning opened up like a broken code and I realized the words must be read backward as in a mirror. It would upset her if I went when she must pretend nothing had happened. I looked at her quizzically as though I'd discovered she had been always speaking a foreign language, and the rest of the evening watched her like a stranger come to stay.

The dark came early, and the Prussian turned on all the lights in the parlor and left a trail of them burning after her in the dining room and hall, the kitchen, and up the stairs, where she had gone to kiss Rose good night. Even after the Prussian had locked up and gone to bed, my room was aglow with enough light from those left on that the curve of mirror was filled with dull silver far inside it.

I closed my eyes, afraid I would see Edwina standing on air outside my window or reflected in the glass there. Inside the dark behind my lids floated reds and blues, and my vision filled with snatches and pieces. Of purple-black bruises and pale feet like fish. Of bones snapping and a wheel running over a hand. The Old One's eyes held me like the sea inside the rocking waves. Salt water burned against my eyes, and I saw clearly as if my lids were transparent. I could not stop seeing. All around, the threat of the Old One's gift seemed to shimmer, and her words hung in faint but unmistakable vibration in the air.

The feeling came like a snake. The Old One's power was true, and the Prussian's nightmares became visible things: the blue corpse of her mother and the eyes of the dead calf coated with flies. Eventually she would see Ed stepping out in front of the horses, had already seen the faint ghostly outline of that vision. Ed, raising her hand to touch their noses, the farmer had said, as if she had just noticed them coming on her. Ed, reaching out to plead for the animals to stop. Not a suicide, but a request for mercy.

At three I went to Rose's nursery. She was awake and looking out the window.

"There are animals outside crying."

"No, just your family awake and restless."

"Something else too."

"There are no animals, Rosie. That's just a story."

"I'm sure, Anna." She hugged my arm. "They're looking for their fur and babies."

"There is nothing here to hurt you."

"They can get in through the glass. They will break the windows, Anna."

I stroked the hair back off her forehead. The Old One would tell her the selchies were looking for Edwina to take her with them and we must open wide the windows to let them in.

"If you close your eyes and go to sleep, I'll go outside to make sure there is nothing there," I lied.

Rose nodded and lay down for me to cover her. She closed her eyes so tight the skin wrinkled like an old woman's.

"That's good," I told her and started back to my room, but there was something restless and unsettled in the house, and I turned downstairs instead.

The steps were cold, and I stopped on each tread, thinking here Hailus Tucker had stood, and here Edwina with him, and here the Prussian holding an imaginary baby and watching herself in the mirror. I made myself look in that mirror and saw a dark shape. I made myself stand and look, though terror filled me that I would see

Edwina in the glass behind my shoulder, reaching out to touch me.

But there was only my form, moving when I did, though I would swear there were others, invisible around me. I turned off the parlor lamps and shivered from what I told myself was cold. To prove I was not afraid, I opened the front door and stood looking at the empty lawn for the creatures Rose had heard in her dreams. I imagined Edwina walking out of the darkness toward me. Then for the first time I admitted I would never see her again, not as she had been.

The feelings I had put off all day now surrounded me like the dark that reached out past black nothingness. I sank in them, and there was no bottom, no surface, no warmth. Her death was endless and final. And then, though I did not want to give in to that death, it took me over and carried me through the storm of itself until I felt raw and bruised and turned inside out with my silent crying. Edwina was dead and gone like a part of my own self. I crouched barefoot on the cold porch until that knowledge burrowed itself into the center of my bones and I felt it burning there.

Then my teeth began to chatter and I trembled so violently I could not stop. I went inside, and when I reached into the closet for a coat or shawl or sweater, my fingers touched the Prussian's seal coat, the pelts rich and deep and softer than buttered silk. I held it against my face, the softness brushing the length of my body, and wrapped it around me until my trembling stopped, my fingers running just over the tips of the fur.

I could not stand the dark, could not let Edwina be lost in it on her first night dead. I brought the candelabra from the mantel and set it in the open doorway. I lit the candles, and though the Prussian forbade us to leave fire burning, I left those nine in the wide-open door.

"Ed," I called softly. "Edwina."

There was no answer, of course, no movement, no vision. It was a foolish thing to think she could see the light or that it would help her, even more foolish to speak out loud to the dead. But somehow it was better for me that way, standing barefoot in the Prussian's coat and watching the candle flames dance in the circle of their light.

"I will keep you company. I will make sure the door is open," I told her in case she could hear.

The next morning my parents found me asleep at the foot of the stairs, still wrapped in the coat. For a moment when they first saw me from the top of the stairs, my father told me later, they thought an animal had somehow gotten in, a bear or an enormous dog. But then the Prussian noticed my feet, the bare white toes not quite covered by the fur.

She was standing over me when I awakened, her hands held close to her shoulders in alarm. In that moment sleepers have when their consciousness has not returned and they look around themselves, mindless as babies, I stared at my mother, her fine eyes and burnished chestnut hair twisted in coils about her head, and I thought she was the most beautiful vision that could ever be.

But even before that moment was done, I was aware of how strange its total neutrality, its complete peace. She was having no such moment but looked down at me in horror.

"My God, Anna," she said. "What has happened here?"

Chapter Twenty-two

THE OLD ONE PICKED OUT Ed's burial dress, not black as I'd expected, but with a navy field spilling over with sprays of pink cabbage roses, the neck and wrists trimmed with narrow lace, and ebony combs to catch up Edwina's hair. When I arrived at the cabin, she lay in the bed she had shared with the Old One, still set in the middle of the room. Her hands were crossed at her chest as if she were sleeping, the good hand on top of the one gone black with bruise, Edwina covered all over with the pink roses of her last dress.

I had not asked my parents if I was allowed to miss

school and come here but had dressed quickly and walked past them out the door. Rafferty met me at the foot of the path and without a word escorted me to the cabin. Inside, the Old One sat bolt upright in a straight-backed chair, eyes closed and her crossed feet six inches off the ground. At first I was afraid she had died sitting there, but without opening her eyes she spoke.

"We should sit the watch for three days, but Thomas says I must be gone by then, before the town has time for mischief. So we'll do the best we can by her and I'm gladdened you've come to take your place with us."

Then she went quiet again, Edwina's pale profile in relief against the black of the Old One's dress. The Prussian always said corpses looked just like sleepers, and when I was small I had thought how strange that no one woke them. Now I studied Edwina's body, and though her eyes were closed and she was still, this was in no way sleep. Her face was sunken and gray, her hair in contrast, lurid red like a clown's. Edwina, and no longer Edwina.

As always, I sat with the Old One, both of us quiet and thinking our own thoughts, yet now with miles of space between us and the terrible body between. I wanted the coffin lid to shut down upon that face and the earth to close over it, the grotesque caricature of what had been Edwina. Yet it was still Ed's face, and I looked at it intently to save up for never being able to look at it again.

In the quiet and the restfulness here the turmoil of the past day and a half began to settle like dust and I closed my eyes for a moment like the Old One, drifting in the dark. Then the Old One cleared her throat and spoke.

"Did she come to you in the night, Anna?"

"Who?" I said, again watchful.

At first she said nothing, then she spoke low, as though to herself.

"Pale she was, her hair and skin and clothes all pale and soft-lit like glowworms. When I woke, she were moving around the room slowly, like she were saying goodbye to each thing, or searching for what were lost. I were sleeping on the pallet so she might have the bed her last night here, and when I sat up, she turned and looked as though she were recalling who I might be."

"It was a dream."

"No, child, I know the difference. She did not find her way to you then, or to the wee one?"

"Rose thought she heard animals, but there was nothing."

"You're sure?"

The night before, I hadn't been, but now the proof was before us. Edwina, never about in the night except in our imagination.

"Tell me, child, how you know."

"It's a foolish thing. I lit candles and left the door

open. I called her name and then fell asleep at the foot of the stairs. It seems so stupid to even tell you. I looked for her and thought I felt her around, but it was just because of all that happened."

"She did not pass over you on her way up to the baby?"

I shook my head.

"But you wouldn't know if you were sleeping." The Old One closed her eyes again and nodded. "I must leave, you know."

"Not soon?"

"As soon as she is buried. Thomas has told me, and I agree: they will let me put her to rest, but then we know not what wicked plans they might have for me."

"But where are you going?"

"I cannot tell you secrets I do not know myself. But I must go, Anna, and you must watch for Edwina if she comes to say her farewells. Tell her for me how I love her as my own self and how I will never desert her."

I was so confused then, and so tired I could not think what all this meant. There were no such things as ghosts or spirits. Yet surely not all that had made Edwina and the largeness of her desire was trapped in this white body smelling faintly of first decay.

I felt frightened also, with the Old One moving beyond reach by leaving, the same as Ed had by dying. I wanted to be five years old, held in her arms, the Old One singing and humming me to sleep. I wanted the dry warmth of her skin against mine and to smell the wisp of sugared coffee on her breath while she told the selchie stories in the kitchen where my mother would not go. Yet it was not possible those moments would come again, and I was filled with the death of time past, forever beyond my touch and forever inside me living.

"Can't you stay?" I whispered. "For Rose?"

"You have given your word to take our place, as if you were ours and she yours in return. Do these things for me, Anna. You have promised."

I wanted to tell her she must stay, since I could not do all she had asked. But I felt a long ribbon being drawn through my fingers, pulling her and Edwina with it. Then Rafferty came and spoke so softly to the Old One that I could not understand him, and the men lined up stiffly before the porch, the wooden box propped on end against a tree.

"It's time to close her away, Anna," the Old One said.

She bent over Edwina and straightened a lock of wild red hair. She whispered in her ear and pressed two fingers in the middle of Edwina's forehead.

"It is done," she said, coming to stand before me. "I will take the head of the procession if you will take up the rear." She reached to press her fingers against the center of my forehead as she had done for Edwina, and I felt her touch after she had taken her hand away.

"I rue our parting, child, but there's no helping it."

"Are you saying goodbye now?"

"To make sure we have the time to say it."

"Will you be back?"

"In some ways I will never leave. I cannot say about the other. But do not fear, Anna, neither what you find about nor inside you. Do not fear."

Then she was gone, leaning on Rafferty's arm up the path to the waiting hearse in front of Lucy Minchion's. The men took up the coffin, arguing which of them should stand where. In a minute Ed would be closed inside, and the thought filled me with panic, as I pictured myself shut inside the darkness with her. Though I had not before touched anything dead, I laid my hand over her hands and was shocked at how cold and hard they were. I had wanted to comfort her, but now I wanted comforting myself.

The men lifted her. *Like some dead thing*, I thought, and then, *of course*. The four of them were awkward and wavered under her weight, one swore at another to be careful, and all wiped their hands against their suits when they had finished touching her.

"Get me the nails for the lid," one said.

"Wait," I told him. They had left one corner of her

skirt pulled over the edge and her hands disarranged. I straightened these and her hair also. They were lifting the lid on, had already blocked her from my view, when I told them to wait again. The doll she had made for Rose was wrapped in flannel on a table in the corner, its blue eyes staring. I thought to put it in Edwina's arms, when I saw the lock of Rose's hair woven into the yarn, the soft brown baby hair entwined with blue ribbon.

"Go on," I told them. "I've changed my mind."

They nailed the lid tight, and I followed them up the narrow path, the trees slapping and our feet stumbling against the underbrush. At the cemetery, mourners lined up next to the mound of earth and the grave it would fill. Grown children the Old One had delivered: not all, but the ones who had chosen to stand by her. The Hannachs were there, Paul with a cane and baby Anna Selchie in her mother's arms. Farmers with brown faces and white foreheads, women awkward in their Sunday clothes, and Ray, the man whose team Edwina had been run down by. All these but not my parents or their friends.

While the minister finished his sermon, the Old One stood at the foot of the grave and said her own prayers in Gaelic. The men lowered the coffin on ropes and she tossed in a handful of dirt, the clods hitting soft and hollow off the wood like first raindrops. Then she turned from her place to give room for the next mourner, and we filed up, the earth smelling cold and metallic. I threw my handful of dirt on Edwina's coffin and wondered how death, as clear as air, had found the shape and force to bring her here.

When I returned to my place, the Old One was gone, only Rafferty standing like a guard between the funeral party and the gate out to the road. The minister quickly finished, and the mourners fled.

"So," Rafferty said. "It's done now."

"You helped the Old One get away, didn't you?"

"It is my way, you know, to be perverse. When the town finds the chicken's flown her coop, they'll throw a perfect fit and your mother will never get over it."

"Be serious for once, Rafferty."

"I am serious, and it was serious business we were about here. But it's done, and all that's left is to order the headstone from Des Moines, one so big it'll look like the Taj Mahal sitting out here on the prairie."

He crossed his arms across his chest and strolled around the grave, studying the way it was situated.

"You know what they're planning, don't you? To leave this spot unmarked and forgotten except in the sexton's records, to let the grass grow and the earth flatten. But I'll have them roll a granite boulder over that hole, carved out with a madonna and flying angels blowing trumpets and an inscription so large they'll be able to read it from the next county. 'Edwina Selchie. Simple as a dove. Trampled by horses,' in letters carved so deep their children's children will still read and ask about it."

He kicked at the dirt, and I didn't know what to make of him, pacing off the length and width of the plot. I was so tired and the scene so unreal, Rafferty measuring Edwina's grave under one of those pure September skies, perfectly blue and clear. I wanted the Old One to explain what had happened. I wanted Rafferty to tell me what to do. Then an image of Edwina in her grave flashed before me and I put up my hand to brush earth from my face. Rafferty stopped and looked at me from under his hat brim. "I didn't actually expect you to be here, you know."

I shrugged.

"And now what are you going to do?"

"About what?"

"About going back to them. You left to come here, you must go somewhere afterward."

"I'll go home, of course. Where else would I go?"

"Anywhere. At home you'll just trade yourself for the price of the rent, no doubt."

"What do you mean?"

"Exactly what I said. You'll become the obedient daughter, even though you know exactly what commands your parents are capable of."

I backed toward the gate. "I have to go home. They are expecting me."

"And what will you talk about with those parents from now on? Will you ask them why they let Edwina Selchie come to this? Or will that always be some rotting thing you keep in the corner, pretending it doesn't stink?"

I stared at the black hole of Ed's grave. Rafferty came closer to me.

"You know you will always see it. Always." He spat. "You are your mother's child. Every time I think you're not, you turn and prove you are."

"I came here."

"But you're going back as if nothing had happened. We've already had this conversation, you and I."

"I don't know what to do."

"Edwina Selchie's dead, and you will say nothing?"

"But what?"

"After all this you're not full of words you want to shout at them?" He grabbed me by the arms, his gray eyes stormy. "Even I am full, after this."

"Why are you doing this to me now?" I cried at him. "I don't want to hear. It is too much."

I tried to hit my fist against his chest, but he held me still, so close to him that I saw another eye in the middle of his forehead.

"That is my job, Miss Berter, to be always around in places you don't want and at times you don't wish, telling you what you would give your arm not to hear. Now it is time you went home."

He pushed me away, tugged his hat brim down tighter, and walked toward the gate, past two men coming with shovels. They began filling the grave, and I winced at the sound of the dirt hitting the coffin and then of earth against earth. I did not want to be here, but I did not want to go home, where Rafferty's words would chase me through the house and I would not be able to shut out the sound of his taunting.

When the men had mounded up the dirt, they smacked at it with the flat backs of their shovels, and after they left I stood alone at the foot of the grave and stared at the blank brown earth, expecting some answer to be written there or some voice to speak. But all was silence, and I saw Edwina as the drifter in the Old One's vision. I told myself again, Edwina is dead, but she moved through in my mind in ever changing, ever constant orbit, glowing softly like the moon.

All the way home, my thoughts came in fits and starts, and where I wished answers I found only space and air. What I would say to my parents and how we would act toward one another I could not imagine.

But the Prussian kept herself occupied in private rooms and with duties that would take her out of the house, and my father stood his distance, waiting for me to be ready to speak. For more than a week we avoided being with each other for any length of time or leaving any silences when we were at table. I did not try to change this mode, afraid as I was of breaking beyond repair the terrible fragility of the household. Though I could not explain how, the world as I knew it, all that gave me nurture and protection and life, would shatter if I spoke the Selchies' name to my parents.

Still I could not get Rafferty's words out of my mind, nor convince myself they were not true. I still grieved for Edwina and the Old One, for Rose and myself and all that was lost. I lay down at night, my mind busy with a scramble of images, and when I could not make them still or sensible, I cried in frustration and slept with my shoulders hunched and eyes closed tight against Edwina's presence. When Rose cried out in the night, I would not go to her, and during the days I was glad of school to occupy me. I could not tell if my house was prison or haven, but depending on the moment it felt like both and I huddled inside it even as I wanted to break out. This great silence was filled with the sound of my own voice arguing with itself, telling me the Selchies were gone. Yet they stayed closer than ever before. They whispered in my ear and rode inside my heart. They came flickering in images that appeared upon the air, and I was never without them.

"Do not fear," the Old One had told me.

And so one evening I stood at the doorway of my father's office and when he looked up I asked him, "What do you know about Chicago?"

"Chicago? Do you plan to travel there?" He blotted the entry he'd just made in the ledger.

"I came from there, didn't I?"

He pushed his chair back and pressed the tips of his fingers together.

"What do you want to know?" he said finally.

"About where I came from."

"From an orphanage, St. Ann's, run by the Sisters of Mercy."

"I mean the people before that."

"I don't know." He turned his palms to the ceiling.

"Are you telling me the truth?"

"Of course, Anna, why would I lie?"

"You never told me this before."

"Your mother was afraid. She believed if you knew, you would not love us as the true parents we wished to be."

"But the ones before you?"

"Children are left at St. Ann's by parents who cannot or will not take care of them. Often the Sisters themselves do not know who has brought a particular baby, and I believe that was the case with you, Anna.

"But even when names are known, they become part of a confidence the nuns will not disclose. They insist the old life of the child ends when the new parents take her and what has been remains a secret."

"That's all you know?"

"All but that I could not love you more deeply than I do, Anna, that there has never been a child born in any circumstances more special to me than yourself. That is the truth. I swear it."

We both held very still and his words sang in the air between us, ties that were unbreakable, and I heard again the Old One's words, stronger now: "Do not fear."

Two weeks after Edwina's burial Douglas Selchie returned, weeping in our parlor and twisting his hat in his fists. I did not feel sorry for him. His show came too late and was not believable. The Prussian received him, but my father seemed disgusted and when Rose asked who the strange man was, he told her no one worth bothering with.

Two weeks later Hailus Tucker's mother wrote, announcing her son's engagement to a debutante of the season before. The Prussian began reading the letter out loud to Father, but he stopped her and said he never wanted to hear that man's name mentioned in our house again. She sat looking at the words of the letter as if she were trying to make out what they said; then without arguing, she folded the note inside the envelope and let it slip from her fingers onto the floor.

All this while I thought of telling Rose her story, the way the Old One had charged me to do. But as soon as I began to speak, I was no longer sure exactly what I had thought was so important to tell her. My voice did not sound like my own, cracking and breaking as it did, and I lost my nerve before the first sentence was completed. I thought of disguising it as a fairy tale, or a fable full of animals, or a story that had happened to someone else, but all seemed wrong except the plain truth, which in turn was too tangled and unhappy to tell a child so small as Rosie. So I read my sister stories that had nothing to do with her. I promised myself I would tell her when she was older or when the moment was right, but all the while the voices of the Old One and Rafferty nagged at me and I felt Edwina all around.

Gradually the Prussian seemed to relax and return more to her normal ways, but she still left on too many lights and avoided me while she and I were home alone. I was not yet ready to talk about what had happened to Edwina and my part in it. But though I could not say any of the words I wished, I could not give up the compulsion that I must say them and those words and all their variations rang constantly in my head until I could not hear clearly any other thing. I repeated and rehearsed them. I tried to memorize the order in which they should be said. I sat with the Prussian and my father at dinner, convinced I would speak before the meal was over. Yet I remained silent and the longer my silence, the louder the words roared until I lived in their constant storm.

Then one day late in Indian summer when great flocks of birds rose together from the trees, shifted, and circled

back on themselves like dark turning waves, I returned
from school and let myself quietly in the front door. Rose
was prattling on to the Prussian in the parlor, and I stood
listening in the hall. At first her voice was a murmur,
drowned by the sound of my own breathing, her talking
on and on as she was wont to do. Then distinctly she
said, "Where are those people we used to see?"

"Which ones, darling?"

I moved closer and leaned my head against the back
of the open parlor door.

"The ones with the rabbit skins and empty turtles.
Anna's friends."

"They moved away."

"Why?"

"They didn't want to live in New Marango anymore."

"Why not?"

"They didn't like it."

"Why?"

"I don't know why, but they didn't, and so they
moved so far away that they'll never come back. We'll
never see them again so we might as well forget them
and leave room in our minds for better things."

Then Rose became enthralled with the idea of only
so many ideas and memories fitting inside her head and
began asking a thousand questions about that. But I could
not stand the Prussian's lie, the trickery and deceitfulness
of it used to force the Selchies' absence in memory as

well as presence. Out of the confusion of feelings that I had not been able to make sense of, anger suddenly came clear, and then indignation. I went in the parlor and sat in the chair opposite the Prussian.

"I did not hear you come in," the Prussian said, looking up for a moment from the embroidery in her lap.

She wore a rust-colored dress with round horn buttons, the fabric the same reddish tint as her hair in the late afternoon light. Rose played at her feet, clumsily trying to string large wooden beads on a cord, and it seemed impossible that anything evil or monstrous had ever gone on in this house. Yet I knew and could name what had, though I wanted with all my heart to believe her lies that allowed this scene to seem so innocent and good.

"What you told her was not true," I said, but my voice broke and I had to clear my throat.

"What was that?"

"They didn't go away as you said."

She put down the sewing hoop and needle and studied me carefully. "A child cannot understand everything, nor is all news fitting for her ears."

I hesitated. She was right, of course, in her way that made just enough sense to confuse the issue.

"But you lied to her," I said. The blood drummed in my ears as if I were underwater, and I was shocked that the Prussian looked at me so calmly.

"Not in front of Rose, please."

"Why not? That is the point."

"Rosie," she said, "take your blocks in to Malina and ask her to help you string them."

Rose went out, dropping wooden beads as she went, and the Prussian turned to me again.

"But they are gone. What difference to her how they left?"

"You told her to forget them."

"As I tell you and have told you before. They have no part in our lives, and there is no reason to complicate matters."

"She has a right to know."

"Know what, Anna? Tell me your grand plan, since you seem to know everything." The Prussian brought her hand down flat against the arm of the chair.

"Know who her mother is and how she came to be your daughter, the same as I have the right to know what you have not told me."

"I intended to tell you later."

"How much later? You have already waited sixteen years."

The Prussian picked up her sewing again, wrapping the needle seven times for a French knot and studying her own deliberate motions.

"You make things so hard, Anna. Why cannot you accept what is before you and be satisfied?" She pulled the thread up for another knot, though I wanted her to look at me.

"Because there is more, and it changes the rest."

"What is changed? You and your sister live in this house with your father and me. Nothing is changed, and we've worked hard to give you that constancy. Trust me, when you are older you will see that this is best."

"But what of the others? What about what happened to them?" My throat was thick, and I forced myself to go on. Always with her it was so easy to find excuses not to.

"What about them?" The Prussian spoke sharply now and her voice rose to match mine. "A madwoman attacks the house with an ax and then throws herself in front of a galloping team and you blame me? Is that what you're about? Your father and I were the ones trying to get her to where she could not harm herself, or don't you remember that? It was you, Anna, who let her loose that night, and when Pandora opens the box she's been forbidden, all manner of trouble is bound to fly out."

We sat looking at each other in quiet. She put her sewing on the table, leaned back in one corner of her chair, and crossed her arms. Now her voice calmed into the tone she used for lecture.

"Your father and I have tried to be gentle with you these past weeks because we feared you would blame yourself for the woman's death and become despondent.

But you force me to be blunt, Anna. You have concocted some fantasy about my implication in the accident and my responsibility to confess what I didn't do. I cannot stand for that.

"We've given you enough time to get over what happened. Now stop moping around the house and letting your imagination run wild with you. The mourning period is over and it is time to return to reality."

Then I felt for a moment that truly I must be mad and that all I knew or remembered was only hallucination. There was nothing solid and dependable here, not even the great earth I stood on, and if I tried to cling to anything about me, my hand would pass through the object I reached for as if through air.

"None of that is true," I said.

"There is no sense in discussing this when you are not yourself, Anna."

"But it's not true. You took her jobs away, and you wouldn't let her visit Rose."

"You don't know the whole story, and without all the facts, you simply cannot make a correct conclusion. Isn't that right?"

She got up then, adjusted the cushion of the chair, and started toward the door. "Supper will be at the usual time. I'll talk to your father in the meanwhile."

"No, wait," I called after her.

She stopped and turned.

"I don't believe you ever intended to tell me what I found out for myself, just as you won't tell Rose."

"I will, if she asks."

"How will she know to ask?"

The Prussian shook her head.

"This has been a terrible time for you, Anna, but we will help you get back to your old self. We would do anything for our daughters, you know that."

Then she was gone, and I sat dumbly wondering if truly I had perceived what had happened so differently from her that my senses could not be trusted. If we both looked at a person and each saw a different form, who was to tell which of us was correct, or if both had been mistaken? Had Edwina been madwoman or victim or both or neither? Or was it only another of the Prussian's tricks, pretending to see only what she wished me to believe?

Nothing to trust but my own senses and sight.

Of the Old One charging me with Rose's care and of Edwina limp and broken. Of my mother's eyes that always held some secret from me and of selchies swimming in their ancient sea, rising up in the green vault of ocean and flying across the infinite water sky.

So closed here, all shut in rooms like Edwina in her box. I could not stand the thought and stopped at the kitchen door to watch Rose playing under the table as I used to do. Rose with something about Hailus in the passage of her face about her nose and something of Edwina in her chin and mouth. Rose's face the way I saw it. Rose Berter and Esther Selchie. Another shape deep inside I could not yet see but only sense, a soft face with rich fur slicked back wetly and memories of deep ocean water, dark and green.

I rubbed my hands over my own face, feeling with my fingertips the curve of bone around my eyes, the strong line of jaw and hump of nose. Seeing my face by touch and not recognizing it in any way as the face that had looked back at me out of reflections. Even as I went up the stairs and turned to look in the long mirror, the young woman who returned my gaze was puzzled by what she saw, another young woman she had never seen before, another Anna looking up through the water that held her.

I stood at the Prussian's door. She was seated at her writing desk, her back to me, though she must have sensed my presence.

"I will tell her," I said. "You know I will someday."

I thought I saw her shoulders tense, but that was all and I could not be sure.

"She must know who she is, so she will recognize herself."

Still the Prussian would not reply, sitting so distant

from me that I could not help but know how separate and different we were. After long silence, I left my mother there alone, so far away I could not reach her, and swam for that place she would not go, the place that felt to me like home.

Coda

*F*ROM THE SILVER-GREEN WATER where the Prussian cannot reach me, I tell Rose the seal stories and sing her their songs. About selchies in their emerald silence, sliding slick and fast down the fathoms and over the mountains beneath the deepest sea. About the sickness that causes them to pine for land so deeply that they would give up their pelts and home. About the humans who would kill them.

At first I was awkward and spoke in another's voice. My stories were short, and I did not know what came after. But I kept on, for Rose's sake. When she is grown and finds all the parts of herself that are not like my father or the Prussian or anything else familiar, she will at least know how to trace those parts back to before time. She will know that she is not freak or traitor, but that she came from more parents than two and how her world is wider because of it. She must know these things, I believe, so she may see herself clearly.

Because of this I told her the stories, in the beginning only when our parents were out of the house. But soon, when I put her to bed, Rose would climb into my lap and we would begin, Father and the Prussian finishing their coffee right below our feet. As I became more used to swimming inside them, the stories became longer and more complex, their meaning more surely about what had happened even as their appearance turned more foreign and strange.

Now I come like moonlight, and my voice is water.

I tell Rose about the half-selchie baby the selchie woman is killed for, and how that mother, forbidden to return to the sea, swims in the air around us. I tell Rose how the great-grandmother of that child comes each day and listens for her.

"She streams up from water so deep no human can go there and raises her head above the waves and waits there, listening for her great-granddaughter's voice. If ever she hears that call, she will swim onto the shore and leave her magic coat full of power there. She will take that risk and come for the child. And if that child ever finds the land wanting and wishes to return with her, she has only to sing her want, and the selchies will carry her home with them."

"Won't she be drowned, Anna?"

"They'll bring her mother's coat, and when she puts it on she will have the power to dive so deep into the green water that she can go wherever the seals take her."

I tell her how it feels to hurtle through that water and to fall into it and be caught up by it. When I watch her play in her bath or in the water she washes in, I see how she moves her hands like swimming and how her eyes are seeing what is far away. I know she has turned herself into another creature, if only for that short while, and it is too late for the Prussian to take this back from her.

And somehow the Prussian knows this, too, and leaves us alone. It is her old trick of ignoring what doesn't suit her, and we use it to our advantage. But I believe that when she watches Rose and me together, the power of the Old One's curse is at work and the Prussian sees not her own two daughters, as she would like, but two changelings in the place where she would not go.

The Prussian locks the doors at night and bolts the windows, as if closing the house tightly will keep out all she fears, keep in all she loves.

But Rose and I drift out on tides to beyond the breakers, and we see the Prussian as very small and helpless on the shore. Each time we leave her there, it becomes more apparent how sad and regretful she is of our leaving. I have the sight also and see she is afraid of swimming and ever will be. We leave her, and she cannot stop us.

That is the great secret I have learned. That she has the power to frighten but not to force. I am the only one who can stop myself from doing what she would not have me do. That was her trick, to fool me into thinking it was she when all along it was that other Anna.

I learned it slowly, when I mentioned Edwina and the house did not crash down upon me, when I first told Rose the stories and was not destroyed. I saw the Prussian watching me, only watching, and I wondered when she looked at me, what did she see? Surely not Anna becoming more like her mother each day. Instead she sees me sitting with my knees hugged to my chest, waiting and telling Rose stories as I wait. For now I stay with the Prussian. She is my mother, and I love her as best I can.

But I am not hers, and I have other places to go. It is what I whisper in the stories: it is the power of the sea. As the Old One told me when I was Rose's age, I tell Rose now, how Iowa looks like the wide rolling sea, how the endless fields of ripe wheat and young corn move in the wind over the gentle rises of the land. The sky stretches forever, the way it does over ocean, and the hawks turn in slow circles like frigate birds on salt breeze.

I tell Rose this: how the selchies swim through moonlight on waves like white fire and how that fire moves inside the water and changes shape as the water moves within itself. The whole surface of the ocean becomes lit from within, and the light rides on the swells, diving deeper as the waves rise to break. As far as one can see, the water is alive with light, the reflection of the full moon changed to fit the changing shape of the water and riding within it.

I think of this and let myself fall. The water carries me up and rocks me. I cup the fire in my hand, and it does not burn, yet all around, the sea is white with moonflame. I am safe here, this place of birth that came before the time I was born. I am home now with Rose. We will swim in this sea forever.